A Sad Soul
Can Kill You

A Sad Soul
Can Kill You

Catherine Flowers

URBAN
CHRISTIAN

Urban Books, LLC
97 N18th Street
Wyandanch, NY 11798

ISBN 13: 978-1-62286-805-6
ISBN 10: 1-62286-805-6

First Trade Paperback Printing June 2015
Printed in the United States of America

10 9 8 7 6 5 4 3 2 1

Distributed by Kensington Publishing Corp.
Submit orders to:
Customer Service
400 Hahn Road
Westminster, MD 21157-4627
Phone: 1-800-733-3000
Fax: 1-800-659-2436

A Sad Soul
Can Kill You

A tale about redemption, deliverance, and healing

Also By Catherine Flowers

Yesterday's Eyes

Dedication

This book is dedicated to those with burdens unreleased, wounds unseen and unhealed. By God you were created—not to walk in sadness but to stroll in gladness with your head held high, trusting in Him with every step you take.

May you surrender to Jesus and receive the gift of salvation, joy, peace, and everlasting life. For these things and much more are yours to claim when you submit to Him and walk in the glorious light . . .

All scripture is taken from the NIV and is italicized for emphasis only.

Acknowledgments

As always, to God be the glory. His magnificence reigns! I thank Him for the gift of writing. I would also like to give thanks to Joylynn Ross, acquisition editor at Urban Christian, for her advice, patience, and wisdom. Thank you to my editor, Maxine Thompson, of Thompson's Literary Agency, whose expertise remains an invaluable source for me. Thanks to Alanna Boutin for her copy editing expertise. And to everyone else who played a role in bringing this novel to fruition, I say, "thank you," once again.

I certainly can't leave out my mother, DeLois Brown, who has been my self-appointed promoter from the very beginning . . . Thanks, Mom! And a magnificent thank you goes to my big sisters and a host of other family members (you know who you are) who supported me when I first began this journey of telling tales with a keyboard and a thought!

Finally, I, of course, want to thank my biggest supporters—my children: Walter, my eldest, who continues to encourage me in my writing ventures; Fatima Manson, who while making her own way in the literary world as a freelance editor, saw room for improvement in the early stages of this novel; Nick, whose encouragement resonates whenever we speak; and Kiana, my youngest, who advised me on the "proper" use of Internet dialect. Ty . . . lol!

Preface

"Be alert and of sober mind. Your enemy the devil
prowls around like a roaring lion looking for
someone to devour."

(1 Peter 5:8)

"The human spirit can endure in sickness,
but a crushed spirit who can bear?"

(Proverbs 18:14)

Preface

Prologue

Tia pulled the hood of her coat on top of her head and got out of her car. She shuddered as she moved swiftly up to the door. She stopped to catch a glimpse of herself in the reflection of the large office window. The white fur that trimmed the hood of her coat made her think of the storybook character, Little Red Riding Hood . . . only Tia wasn't going to Grandma's house.

Just as she put the key in the lock, the door swung open and Scamp, the nickname she'd given him, stood before her.

"Hello," Scamp said expectantly.

She smiled nervously as she entered the sparsely furnished room. The only source of light was an old bronze lamp mounted on the wall. Its silhouette cast an indistinguishable shadow over the built-in desk below it. A chair accompanied the desk, along with a queen-size bed as the room's only décor. Tia noticed a Bible prominently displayed on the center of the desk, and she quickly looked away.

Scamp closed the door behind her as a feeling of disappointment slowly began to creep into her. She hadn't expected to walk into a luxurious suite, but she'd expected a little bit more than these shabby surroundings.

He removed her coat, throwing it across the chair. She smoothed the layered sections of her hair down with the palm of her hand and looked around the room again. She sighed heavily. *This room was little more than a meeting place for—*

"I've missed you," Scamp said as he gave her a big hug.

He hovered a full eight inches over her five foot four-inch frame, and Tia closed her eyes and let her head rest on the center of his chest. She allowed herself to enjoy the pleasure of his embrace, and the light, airy scent of cologne that wafted from his shirt made her forget the disappointment she'd felt when she'd first walked into the room.

She remembered how they'd first met right after the New Year—a little over a month ago.

"Excuse me," Scamp had said to her while she had been picking through a bushel of apples in the produce section of the grocery store, "don't you live on Cooper Circle?"

She'd looked up, startled by his approach. She had been prepared to brush him off when she looked into his hazel eyes, and whatever she was going to say disappeared from her thoughts.

"The cul-de-sac," he'd said. "I live one house down from the entrance. I've seen you driving by on occasion. You have a daughter, right?"

At first she'd been hesitant to answer since she wasn't in the habit of divulging her personal information to every stranger who approached her. "Yes," she'd finally answered.

She remembered how awkward she'd felt just standing there talking to him. Now she couldn't decide which felt more awkward—standing before him in the grocery store or standing alone with him in this room with her head resting on his chest.

She remembered inhaling the sweet scent of his cologne he'd had on in the store; it was the same scent he wore now, and she should have known then that she might be in trouble.

"Well, I just wanted to introduce myself," he'd said smiling. *"If you ever need anything,"* he'd winked at her, *"I'm your man."*

She remembered calling out to him as he walked away, jumping at his bait. "Need anything like what?"

"Well," he'd said as he'd slowly walked back toward her, *"I give good massages. That's my specialty."*

Scamp released his embrace, and Tia opened her eyes.

"You look good," he said softly. He held her hands and stepped back to look at her small, petite frame. "I always did love me some chocolate," he said smiling.

Tia fumbled with the belt she wore around her tailored blouse, and then slowly gazed at the brown skin on his face before finally looking up into his hazel eyes. "Thank you," she said.

He motioned her to the bed. "Sit down and relax."

She sat on the edge of the bed and watched as he walked over to the window and closed the beige curtains. He returned to the bed and bent down to remove her shoes.

"Lay back," he said as he gently placed her legs on top of the bed. "Relax and tell me about your day."

Tia positioned herself on the bed and leaned back on the pillow. "Well," she sighed, "it was a pretty slow day, thank goodness. I could even say it was a boring day, but I'm not going to."

He began unbuttoning his shirt. "Why not?"

"Because tomorrow is another day, and we never know what's going to happen at the hospital."

"Yeah, but you're a pretty tough nurse." He stood up and removed his shirt, exposing his slightly protruded abdomen. "You can handle it."

"I guess," she said.

"You can," Scamp said as he placed his shirt neatly across the chair on top of her coat. "You can handle that . . . and more."

She gazed at the thinning mass of brown and gray hair that adorned the sides and back of his head. The multi-colored strands were also present in greater numbers on the center of his chest, creating a triangular mass of thickness. "I'm just tired of the drama," she said.

He sat down on the bed. "Are we talking about the same thing?"

"Are we?" she asked.

He removed the belt from her blouse and changed the subject. "Turn on over, girl," he said as he eased her onto her stomach. "Let me give you a massage."

She turned onto her stomach and felt his hands stroking the back of her neck. She closed her eyes as his fingers slid under her blouse and pressed against her flesh, slowly gaining momentum, and then descending to her back. His hands traveled down the length of her waist, and then back up again, kneading her flesh the way a baker kneaded dough.

She turned her head to the side and opened her eyes. The leather-bound Bible sat directly in front of her, its contents tugging at her conscience. She turned away, not only from its image but from the truth she knew it held.

No, Tia thought, she wasn't at Grandma's house. But Scamp definitely was the big bad wolf, and by the time he whispered, "Turn over. It's time to do the front," the fire burning in Tia was in full force.

Afterward, Tia lay next to him in bed, inhaling the industrial scent from the stiff pillowcases that had infiltrated her nostrils. She looked at the off-white curtains hanging from the window and noticed a brown stain embedded in the fibers of one of the panels. The blemish coincided with the way she now felt inside. A sudden gush of sadness engulfed her as she listened to Scamp sleeping soundly.

She eased out of the bed and got dressed quickly. Too bad those hands hadn't belonged to her husband, she thought as she walked out of the hotel room.

Chapter One

"Code blue," the commanding voice on the overhead paging system said with clarity. "Fifth floor, room 524!" The operator repeated it. "Code blue, fifth floor, room 524."

Tia Sparks had just started her Wednesday morning nursing shift at Victory Memorial Hospital on the south side of the city of Chicago. She'd entered the elderly patient's room to find him unresponsive and with no detectable pulse. After she'd called for help, she'd immediately begun CPR until the resuscitation team had arrived and taken over.

Tia had delegated herself to crowd control while the doctor and ICU nurses continued their efforts to revive the patient. She watched as IV lines were started and heart-monitoring patches were placed on precise areas of his upper body.

"Clear!" the doctor shouted as he gave the patient a jolt of electricity from the defibrillator.

Tia watched as the patient's body bounced slightly on the bed. Seconds passed with no detectable activity.

"Clear!" the doctor shouted out again.

There was still no response, and shortly thereafter, all resuscitation efforts were stopped and the patient was pronounced dead. Tia stood in the doorway, watching them prepare to transport the patient off the floor. She wondered if he had been discovered sooner would their efforts to save him have made a difference.

Suddenly, the memory of her extramarital encounter came flooding back to her. It had only happened once, but she convinced herself that she did not want the fire burning in her to be extinguished. She rubbed her shoulder. Good or bad it was the only indication that she was still alive.

She walked slowly back to the nurse's station and entered her notes into the computer, then she headed back down the hallway to check on her other patients. She reached the end of the brightly lit corridor and stopped in front of room 523. It was situated directly across the hall from the room where she'd called the code just a little while earlier. She tapped lightly on the closed door, and thought she heard someone crying.

"Come in," the woman answered weakly.

"Good morning," Tia said closing the door behind her. "My name is Tia. I'll be your nurse today."

"Good morning. I'm Francis, but you probably know that already," she said, pointing to the chart in Tia's hand. "At least I hope you do," she mumbled.

Tia stopped at the sink next to the door and washed and dried her hands. Before putting on a pair of latex gloves, she walked over to the window and opened the blinds. Although it was a frigidly cold and cloudy day, the sun revealed itself intermittently, allowing its light to infiltrate the room. "Let's get a little light in here," she said.

Francis's mottled hand shook as she dabbed at the corners of her eyes with a tissue.

Tia looked down at her weathered face. "Have you been crying, Francis?"

"No," she said, rubbing the side of her face. "I'm just a little tired, that's all. And I usually go by Franny."

Tia looked at the almost empty IV bag of normal saline that had been calculated to run slowly through her patient's veins.

"I'll be changing your IV when this bag is finished," she said.

"Are you a nurse?" Franny asked.

Tia looked down at her navy and white nurse's pin; the gold trim surrounding it glittered from its position on her right collar. Just below the pin was her name badge with the initials *RN* in bold, black letters large enough for even the faintest eyes to see. Never mind the fact that she'd just told her who she was. She looked at the woman's gentle but tired-looking face. "Yes," she said softly, "I am."

"What was all that commotion a bit ago outside in the hallway?" Franny asked.

"Just a little situation," Tia said as she placed her stethoscope in her ears, and then placed them on the left side of Franny's chest. She listened as the faint beating of her heart decreased, and then escalated like a motor being revved up.

Tia thought about her own heart and how the beating of it increased every time she heard the baritone of her lover's voice. It was like a musical opus, and it had slowly made its way to the core of her body where she'd invited it to mingle with her soul.

"Is everything all right?" Franny eyed her suspiciously.

"I'm not done yet."

"No, I mean with the patient across the hall."

"Oh," Tia said. "Well, I can't talk about the condition of other patients; privacy rules, you know."

"Oh, I see."

"Can you sit up for me please?"

Franny slowly raised herself to a sitting position. "Did you go to college?"

Tia smiled. "Yes, I went to college. You can't get a nursing degree unless you do."

"I was just wondering," Franny said. "You look a little young."

"Well, I guess that could be a compliment," Tia said. She placed the stethoscope against Franny's back and listened to her lungs as they made a whistling sound when she inhaled. Each time her lungs reached their capacity, Tia instructed her to release the air and the sound reminded her of wood crackling in a fireplace. She pulled out her pen and began making notes on a sheet of paper attached to a clipboard.

"How old are you?" Franny asked completely dry-eyed now.

"I'm thirty-two."

"Oh, you're just a baby," she said with a weak smile. "But you remind me of a girl who took care of me once before when I was in the hospital. Her name was Mary. She was real nice."

"You were a patient here before?" Tia asked flipping through her sheets. "I didn't see that in your records."

Franny looked down at her gown and began fumbling with the collar. "Uh, no," she stuttered, "I . . . I was at another hospital."

"Oh." Tia stared at her for a moment before she continued writing notes in her clipboard.

"I really liked her though," Franny continued.

Tia thought she detected a sound of sadness in her voice. "How young was she?"

"Oh, I can't remember." Franny waved her hand in midair. "Maybe twenty-five, thirty . . . somewhere around your age, you know."

Tia stopped writing and looked at her. "I thought you said she was a girl."

"Honey, when you're sixty-eight years old like me, that age *is* a girl." She laughed a short, weak laugh. "I wish she would have been my own girl. I never had a daughter."

Tia looked at her. The way Franny smiled and dabbed at the corners of her eyes reminded her of her own grandmother, Mavis, back in Milwaukee. Her relationship had started out rough with her grandmother who had taken her in after her own mother, Ida, had been sent to prison for the negligent death of her brother. Tia had been six years old at the time, and she could barely remember her brother who had been just a baby.

But she remembered her grandmother and how ferocious she'd been. Over the years, though, Tia had seen a steady decline in her grandmother's health, and she couldn't help but wonder if it had been due to the stress of taking care of her husband, Henry, for three years before he died.

Although Mavis and Henry had separated prior to him getting sick, they had never divorced. And after Henry had a stroke, Mavis moved back into the house and took care of him until he died. Now that Mavis was getting up in age, Tia was glad that her own mother Ida, who had since been released from prison, was there to watch over her.

"Can you lay back down for me, please?" Tia said softly.

Francis slowly slid down onto the bed until she was flat on her back.

"Do you have any sons?" Tia asked as she pulled the covers down to take a look at her lower legs.

"I have one," she said flatly.

Tia pressed on her leg gently. The varicose veins decorated her swollen limbs like swirls of green licorice.

"Are your legs still hurting?" she asked.

"A little."

"I read that you came into the emergency room two weeks ago complaining of leg pain."

"Yes, I did."

"What happened? Did you do your follow-up?"

"I wanted to. But before I could make an appointment to see the specialist, I was back in the ER the next day 'cause I couldn't breathe!"

"Yes," Tia said flipping through her paperwork. "I see they ended up admitting you to the cardiac unit for a full workup. Now," she closed her chart, "you're here on our subacute unit."

"What kind of floor is this anyway?"

"Well, it's supposed to be for patients who are stable enough to leave the floor they were admitted to but who aren't quite strong enough to go home just yet."

"Do you think I'll be going home soon?" Franny asked softly.

"We'll have to see what the doctor says." Tia tucked the covers neatly back around her. "Your lungs still sound a little wet so the doctor will probably want to continue your respiratory treatments for a few more days. But if they clear up, that might be a possibility."

Francis turned on the television set perched on the wall directly in front of her bed.

"So, how old is your son?" Tia asked.

"He should be around fifty-one I think."

Tia smiled. "You don't know?"

"Well, I didn't really raise him." She rubbed her shoulder. "It's a long story, you know."

Tia finished documenting her assessment and looked at her. "You're probably ready to go home, huh?"

Francis shrugged. She pointed to the television set. "You know that's a shame about what's going on over there in Africa," she said.

Tia looked up at the latest news scrolling across the bottom of the television screen. More deaths in West Africa have been attributed to infections caused by the Ebola virus. "Yes," she said sadly, "that is a shame."

"Yeah," Franny grabbed a tissue from the table next to her bed. "All those people dying and their children left without a mother or father. That's some kind of torture," she said as she began to cry.

"Oh, don't cry," Tia said rubbing her shoulder. "You're right. It is torture. The only thing we can do is pray for a cure."

Pray. Tia remembered how she'd begun praying when Scamp had started massaging the soles of her feet. "Lord," she'd prayed between moments of euphoria, "please don't let this happen." But even as she prayed, Tia knew she had waited too late to call on God. The flickering flames of temptation that had danced around in her had, by that time, already begun to burn out of control.

Tia looked down at Franny. Her tears had been reduced to sniffles. "Are you going to be all right?" Tia asked.

Franny nodded.

Tia stared at her for a few more seconds before she realized she was not going to answer her question about going home. "Well," she said, touching her shoulder gently, "I'll be back to change that IV in a little while. If you need anything before then just call."

"I will," Franny said.

Tia walked back over to the sink and tugged at the outer rim of her latex gloves until she had pulled them down and off. As she washed her hands, she thought about all the patients she'd taken care of who were similar to Franny in that they never followed up with the doctor's recommendations.

Victory Memorial Hospital had once been deemed a central dumping ground for the majority of city residents. But since the restructuring of its financial plan, the hospital had expanded not only in space but in technology as well.

Now its specialty services were offered to all of the counties surrounding the city of Chicago, and Tia hoped Franny would follow up with the doctor's referral and take advantage of the services being offered to her once she was discharged.

Her thoughts shifted back to the memory of Scamp's fingers and the massage he'd given her the night before. She turned off the faucet and sighed. Even if she had wanted to, she wouldn't have been able to put out that fire. There was no amount of water that could have doused the inferno that had burned within her.

Lorenzo, her husband, had neglected her needs for so long that the slightest bit of attention from another man was enough to cause her to subconsciously hunt for more. Scamp had made whatever she was looking for easy to find. When he'd introduced himself in the grocery store that cold day in January, Tia had initially been resistant. But when he'd let it be known that he could give a good massage, her interest had been piqued.

Once she'd looked into his hazel eyes, it was as if she had become hypnotized. She became blind to the consequences of what their meeting would eventually lead up to, thinking only about the opportunity standing before her . . . an opportunity she was desperate to take advantage of.

Tia snatched a paper towel from the wall dispenser in Franny's room and began furiously drying her hands. They had been washed clean, but what about her soul? She threw the used paper towel into the wastebasket and walked out of the room.

Chapter Two

Lorenzo Sparks stood nervously in the middle of his parents' kitchen, staring at the stainless steel toaster on the countertop behind his mother. The small appliance glistened in the setting sunlight that filtered through the window, and he was thankful for the rays that bounced off its metal rim. It created a blinding effect and gave him a reason not to look directly into his mother's disbelieving eyes.

"Son, are you sure?" his mother asked feebly. "Are you *sure* that's what happened?"

Lorenzo glanced at his father. "Yes," he said. "He took me up to the attic and told me to take off my pants—"

"That's enough!" Lorenzo's father yelled.

The sudden loudness of his voice caused Lorenzo to jump. He jerked his head just in time to see the hostility in his father's eyes.

"I won't sit here and let you smear my brother's name!"

Lorenzo lowered his head as his father stormed out of the kitchen.

The crushing silence that followed was soon interrupted by the swishing sound of bundled straw sticks as his mother began sweeping the already immaculate kitchen floor. He watched her as she swept invisible crumbs of debris into a neat little pile. She scooped them up into the dustpan, and then deposited them into the wastebasket where they would be escorted out with the rest of the trash.

Lorenzo knew then that relinquishing the weight of what had happened to him twenty-seven years ago had been a mistake. The apathy and hostility in his parents' eyes told him so. It confirmed what he'd always feared, and what the perpetrator—his uncle—had told him would happen if he ever told anyone.

They would not believe him.

And they didn't.

The realization that his parents wouldn't or couldn't accept the truth made the burden he'd carried for so long all the heavier. Lord, would he ever be able to release this load? His shoulders slumped as his heart began to swell from the inward pain he felt. Would he ever be free?

"I guess I'll be going," he said awkwardly.

His mother continued with her make-believe cleaning.

Lorenzo slammed the door behind him and shuffled quickly to his car. With every step he took, he wished he could take back the words he'd just spoken to his parents. The car rocked gently as he squeezed his large frame behind the steering wheel. He let the engine idle while he turned on the CD player. The lyrics from a popular Gospel artist filled the surrounding space:

> *"Lord at thy feet I fall, and Lord I surrender all, and if You can forgive me of my sins. . ."*

Lorenzo turned off the radio and sighed. He put the car in gear and headed toward the interstate.

His parents lived in an upscale suburb on the North Shore of Chicago, almost parallel to I-94. As he drove along the highway, the views quickly transitioned from suburban neighborhoods to grungy residential to industrial by the time he made his exit.

He drove toward Lake Michigan, passing through an eclectic neighborhood of auto shops, liquor stores, restaurants, and churches until a winding road led him directly to the lakefront. He parked his car on a nearby parking lot and turned off the ignition.

As Lorenzo got out of his car, he looked up at the smokestacks from the factories nearby. The stream of soft gray smoke paled against the night sky that was illuminated by the city lights. There was not a single star in the sky as he watched airplanes returning from unknown destinations. He closed his eyes and prayed. *Just make it better, Lord. Please make it better.*

The flashing red light from the pier danced about his face. Why didn't his parents believe him? Why . . .? He stopped and opened his eyes. There was no use in starting another internal dialogue.

He shuddered as he pulled the collar of his coat up around his neck. Then he started walking until he found himself standing directly in front of the lake. It had been an unusually cold winter, and the temperatures for the first week in February had fluctuated between 25 degrees above zero and -25 degrees below with the wind chill factored in.

The picnic tables had all been lined up neatly against a toolshed that stood deserted for the season, and mounds of snow that had been plowed from the walkways surrounded the benches, trees, and any other area that was not in the direct path of would-be pedestrians. Off in the distance he thought he saw someone running; his dark outfit a mere silhouette.

He stared at the frozen water; its exterior decorated with never-ending patterns of cracks and curves. He could hear a soft, steady rumbling just below the surface where the water had not completely frozen. It was as if the massive body of water moved in unison, rushing to reach an unknown destination. He stood listening until the sound began to blend in with his own thoughts, until like the horizon, he could not tell where one ended and the other began.

It had been twenty-seven years and Lorenzo was still reliving the memory of what happened to him when he was eleven years old. Each time he recalled the incident it induced a kind of internal explosion within him, and the internal void he lived with became a gaping tear. It was a tear with shredded edges that continued to expand, and Lorenzo could not mend it.

He remembered the subtle curvature of the man's (whose name he refused to speak out loud) mouth, and the lies he'd used to bait him back then.

"I'm telling you, little man," the perpetrator had said to Lorenzo, "this is 1987. You better get with the program."

Lorenzo recalled the perpetrator's finger poking into his blue jean-covered thigh while he talked.

"I know what I'm talking about," he continued, "and you need to let me help you. Your girlfriend is gonna need you to tell her what to do. How are you gonna tell her if you don't know? You don't wanna look like a chump, do you?"

Back then, Lorenzo hadn't known what a chump was, but he remembered shaking his head slowly, thinking it was probably something he would not want to look like.

"And," the perpetrator added with persistence, "if you let me do this now, it won't hurt you later when she's doing it to you."

"But I don't even have a girlfriend," Lorenzo remembered saying as he watched the perpetrator blow transparent circles of cigarette smoke into the air.

"But you will," he'd said. "You will."

"And boys can get hurt?" Lorenzo had asked.

"Oh yeah," the perpetrator said, baring his crooked, mushroom-colored teeth. "Guys get hurt too."

Before anything happened, Lorenzo attempted to verify the accuracy of what he'd been told. He'd asked his mother if it was true that "doing it" with a girl for the first time was painful for the boy. The sound of shattering glass from the plate his mother dropped was still vivid in his memory.

"Where'd you get that information from?" his father had asked, looking at him as if he'd lost his mind.

Lorenzo had opened his mouth to tell, but then he remembered he'd been sworn to secrecy by the perpetrator. "Nowhere," he'd answered. "I was just wondering."

"Well, wonder yourself on upstairs," his father had said sternly. "You ain't got no business thinking about stuff like that. Go on upstairs and read a book. Get your mind out of the gutter."

Several days later, when the perpetrator knew no one would be at home except Lorenzo, he came to the house. He took Lorenzo up to the attic, reminding him along the way about his vow of secrecy. He told him to lie down on the dusty wooden floor, and Lorenzo, surrounded by items long forgotten or no longer wanted, silently wondered why the thing being done to him for his own good had to be kept a secret.

Just a few days later, the perpetrator wanted to "help" Lorenzo again, and had carried him into the downstairs bathroom. But Lorenzo had begun to sense that something was not right with this kind of "help." He remembered struggling and kicking until the perpetrator had given up. That had been the last time Lorenzo allowed himself to be in the same room alone with the perpetrator. Still, the damage had already been done.

He had wanted to tell someone what had happened, but his uncle had convinced him that if he told it would be Lorenzo who got into trouble. And so, believing yet another lie, Lorenzo kept the secret and grew up convinced that it had all been his fault.

He shuddered as he remembered lying in the attic, frightened and confused while the perpetrator "helped" him to become a better boyfriend for his nonexistent girl-friend. The intricate patterns formed by the cobwebs in the corner of the ceiling were still etched in his memory. And Lorenzo wondered how long they had been there, hidden in plain sight.

He looked around the deserted lakefront. He had no idea how long he'd been standing in that one spot, but the numbness in his cheeks let him know it was time to go.

Chapter Three

Lorenzo left the lakefront and drove until he saw the petite gray and white house nestled between a boarded-up tavern and a dilapidated storefront. Empty plastic bottles, paper, and other debris littered the curbside, and he parked his car under the one streetlight still working. He carefully checked out his surroundings before getting out of the car, and then he walked swiftly up to the wooden door.

He knocked once on the unfinished surface, then three more times in rapid succession. The stench of sweat and smoke greeted Lorenzo as a tall, muscular man opened the door just enough for Lorenzo to squeeze through. The man turned his clean shaven head toward the basement of the crack house, and Lorenzo walked down the rickety stairs that creaked each time he placed his full weight of 380 pounds on them.

As it always did, the battle between his flesh and mind waged on. With each unsteady step he took, the morality of his mind fought to be heard over the lustful persistence of his flesh. Lorenzo licked his lips. He needed this, and that was all there was to it. He hurried down the steps, eager to become immersed in the darkness that kept his soul in captivity.

As he entered the dimly lit basement, the intermingling odor of feces and urine quickly clung to his polyester jacket like a leech. He turned the corner and entered another semidarkened room where men and women, young and old, had all found a space where they could disappear right in front of his eyes. Lorenzo intended to disappear as well . . . just as soon as he got what he came for.

Although he had entered a crack house, the rock hard substance was not what he had come for. Opiates, in the form of painkillers, were his drug of choice. He continued down the grim hallway until he reached the last room on the left where the drug dealer sat behind a tattered and stained folding table.

This drug dealer was a jack-of-all-trades with a menacing demeanor when it came to assisting others in the destruction of their lives; little by little, one hit from the pipe—or in Lorenzo's case, one pill at a time. But Lorenzo couldn't see any of that. He couldn't see beyond his misery or how much he wanted the pain to stop. All he knew was that the handful of pills he was about to purchase would make all of his unpleasant feelings go away.

"What you want?" the dealer asked Lorenzo without looking up. He was surrounded by three other menacing figures who did all the looking for him.

"The usual," Lorenzo said as he quickly placed four twenty-dollar bills on the table. The tug-of-war within him continued as did his pain. He wanted to leave, just run up the steps and out the door, but his misery would not allow him to do so . . . not until he had gotten the pills.

The dealer snatched the money from the table, and then reached into a mop bucket underneath the chair he was sitting on. "Here you go," he said as he slid a small plastic bag across the table.

Lorenzo grabbed the tiny bag with four round pills inside, and turned to leave without saying a word.

"See you next time," the dealer said.

The condescending tone in his voice may as well have been an arrow piercing straight through the center of Lorenzo's soul. He stumbled past the lifeless shadows lurking in the murky environment. He made it to the steps and left the same way he had entered.

The nagging pull at his conscience, combined with the arrow still penetrating his soul, was too much. Lorenzo took two of the pills out of the bag and swallowed them before he'd even gotten to the car. Later, he would take the other two and everything would be all right. At the very least, the void in him would be gone, and that would be good enough.

He started the car, hoping the pills' numbing effects would kick in by the time he got home. As he drove, he thought about all the years he'd been trying to convince himself that everything was all right, that *he* was all right. His self-persuasion had never really worked, and the events of today had been an accumulation of just how wrong everything truly was. It had ended with his visit to his parents' house, but it had started that Wednesday morning with his wife, Tia.

He'd been lying in bed next to her, trying to think of something to say that would make amends for what had happened. He was trying to find a way to apologize again for the physical spasm of emotion he'd been able to conjure up, but that had ended seconds after it had begun. What could he say that he hadn't already said before?

He remembered studying the limbs on the birch tree outside of his window, noting how still they remained under the weight of the fresh February snowfall. And then finally the words had come. "You're my soul mate," he'd spoken softly to his wife. There. He'd finally said something loving.

But Tia had remained stone-faced and silent.

Lorenzo had taken a deep breath. "You know that, don't you?" He'd forced himself to look down at her. The pasty white streak traveling down the right side of her dark brown cheek let him know she'd been crying.

"No, I don't," she'd answered coldly. "How can I?"

He'd gotten out of the bed after that and had gone back into the living room where he'd begun sleeping at night, preferring the company of a television set to that of his wife. Sometimes, Tia would come to him in the middle of the night and try to get him to come to bed. Lorenzo would pretend not to feel her shaking him or he would mumble "okay" just to get her to stop, but daylight would find him right where she had left him.

It didn't bother him that months had gone by since he'd last made love to his wife. And he didn't care about the wall of resentment he was creating between them because of it. After awhile, Tia stopped getting out of bed to wake him. And Lorenzo didn't care about that either.

The pills had not kicked in yet, and the familiar sensation of emptiness returned to Lorenzo. He parked his car in front of his house and waited for the dull emotional pain that he knew would follow. This time he tried to convince himself that the pain was not really present. But it was, and it would not be dismissed simply by his denial of its presence. He got out of his car and slammed the door shut. His pain was real, and it had become quite unbearable.

Chapter Four

The crescent circles forming at the top of Franny's pale blue gown grew bigger and wetter. She waited until she could no longer hear the fixed rhythm of Tia's synthetic heels hitting the hallway floor outside of her room. Then she released the full volume of her tears. She wasn't crying because of the Ebola outbreak in West Africa. She was crying because of the predicament she was in.

It had been two weeks since she'd driven herself to Victory Memorial Hospital and shuffled up to the registration desk complaining of leg pain. After an assessment of her swollen legs was done by one of the emergency room doctors, she was told that she needed to be seen by a vascular specialist.

The doctor suggested she follow up with her primary care physician the next day for a referral. But the next day found her back in the emergency room—this time complaining of shortness of breath. The doctor who had treated her hours earlier asked her if she had contacted her primary care physician like he had advised her to do.

"I didn't have a chance to." Franny's voice had quivered. "When I woke up this morning, I could hardly breathe!"

She remembered following the doctor's eyes as they traveled up to her gray disheveled hair, and then back down to her stained blue dress, and she wondered if he noticed that it was the same dress she'd worn the night before.

"We're going to admit you for a full cardiac workup and a consultation with a vascular surgeon," he'd said before leaving the room.

Well, at least she'd had somewhere to stay temporarily. Now, they were talking about the possibility of releasing her in the next few days. Where would she go? She'd been sleeping in her car for weeks, but she couldn't keep doing that. It had gotten far too cold.

She turned to the news channel on the television set. A young man was reporting on the status of homeless shelters in the surrounding area.

"Due to the extremely cold weather," the reporter said, *"all shelters are full. But one shelter has decided to keep their doors open all night."*

Franny watched as he walked into a small building with his cameraman right behind him. The uninviting room was already half-filled with men and women who were lounging on plastic chairs reading newspapers. Some of the women rummaged through stacks of clothing laid out on a white vinyl table that had been pushed against the wall. Quite a few of the men had congregated in front of the steam radiator, eager to thaw away the cold that had set up residence in their bones.

"Love and Faith Rescue Mission has extra seating set up," the reporter announced as the cameraman spanned the room to reveal multiple rows of chairs situated in the large space. *"They'll be extra blankets, hot coffee, and cocoa as well,"* he added.

Franny did not want to spend the night sleeping on a chair. She didn't want to spend the night in a shelter at all. She dried her eyes and took a few moments to regain her composure. Then she picked up the phone and called her estranged son, Homer.

She'd gotten pregnant with Homer when she was seventeen years old. The eighteen-year-old boy who'd gotten her pregnant had joined the army shortly after she'd told him the news. The year was 1963, and it had been gut-wrenching for Franny to find herself pregnant and unmarried.

Even now, fifty-one years later, she could still remember the terrible ache in her heart after Homer's father went missing in action. She never saw him again, and her heart was left feeling like there was a vice grip around it. Somehow, she knew she would never be the same after that.

Charlotte, Franny's mother, had made the decision to send her daughter away until after she'd had the baby. So Franny had stayed at a facility that offered pregnant girls the opportunity to continue their education while providing a reprieve for them during their pregnancy.

When Homer was born, and Franny saw the curled up claw where his left foot should have been, the vice grip around her heart was replaced by a fracture, which caused her heart to crack and shatter. The deformity was more than she could handle. It was the last straw.

She left Homer with her now-deceased mother shortly after he was born and enrolled in an out-of-state university. In the beginning, she called weekly to check on Homer's well-being.

"How's my baby?" she'd ask her mother.

"He's doing fine," Charlotte would reassure her.

"How's he doing with that foot?"

"He's making a lot of progress in therapy."

"Is it still balled up?"

Each time Franny asked that question, she always hoped to hear her mother say that Homer's foot had somehow miraculously uncurled itself and had become a normal-looking foot. But that was never the case, and her heart sank each time she heard the answer.

"Yes," Charlotte had said. "It'll probably stay that way, but Homer is going to be just fine."

As time passed, her weekly calls became every other week, then once a month. Soon, months went by without her calling to check on her son. And for every month that passed without her calling was a month she managed to subdue the guilt inside of her just a little bit more.

She never told any of her college classmates or her roommate that she had a son. And by the end of her freshman year, the facade had become her reality. The guilt—having been hushed into silence—became temporarily nonexistent.

The financial aid Franny received from the government was not enough to cover all of her expenses, and Charlotte had refused to help her.

"I'm taking care of your son," Charlotte had said. "That's my help, and that's all the help you're going to get from me."

So Franny had gotten a job through the campus work-study program, and divided her time between studying and working to supplement the cost of her tuition. After graduating, she'd worked for a short time as a nanny, taking care of another woman's son and daughter.

The irony of what she was doing had not escaped her. There she was taking care of someone else's children while rejecting her own child. *Men do it all the time*, she'd told herself. *They make babies, and then leave babies.* Including her son's father. And it was this way of thinking that allowed her to continue living without having any physical contact with her child.

Eventually, she began working for the Department of Health and Human Services as an administrative assistant. The job paid well, and she was able to save a great deal of money, some of which she sent home to her mother every week. Still, she had not returned home to see her son.

On Homer's fifth birthday, Charlotte called Franny. "When are you coming home to see your son?" she asked.

"I've been so busy," Franny had said. "I'm trying to make plans now, but it's so hard. How's he doing?"

"Well, he gets teased about his foot sometimes," Charlotte said, "because of the limp, but other than that he's all right."

Two more years passed without a visit from Franny, and on Homer's eighth birthday, Franny received a legal document from Charlotte requesting to become Homer's legal guardian.

"You don't spend no time with the boy," Charlotte had said, "so you may as well sign them. If you don't, I'll just take you to court."

It didn't take Franny long to accept her own justification that she was not giving her son away but was leaving him in a stable environment with his grandmother, a blood relative.

After making Charlotte Homer's legal guardian, Franny began to visit him.

Even though Homer knew Franny was his biological mother, he would always address her by her first name and refer to Charlotte as "Mom."

It seemed to Franny that after each instance of Homer calling his grandmother "Mom," he'd make a deliberate point of looking at Franny. The look of contempt in his eyes made her cringe, and then he'd limp past her to the opposite side of the room and just stare at her.

The visits had become increasingly uncomfortable for Franny, which caused her to keep them short and infrequent. As Homer got older, she would come to visit, and he would be nowhere to be found.

"Where's Homer?" Franny would ask Charlotte.

"I don't know where that boy went," Charlotte would say. "I told him you were coming, and the next thing I knew he was gone."

Eventually, it became easier for Franny to pretend she did not have a son, and that's exactly what she did until Homer came looking for her after he'd graduated from college. By that time Franny had moved back to Chicago, and Charlotte had let Homer know. When he'd asked for his mother's address, Charlotte had given it to him. But when he showed up on Franny's doorstep, she'd quickly realized it was not because he wanted a happy reunion. Homer had made it clear to her that he had not forgiven her for abandoning him. And their relationship had remained distant and strained ever since.

The phone rang three times before Homer answered.

"Hello?"

The deep sound of his voice intimidated Franny. Her heartbeat quickened. "Hello, Homer," she said, trying to control the tremor in her voice.

He paused before he spoke. "Yes?"

"I've been in the hospital," she told the dull voice on the other end of the line. "But I might be released in a few days."

Homer made a sound that was similar to that of pressurized air being released. Then he spoke. "Where will you go?"

Franny was quiet.

"Hello?"

"I'm here," she answered. "I was wondering if you could pick me up when they release me."

"And take you where?"

Franny could hear the agitation in his voice. She took a deep breath. "I was wondering if I could stay with you for a couple of months. I've already applied for senior housing so it shouldn't be longer than that."

"I don't know," he said. "My place is not that big. I mean it's me and Sandra, and you . . . Where have you been sleeping? Why can't you go home?"

She looked around the barren hospital room. The pale gray walls and neutral décor were incomparable to the material comforts she'd had in her three-bedroom, two-bath Cape Cod home; a home that she'd lived in for the past twelve years. But ever since she retired, it had been a struggle to maintain her same standard of living.

The truth was that she had financially miscalculated everything. And the Social Security check she received along with her pension just wasn't enough to pay the mortgage, utilities, and other miscellaneous bills.

If there had been anyone else she could have called on, she would have. Anyone . . . other than her son who she knew still held a grudge against her. But there was no one. Franny had never married, and while she'd made acquaintances through the years, she had never maintained any lasting friendships. Now, being homeless had only caused her to shun the few acquaintances she had.

She looked around the drab room again. Yes, Lord. She would love nothing more than to go back to her home. But what she wanted to do, and what she *could* do were two different things. The house had already gone into foreclosure, and she had been evicted. She remembered the day she'd come home and found the yellow notice of eviction taped to her front door.

The bright neon color had stood out like a traffic light at midnight, and she remembered the sinking feeling she'd felt in her heart. Franny had known from the color of the paper what the notice meant before she'd ever made it up the walkway. It had been clearly visible not only to her but to her neighbors as well, and she'd quickly snatched it off the door.

She'd had no one close she could call on to help her pack and move so little by little, she had packed her life's belongings into various-size boxes and bins and had professional movers take them along with her furniture to a storage unit she'd rented.

She remembered the panic that had settled within her and would not leave. Thank God she'd had the foresight to see the eviction coming and had already applied for senior housing. But the timing was still off, and she was faced with the reality of having no place to live.

The first week, she rented a motel room, but that quickly became an unaffordable option. She then made the decision to sleep in her car rather than ask anyone for help, and so she'd checked out of the motel room and parked her car on the parking lot behind the motel.

Her first night of being homeless was filled with anguish, discomfort, and fear. And she'd prayed all night for the Lord to be with her and protect her. She'd stayed awake the entire night, letting the car run at intervals as the temperature outside dropped.

By daybreak, her fear had subsided, along with her tears. But something had gone terribly wrong. How had she ended up in a situation like this? She had worked all her life, and this is what it had amounted to?

Franny had felt trapped and alone. Still, she clung to her belief that God was going to work it all out. She told herself that any day the manager of the senior housing complex would be calling her to tell her that an apartment was available. She just had to hold on.

The second and third nights weren't any easier, but she told herself it could be worse. At least she had access to running water and a bathroom at the 24-hour restaurant across the street. But then her leg had begun to swell and ache, and she'd driven herself to the hospital.

It had been so nice and warm in the examining room, and when the doctor had completed his examination and released her, she didn't want to leave. She'd reluctantly returned to her cold car. It had taken everything in her to keep from crying as she'd slid behind the steering wheel and looked at the icy crystals covering the windshield. The following morning, she'd begun to have difficulty breathing, and had returned to the hospital.

"Hello?" Homer yelled into the phone. "Are you still there?"

Instead of answering his question, Franny repeated herself. "It would only be for two months," she said. "Just until I can get into senior housing."

"I'm sorry," her only child continued, "but there's just not enough room."

Franny closed her eyes as she felt the heaviness in her heart make its way up to her throat. She hung up the phone without saying good-bye. What else could she do? The heaviness in her heart would not allow her to speak, and now it was keeping her from moving her left arm.

Chapter Five

Lorenzo turned the key in the lock and opened the front door. He reached into the pocket of his stench-filled jacket and took out the small plastic bag containing the last two pills. After he placed them on the living-room table, he took off his jacket and let it fall to the floor. Then he went into the living room, grabbed the blanket from the microfiber couch, and began folding it. After he was finished, he threw it on the back of the couch and the gust of air it created knocked the wedding picture of him and Tia off the end table.

Lorenzo picked up the courthouse photo and studied Tia's face framed by tiny locks of hair. They stood side by side, and he towered over her as she smiled into the camera. He remembered his parents attending the occasion, stoic witnesses, and then quickly leaving after the ceremony had ended.

It had been a dismal affair with everyone returning to whatever they had been doing afterward, treating the whole thing as something on their to-do list that could now be crossed off.

He gazed at his lean frame in the photograph, and then traveled up to the pathetic smile that was plastered on his face. That smile had made him look like a happy man, and he remembered praying to God that his union with Tia would somehow turn him into one.

He sat down on the couch and thought about when he'd first met Tia thirteen years ago at a War concert.

He'd sworn it had been love at first sight. She had been so beautiful and petite, and he'd loved how his six-foot frame towered over hers at five-foot four.

They had maintained a long-distance relationship for a year, and then shortly after he had been introduced to Jesus, Tia had gotten pregnant. He could still recall her visiting him in Chicago, and how he had begun to share with her what he had learned about Jesus.

"See, we're all broken," he'd said. "And we all need fixing . . . and somebody to do the fixing." That much he remembered saying to her. The rest he knew—whether he'd said it to her or not—was that something was missing, especially inside of him.

"You just have to trust God," he'd said, and now she was going to church every Sunday without him.

When he'd told her they needed to do the right thing, he'd meant it. But needing to do the right thing and wanting to were two different things in Lorenzo's mind. Still, he'd asked her to marry him, and he remembered her saying, "If you want me here, then this is where I'll be."

He continued looking at the photograph he still held in his hand. Their first year of marriage had almost been their last. He'd been controlling and insensitive, and had actually put his hands on Tia once. To make matters worse, she had been eight months pregnant at the time. Lorenzo didn't know what had come over him. It was almost as if he had undergone a complete personality change once they'd gotten married.

He'd slapped her—he remembered that much. But he was unclear about the reason why. He rubbed his forehead. The pills he'd taken earlier were starting to do their job. His mind was getting foggy, and he didn't want to think about anything unpleasant. Still, he sat on the sofa, straining to remember what had happened.

Tia had brought something home from the grocery store. What had it been? He closed his eyes and thought harder. Caffeine. That's what it had been! She had bought a box of caffeinated tea bags—something he'd told her he didn't want her drinking while she was pregnant. He opened his eyes. Had that really been the reason for his inexcusable behavior or had he put his hands on her due to his own inner frustrations?

When he'd almost missed the birth of their daughter, that had been the last straw for Tia. "I can't stay with you the way things are," she'd said to him from her hospital bed.

She was going to leave him. One life had begun while his was ending. He could not be alone again. He remembered getting on his knees in the hospital room, crying as he'd asked Tia to forgive him before praying to God asking for that and much more.

Tia forgave him and stayed.

For a while, Lorenzo was all right. He kept his job as an electrical engineer and went to work every day. He couldn't say that he was happy, but he'd been renewed enough to feel contentment. But Lorenzo had failed to ask for what he really needed, which was healing and deliverance from the abuse he'd suffered as a young boy.

By the time their daughter, Serenity, was eleven years old, his recurring pain had intensified, and he could no longer deny that marrying Tia had done nothing to alleviate it. If anything, it seemed to have gotten worse. His weight had doubled since he'd gotten married, and he couldn't stand lying next to his own wife in bed night after night.

He put the photograph back on the end table. The past two years of his marriage had been blemished with too many resentments, and infrequent and dull episodes of intimacy between the two of them. Their marriage had become nothing more than a façade, and not a very good one at that. On top of all that, there had been issues with his attendance throughout the year and he'd been let go from his job. His only source of income was the weekly unemployment check he'd been receiving for the past six months.

He rubbed the creases in his forehead and turned on the DVD player. A sixteen-ounce bag of raisins drenched in a creamy blanket of milk chocolate lay on the coffee table next to an open bag of previously popped microwave popcorn. Lorenzo grabbed a handful of each and stuffed them all into his mouth as he began watching his favorite movie, *Antwone Fisher*.

Two hours later, the movie ended, and Lorenzo was catapulted back into reality. He stopped the DVD and switched back to the television. A well-endowed female with exaggerated cheekbones spoke loudly with an East Coast accent. Lorenzo tried to focus on what she was saying, but the dream he'd had the night before roared even louder in his memory.

It was always the same. In his dream there was a big open field behind a triangular building. Lorenzo always thought it was a mall. There was only one entrance, and that was through the front door. If anyone tried to enter from the back of the building they would end up in total darkness. Lorenzo would look up to see a big sign that read: WARNING. DO NOT ENTER THROUGH THE REAR! Then the dream would end. It always ended there, and he would wake up feeling clammy and short of breath.

"Why are you always in such an irritated mood?" Tia would ask him.

"Irritated?" he'd shout. "That's an understatement! You," he'd point his finger in her face, "have no idea how I feel!"

"You're right," she'd say. "I don't know how you feel!" Then her voice would suddenly soften. "Tell me what it is. How can I help you if you won't tell me what's wrong?"

Lorenzo didn't know why, but he hated it when Tia softened her voice. It was as if she was trying to play psychiatrist with him or something. Well, he wasn't having it. Not at all. She was a nurse not a psychiatrist, and she needed to remember that!

"I'm not the enemy," she'd said. "I'm your wife."

She'd almost got him with that comment. He'd opened his mouth to speak. He was going to try to tell her his secret when the next thing she'd said messed it all up.

"A real man would know the difference."

A real man? So now she was implying that he was not a real man?

After she'd said that, Lorenzo knew he would not be able to tell her what was wrong. He cringed at the thought of how she might react if she knew he had been molested as a child by his uncle. Would she hold the same look in her eyes as his father had held in his? Would she blame him with unspoken words as his mother had done? Lorenzo had decided he couldn't take that risk. If Tia thought he wasn't a real man, she definitely wouldn't think so after he'd told her his secret.

So he left things the way they were—with his wife not knowing what he had been through or what he could not get past. He sighed heavily. He was so far from being irritated that to feel that way now would have been a blessing. No. Lorenzo was way past irritated. He was done. Defeated.

Game over.

Chapter Six

Fifteen minutes later, Tia walked through the front door of her house. Her German shepherd, Catch, raced around the corner to greet her. He was as loyal as dogs came. He stood up on his hind legs, and the full force of his weight pushed her 115-pound frame backward until there was no space left between her back and the mahogany door she'd just closed. He continued to lavish her with tongue licks and shoulder paws, and Tia thought about how some women often referred to men as dogs.

She looked over at Lorenzo slouched on the couch and—in his case—she wished he would act like a dog, their dog. She gave Catch a final hug and squeezed past his bulky frame.

"Hey," she said to Lorenzo. She tried to make her voice sound light and airy. "How's it going?"

"Fine," Lorenzo answered simultaneously tapping his fingers on the end table.

A stifling silence filled the air.

"Where's Serenity?" Tia asked.

"At the library, I think, or over at one of her girlfriends' house. I'm not sure."

"She's supposed to be home," Tia said hanging up her coat. "It's Wednesday night."

Lorenzo got up and walked past Tia into the kitchen, slightly kicking his jacket on the floor as he passed.

The stench attached to the jacket was activated by the movement, and Tia's nostrils flared. "What's that smell?" she asked, frowning.

"What smell?"

"Like something rotten," she said with a scowl. "You don't smell that?"

"Nope."

She followed him into the kitchen. "Lorenzo, we need to talk."

He didn't respond as he turned on the oven, and then took a slab of beef ribs out of the refrigerator.

"Look, Lorenzo," she said, "something needs to change. I need to be touched, and hugged, and made love to. By you," she added. "My husband."

Lorenzo carefully began removing the plastic wrapping from the meat.

Tia sighed. "What's the problem, Lorenzo?"

"I don't have a problem," he said, half-swirling his neck so that he could look at her briefly. "But if you think I do," he turned away and began cutting through a boney section of the meat, "why don't you just leave?"

"*Really?*" Tia's eyebrows arched as she stood staring at his broad back. "Is that the only solution you can come up with? That I should leave?"

He continued separating the ribs into smaller sections, throwing each one into a pan as he severed the tendons and flesh that held them all together. "Well, you're the one complaining," he said, shifting his weight to one leg.

"Right." Tia placed her hands on her hips. "And why do you think that is?" She waited for him to respond as he put the last rib in the pan, and then began to season them.

"Are you going to answer me, Lorenzo?" She could feel her heartbeat increasing. "I'm trying to talk to you."

He gave the ribs a gentle rub, and she felt a pang of jealousy. So this is what it had come to?—She was competing with a slab of ribs for his attention. "You see that?" She was near hysterics as she pointed to the ribs. "When's the last time you rubbed *me* like that?" Her eyes were bulging. "When's the last time you touched me—period?"

He opened the door to the preheated oven and slid the pan onto the top shelf. "I really don't have anything to say," he said as he closed the oven door.

Tia raised her arms in the air. "Then what am I supposed to do, Lorenzo? I'm still young. I didn't get married to become abstinent!"

He washed his hands, and then turned to face her. His glare pierced her like a frozen dagger. "I already told you," he said, the callousness of his voice adding to the chill already forming within her, "why don't you just leave?"

Tia held her breath. She would not let him see her cry again.

He walked back into the living room and sat down in front of the television set.

She stormed out of the kitchen after him. "Is that what you really want, Lorenzo?"

He was surfing the channels with the remote control, finally stopping to watch the last few minutes of a game show hosted by a popular comedian. "Can we talk about this later?" He waved her away as he chuckled at something the television host said. "Or better yet," he said without removing his eyes from the television, "can we not talk about this at all?"

"I don't understand you," Tia said despising the shrill sound of her voice. "Why are you so irritated?"

He inhaled deeply. "I told you my back has been hurting me, okay?" he lied.

"And what about the other times?"

He turned to face her. "What did I tell you?" he said sternly.

Tia didn't answer. Lorenzo's attempt to make love to her earlier that morning had once again been unsuccessful. Through the years his weight had doubled, and she was willing to take that into consideration for the failed attempt, but there were ways to get around that. And she hadn't believed him when he'd said his back was hurting any more than she'd believed him when he'd said they were soul mates. Yeah, right, she'd thought. Soul mates who aren't mating.

Lorenzo's complaint of back pain had not begun until after he'd been fired from his job as an electrical engineer for a large retail chain. Around the same time, he had started making visits to a doctor who began prescribing multiple medications for him: one to relieve pain, one to relax his muscles, and another to help him sleep.

His steadily declining mood had not gone unnoticed by Tia, and she had pointed out to Lorenzo that he was being prescribed too many different medications, and that all of them caused drowsiness. "I *am* a nurse, you know," she'd said. But her comments had elicited no response from him.

She stood staring at his empty eyes—another change in him—that had become cold and uncaring. "Can't you show me *some* kind of affection?" she asked. "I mean, I cook for you. I clean and wash for you. I'm here . . . ," she spread open the palms of her hands, ". . . for you. Can't you show me *something,* Lorenzo?"

"I don't need a wife to cook and clean for me," he said in the same detached way he'd begun using whenever he spoke to her. "As you can see," he pointed to the kitchen, "I know how to cook. And I certainly know how to clean."

She frowned. "Then what *do* you need a wife for?"

"I don't *need* a wife for anything," he said, swirling his neck again. "Let's get that straight first."

They glared at each other for a few seconds before Tia spoke. "Then why did you marry me, Lorenzo?"

Even though she felt defeated, she was hoping he would say because he loved her, needed her, and honestly couldn't live without her. Instead, he answered her by turning his attention back to the television set as the theme song from the weekly series, *Jeopardy*, began playing.

"You know what?" she said sarcastically. "What one man won't do, another one will. You better remember that."

"Do whatever you have to do," he said quietly, and then turned up the volume on the television set.

"I will," she said as she stormed up the stairs and entered what used to be the bedroom they shared.

She changed out of her nursing uniform into a pair of jeans and a plain white cotton tee shirt and quickly went back downstairs. She clutched her Bible and stopped at the entrance to the living room. "Can you at least come to the evening service with me tonight?"

"No, thank you," Lorenzo answered without diverting his attention from the television set. "I'm good."

"No, you're not good," she said as she stomped back up the stairs to her room. She opened her journal and flipped to the page with the calendar printed on it. She placed an "X" on the eighth day of February, and then she placed the leather-bound book on top of her partially packed suitcase in the closet.

You're a long way from good, she thought as she returned downstairs and slammed the front door behind her.

Chapter Seven

Homer tried to maintain his composure as he stood at his window watching Tia slam the front door of her house and storm down the walkway to her SUV. He watched his neighbor speed out of the cul-de-sac and make a left turn without slowing down or signaling.

It wasn't the phone call he'd received earlier from his mother that had upset him. It was the fact that she actually thought he would pick her up from the hospital, and allow her to live in his home. That's what had him bothered. He tapped his fingers across the windowpane.

His mother had willingly relinquished her rights the day she left him with her mother, his grandmother, and then made it legal when he was eight years old. He was certainly not going to come to her rescue now when she had never been there for him. Let her stay in the hospital or somewhere else, but it would not be with him. That was not going to happen.

He looked up at the mishmash of clouds sprawled indiscriminately across the fading aqua blue sky. There was no break in the frigid temperatures forecast for tomorrow; only more of the same iciness.

"Was that your mother on the phone?"

Homer sighed as he turned to see his wife, Sandra, staring at him.

"Yes," his answer came short and quick.

"What'd she want?"

"She just wanted to see how I was doing," he answered impatiently as he continued to stare at her.

"What's wrong?" she asked frowning.

"I know you're not planning on leaving the house with that top on."

Sandra looked down at the V-neck blouse she had on. It stopped three inches from her neck, barely revealing the edges of her collarbone. She frowned. "What's wrong with this shirt?"

"Well, for one thing, your chest is all out."

"No, it's not," she said softly. "You can't see anything."

His eyes grew big. "Oh, I can see plenty!" he said. "And ain't nobody got time for that."

"Whatever," she mumbled under her breath as she walked out of the bedroom and sat down on the couch.

She tried to justify his comments by telling herself that he only said those things because he cared about how she looked. But a feeling of weariness had been festering in her. It was mentally exhausting to keep rationalizing his controlling ways by placing them under the guise of care and concern. She was supposed to be his wife, not his child.

She turned on the television just in time for the five o'clock news. The anchorman was talking about the payroll tax hike that went into effect in January, and how it had caused an estimated reduction in the average American worker's paycheck by almost $100 per month.

"Man," she mumbled. "Pretty soon nobody's gonna have any money but the rich!"

Homer had followed her into the living room. Although their immaculate ranch-style house was the smallest of the four houses on the cul-de-sac, it was large enough for the two of them.

There was a short foyer upon entering the house which led into a small living room on the right and a hallway on the left. The hallway led to a medium-size bathroom and one bedroom on one side, followed by another larger bedroom on the other side.

The small eat-in kitchen right off the living room had a door that led to a dark and seldom-used basement. Sandra didn't like the basement and never went down there. "It has a dark vibe," she'd said.

Homer was the only one who went into the basement, and he did so whenever he had loads of stained clothing that needed to be washed. He'd throw the dirty clothing into an old washing machine that he had placed beneath one of the two basement windows. Yellowed sheets of newspaper covered the bottom half of one of the windows, and Homer had spent many days standing there watching as his neighbor, Tia, and her daughter, had come and gone.

"We're doing all right," Homer said, bending down to rearrange the magazines on the coffee table. "I have my accounting job, and that's more than enough."

"I know we're supposed to be middle income," Sandra said, "but sometimes . . ."

Homer stood up. "Sometimes what?"

Sandra rubbed her ear nervously. "Nothing," she said.

"No, what were you going to say?" he asked defensively.

"I'm just saying," Sandra chose her words slowly, "that if I got a job . . ."

Homer waved his hand as if he were backhanding a pesky insect. "Don't start," he said.

"I'm not," Sandra said meekly. "I'm just saying."

"Not feeling like we're middle income doesn't have anything to do with you getting a job," Homer said. "The reason it doesn't feel like we're middle income is because that classification is quickly becoming the low income just like they've been predicting in the news."

"Yeah, well, this is Obama's second term," Sandra said with a sigh of defeat, "so I hope something changes."

She continued watching the news as the anchorman began reporting on a follow-up story about three young girls who had been missing.

"The three teenage girls who had been kidnapped eleven years ago," the anchorman said, *"were finally found when one of the girls was heard kicking and screaming at the back door of the house where they were being held captive for more than eleven years."*

"That's a shame," Sandra said shaking her head.

Homer rubbed his head in frustration. "Yeah, but that was nine months ago."

She stared at him strangely. "It just doesn't make sense," she continued.

"What don't make sense is that they're still talking about it," he said as he got up and went into the kitchen.

She looked his way again and frowned. "That's kind of insensitive, isn't it?"

Ignoring her question, he hollered over his shoulder, "When are you going to the store? I'm hungry, and sitting on that couch listening to the news is taking up too much of your time."

"I'm getting ready to go right now," she said. A smirk came to her face as she realized she still had on the blouse that he'd strongly insinuated she change. As she put on her coat, she felt like a child rebelling against a parent, but the realization that she was putting herself in the category of a child made her upset all over again.

She finished buttoning her coat. "It's making me depressed too," she said in reference to the news about the kidnapped girls. She and Homer had only been married for two years, and Sandra was glad they didn't have any children. "Kids just ain't safe nowhere," she mumbled to herself as she picked up her purse.

"Yeah, well, don't take too long," Homer said as Sandra closed the door behind her. He watched from the window until she had pulled out of the driveway. Then he grabbed his laptop and went into the bedroom.

Chapter Eight

Thank God for Wednesday night services, Lorenzo thought as Tia slammed the door behind her. He began his nightly routine of channel surfing until the soft voice of an elderly woman caught his attention. He turned up the volume and listened as she spoke about the hopelessness that so many people were feeling.

"We have an enemy in this world," she said, *"and his name is Satan. Some of you may feel like no one loves you, some of you feel empty inside, and that emptiness is slowly killing you, and you feel like you're already dead so you think you might just as well give up because you just . . . can't . . . take . . . it . . . anymore.*

"Then," she continued, *"the enemy tries to make you believe that it would be best for everybody—especially you—if you just made yourself disappear. Just ended it all."* She looked straight into the camera, and Lorenzo gripped the remote control.

"But don't you do it." She continued staring at him. *"Don't you believe it. I know the pain you're in, and God knows . . ."*

Lorenzo turned off the TV. *Nobody knows the pain I'm in.* He stared straight-ahead at the brown stucco wall. For years, he had yearned to tell his parents what had happened to him. Yet the story had remained untold. Now, after the unpleasant response he'd received from them, he'd decided he was not going to tell another soul what had happened. He wasn't even sure why he'd told them in the first place. Had he still felt the need for his parents' affirmation that he'd done nothing wrong?

Moisture began to accumulate in his eyes. He had hoped that by telling them, his burden would be released; that they would put their arms around him and tell him how sorry they were and how much they still loved him. Instead, he'd gotten just the opposite.

He dried his eyes and returned his gaze to the stucco wall in front of him. Years! It had taken him years to gather enough courage to tell them. And for what? So his mother could question him and his father could all but call him a liar? Lorenzo threw the remote control down on the table. No, he would not speak on the incident again. But what was he going to do about the nagging pain that would not go away?

The timer on the oven began beeping and startled Lorenzo. He got up too quickly and felt light-headed. He put his hand on the wall for support as he walked into the kitchen. He stood in front of the oven for a few seconds before bending down to take the pan of ribs out of the oven.

As he pulled back the foil that had been covering them, the pent-up steam escaped quickly, surrounding Lorenzo with a temporary film of mist before evaporating into the air. He pierced the meat with a fork, twisting it until the flesh began to fall away from the bone. The meat was done. He turned off the oven and returned to the living room.

Like his mother, Lorenzo had also created his own pile of dirt. But instead of taking it out to the trash, he'd become his own receptacle. For years, he'd been depositing all that grime right into his own internal trash bin. Still, the problem with dirt is that it's dirty, and no matter how neat and clean he kept himself on the outside, there was still—just beneath the surface—a garbage bin filled with dirt. And Lorenzo was so tired of feeling dirty.

He opened the tiny plastic bag he'd purchased earlier and took the illicit painkillers out. He had already swallowed two of them right after he'd purchased them. Now he swallowed the last two. He sighed as the heavy pressure from his emotional pain settled into the center of his heart. He had learned to live with the dullness of it, but it was the constant ache that he could not stand.

He would deal with it until it became unbearable—and that would not take too long—then in order to subdue it, he would do what he'd just done, what he'd been doing for quite some time until the doctor had cut him off and forced him to find his medication elsewhere; he would take two of the little white pills to make it all go away.

His secret hope of finding someone who would recognize his plight and free him from his pain was dying. He thought he'd found a rescuer in Tia because she had been easy to talk to and even easier to laugh with. He could vaguely remember the thought swirling around in his head that she might be the one who could put an end to his misery and make everything better. But she could not do for him what he could not do for himself, and he began to resent her because of it. Now, they no longer slept in the same bed and barely spoke to each other.

He began to notice that two pills were not enough to eradicate his pain—they barely numbed it. And he found himself increasing the amount of pills he took more and more.

Chapter Nine

Serenity Sparks watched her mother from across the street as she sped out of the cul-de-sac. She stood peeking through the blinds of her best friend, Cookie's, second-floor bedroom window across the street. She released the blinds when she saw Tia slam the front door of their house and walk hurriedly to her car.

"Is that your mother's car speeding down the street?" Cookie asked over her shoulder.

"Yep," Serenity answered abruptly.

"She better be careful," Cookie said, "driving fast like that."

"I know, right?" Serenity said as she looked through Cookie's pink jewelry box with a ballerina on top. "If that was us driving like that we'd never hear the end of it."

"Uh-huh," Cookie agreed. "They'd probably take our license away."

"Yeah. If we had one," Serenity said. "She's probably late for church or mad 'cause I'm not home to go with her." Serenity hesitated. "She might be mad at my daddy too. But she's always mad about something."

"How come you didn't go to church?"

Serenity shrugged. "'Cause it's boring," she said as she flipped through a fashion magazine. "How come *you* ain't at church?"

"My momma's working late, and my daddy don't feel good," Cookie said. "But I like going to church. Don't you like the youth pastor?"

"He's all right."

"How come your mom's mad at your daddy?"

"Seems like she's always mad at him," Serenity said. "It might be 'cause he's sleeping in the living room. I know she don't like that."

Cookie fell back on the purple and pink polka-dot comforter on her bed. "I wish I could sleep in the living room every night."

"Why?"

"Then I could watch *The Walking Dead* every night."

"Oh yeah," Serenity perked up. "That's my favorite show. Did you see the one about the guy sitting on top of the house eating some pudding?"

"Uh-huh," Cookie giggled. "That was too funny!"

"Ooh," Serenity yelped, picking up a magazine. "Look at this!"

The girls stared at what looked like a picture of a teenage model walking down a makeshift runway inside of a warehouse. Their eyes traveled to the exposed gray heating ducts running across the brown ceiling all the way down to the white lights situated a few inches below them. They scanned the black-and-white checkered floor of the runway, and finally the multitude of spectators all watching the one girl as the cameras captured her in motion.

"I could do that," Serenity said making a small bubble with her chewing gum, and then popping it.

Cookie looked at her friend who was mesmerized by the picture in the magazine. "You think so?" she asked.

Serenity got up and walked over to the L-shaped desk in the corner of Cookie's bedroom. "Uh-huh," she said as she sat down and turned on Cookie's computer.

There had been no school for most of the district due to a national teachers' conference, and the two girls had spent most of the day in Cookie's bedroom experimenting with eye shadow and foundation that Serenity had stolen from her mother's vast collection of cosmetics. Her mother's assortment was so huge that she had to keep them all in a bin underneath the bathroom sink.

Serenity and Cookie's thirteen-year-old faces did not require the layers of mocha and beige foundation each girl had on, and the thick line of black eyeliner that Serenity had applied to her eyelids, made her light brown eyes look hard and gothic.

Serenity clicked on the guest icon on the computer. Once the desktop appeared, she clicked on the browser.

Cookie looked at her. "Don't forget to wash your face.

"You know I won't," Serenity said twirling around in the chair. "My mom would have a fit if she saw my eyes."

"I'm surprised she let you put that red color on the end of your bangs," Cookie said.

"It's just cherry Kool-Aid," Serenity said patting down her dark brown bangs. "I told her it'll rinse out." Serenity left out the part about how Tia had warned her that if she did it again she was going to cut all of her hair off. *"And there'll be nothing left to dye," Tia had said sternly.* "You better wash your face too," Serenity said eyeballing Cookie.

Cookie looked at the computer. "Did you remember to go private?"

"Oops," Serenity said and quickly exited the chat room she had just entered.

"You can't be forgetting to do that," Cookie said. "I told you my dad checks this computer sometimes."

"Sorry," Serenity said as she moved the mouse up to the top of the computer screen, opened the drop-down box, and then clicked on Private Browsing.

The last few times she and Cookie had visited the chat room, Serenity had forgotten to sign in under Private Browsing, but she hadn't told Cookie.

"Is Saucer on?" Cookie asked.

Serenity signed back in to the online chat room, teen2teen.com, that she and Cookie often visited and looked for Saucer's screen name.

Saucer was a boy Serenity had met in the chat room several weeks ago. When he'd uploaded a picture of his face to her, the color of his skin made Serenity think of a milk chocolate bar, and his eyes—big and round—resembled a saucer. "A chocolate-brown saucer," she'd giggled to Cookie. And so that's what she called him.

She knew her parents would not like her talking to a boy—especially one that she met online. But Saucer was always saying lots of nice stuff to her, and he even wanted to take her shopping and buy her pretty things.

The screen name, iluvhotgurlz13, suddenly popped up on the screen. "Ooh," Serenity squealed, "there he is!"

Cookie looked at the time showing on the bottom of the computer screen. "Hurry up," she said. "You don't have much time!"

Serenity sat down and started typing.

> Serenity2cute_13: Hey
> iluvhotgurlz13: Hey 2 cute :) how r u?
> Serenity2cute_13: Fine :)
> iluvhotgurlz13: I bet u r lol. When r u gonna send me a pic?
> Serenity2cute_13: idk soon, lol
> iluvhotgurlz13: U don't kno when?

Serenity looked at Cookie. "What should I say?"
Before Cookie could answer, a message popped up.

> iluvhotgurlz13: u should meet me at the mall

"Ooh!" Cookie squealed. Serenity's mouth opened wide.

Serenity2cute_13: lol, my mom's not gonna let me go 2 the mall
iluvhotgurlz13: u cant go 2 the brookridge mall?
Serenity2cute_13: nope
iluvhotgurlz13: what r u? a baby? lol
Serenity2cute_13: I aint no baby
iluvhotgurlz13: jus tell ur mom u going to the library or sumthin. We might end up there, lol

Cookie stood next to Serenity, looking over her shoulder. "Yeah, that's a good idea," she said as she pulled her gum halfway out of her mouth and began twirling it around her finger. "And tell him he can see what you look like when y'all meet."

"I don't know," Serenity said to Cookie with a worried look on her face.

"What? You scared?" Cookie asked.

"No," Serenity said rolling her eyes.

"Then what?"

Serenity turned her attention back to the computer.

Serenity2cute_13: wen?

There was no activity on the screen.

"What happened?" Cookie asked.

Serenity looked at the bottom of the chat box and saw "iluvhotgirlz13 is typing . . ."

"He's typing," she said.

"Well, he better hurry up. My dad put a timer on this computer, and it's gonna go off at seven thirty."

"Seven thirty?"

"Yep. So we ain't got much time. It's seven twenty-five now."

The girls continued to wait for Saucer to finish typing. Cookie put the finger with the twirled gum on it into her mouth and pulled the gum off with her teeth. She looked at the time on the computer, and then glanced toward her bedroom door. "Come on," she started rotating her hand in a circular motion. Finally, he responded.

> iluvhotgurlz13: The mall is gonna be crowded, lol. How bout u meet me across the street?
> Serenity2cute_13: where?
> iluvhotgurlz13: on the parking lot in front of that pizza restaurant that closed down

Cookie looked at the clock on the computer. It read seven twenty-eight. "The computer's gonna shut down," she said.

Serenity quickly typed her response.

> Serenity2cute_13: wen?
> iluvhotgurlz13: Sunday

"You gotta get off," Cookie said.

> Serenity2cute_13: g2g

Serenity signed out of the chat room. The two girls looked at each other and giggled.

"You gonna meet him for real?" Cookie asked as the timer began shutting down the computer.

"Maybe," Serenity said. She began swirling around in the chair and almost knocked the lamp off the desk.

"Be careful, Serenity, dang!" Cookie said catching the lamp just as it began to fall.

"Sorry," Serenity said as she got up from the computer and went into the bathroom to wash her face. A few minutes later, she returned with a youthful face void of all makeup. She put on her coat, and then walked over to where she'd left the fashion magazine and picked it up. "Can I take this home with me?"

"I don't care," Cookie said. "But bring it back."

"Thanks," Serenity said, tripping on the edge of the rug as she opened the bedroom door to leave.

Cookie rolled her eyes. "Girl, if you gon' be a fashion model you better stop all that trippin'. You gon' kill yourself before you even get started."

"Whatever," she said as they both went downstairs.

They entered the living room where Cookie's parents, Tony and Shari, were sitting next to each other on the love seat.

"Hey," Shari said. "What have you young ladies been up to on your day off?"

"Nothing," Cookie replied. "Just hanging out."

"How was your day, Mrs. Wiles?" Serenity asked.

"It was okay. I had to work a little later than usual but it was fine." Shari rose from the couch. "Did you want to stay for dinner?"

"No, thank you," Serenity said. "I think my mom probably wants me home now."

"Okay. Well, tell her I said hi."

"I will." Serenity turned to look at Cookie. "See ya later."

"See ya," Cookie said as she closed the door.

Serenity knew Cookie was only joking about her clumsiness, still it made her heart sting to be teased about it. She pulled her hood over her head as she carefully walked down the steps and headed to her house across the street.

Homer signed out of the chat room and stood up. He looked out his bedroom window and rubbed the back of his neck as he watched Serenity walk past his house. The skinny jeans she wore clung tightly to her long slender legs, and he estimated her to be around thirteen or fourteen years old—the same age as the girl he'd been chatting online with earlier.

Homer liked meeting young girls in chat rooms, and out of all the chat rooms he visited, teen2teen.com was his favorite. He could be anybody he wanted to be, and they never questioned him. Sometimes, he would send a picture of a handsome seventeen-year-old boy to the girls and tell them it was him. Other times, he pretended to be a young girl who was the same age as they were.

It was all in good fun and the bonus came when some of the young girls agreed to meet him at different locations. They were so gullible. Or were they? Homer believed some of the girls knew just what they were doing and were just playing the game along with him. No one could be that naïve, he thought, teenager or not.

Like the young girl he had just finished chatting with— the picture he'd sent her had been of a boy clearly older than the eighteen years Homer had said he was. Still, the girl in all her eagerness had believed him without question. Homer was looking forward to meeting this one. He had special plans for her.

Chapter Ten

Shari looked at Cookie as she closed the door behind Serenity. "Do you have any homework?"

"Yep."

"Is it done?"

Cookie shrugged.

Shari shook her head. "What does that mean?"

"I'm gonna do it."

"Uh, excuse me. Don't you have school tomorrow?"

"I'm gonna do it right after dinner, Ma," Cookie said as she headed for the kitchen.

"All right," Shari said in a tone that implied harsh consequences if Cookie didn't get it done.

Shari turned her attention to her husband who was scrolling through job postings on a career Web site. She knew his focus was not on the conversation she and Cookie had been having. At that moment, she knew his focus was on finding a full-time job in his field as an alcohol and other drug abuse counselor.

Funding for the Christian-based treatment center where Tony worked had been decreased. As a result, the center had to let some employees go. Many of the counselors were kept, but their hours had been decreased and Tony was one of them. He stayed on because a part-time job was better than no job at all. But their bills were piling up, and he needed to start looking for full-time employment.

Tony's hope was to find a counseling position with another Christian-based treatment center. As a born-again Christian and a member of the First Temple Church, he wanted to continue sharing the Word of God with those dealing with addiction. And a counseling position at a Christian-based treatment center would allow him to freely do so.

Tony knew that an addict could not fight the demons of addiction alone, and he didn't want his clients to stop at the recovery mark. He wanted them to be permanently delivered—just as he had been. He could testify that God was the ultimate deliverer because He had delivered him from an addiction to crack cocaine twenty-two years ago. And he had been clean ever since.

As is the case with any addict, it had not been Tony's intention to become one. He didn't have a sad story to tell. There were no horrific episodes of child abuse, no neglect, or extreme poverty. There was nothing he could blame for the poor choices he'd made other than just that—the choices he'd made.

He had grown up in a two-parent household. His mother and father had raised him to know Jesus, and had loved and nurtured him along with his two older sisters. But Tony had been a follower not of Jesus but of the wrong crowd. When he was eighteen years old, he allowed the negative behavior of his friends to rub off on him, and he became a rebel without a cause.

Whatever his cohorts did, he did. He became a thief, a liar, and when he foolishly experimented with crack cocaine, he became an addict. And the unpretentious life he'd once lived was disrupted for five years.

Unfortunately, Tony's life had not been the only life he'd disrupted. His parents and sisters suffered right along with him; their days and nights filled with untold anxiety each time he went on a binge and disappeared for days at a time.

"Can't you see what you're doing to your mother?" his father had asked pointing to her shrinking body. Tony's mother had always been a full-figured woman, but the worrying she did about the safety of her son had caused her to slowly lose weight.

He still remembered the day his father had lost patience with him and had forbidden him to come back to their house.

"We didn't raise you this way," he'd said full of anger. "If you want some help, act like it and we'll help you. If you don't, stop coming around here worrying your mother like you do."

Tony's two sisters understood the ways of a crack addict as well, and although they loved him dearly, they were wise enough not to let him take advantage of their emotions which even he admitted he would have done had he been given the opportunity.

When he'd asked if he could stay with either one of them, they'd both said, "No."

"Clean up your act!" they'd yelled between tears. "Get it together!"

He remembered standing in front of them wondering why they were crying. *He* should have been the one crying because what they hadn't understood was that he didn't have the power to get it together. He *couldn't* clean up his act. He'd tried. Many times.

He'd uttered prayers to God for deliverance. But they had been heartless prayers because his thoughts had been consumed with how and when he could get his next high before the high he was on wore off. Back then, the longest Tony had gone without using had been two days.

While he was in bondage to his addiction Tony had done some things he wasn't proud of—like the time he'd snatched an elderly woman's purse from her shoulder. He'd been following behind her as she'd walked slowly down the sidewalk. When she stopped at the crosswalk, he ran past her, snatching her purse as he passed.

He had pulled the purse from her shoulder with so much force that he'd caused her to fall forward, hitting her head on the pavement. But he hadn't looked back as he'd heard her scream, and he'd been gone before anyone had a chance to catch him or identify him.

Later that night, he remembered watching the news and hearing the story about an elderly woman who'd had her purse snatched, and how she'd suffered a concussion and a broken arm in the process.

There had only been fourteen dollars in her purse, and for a long time afterward, Tony would hear the woman's screams even after he had consumed enough drugs to eradicate any sensitivities he may have had left. Sometimes, he would have drug-induced auditory hallucinations, and he couldn't tell if the screams he heard were that of the woman or of himself.

It wasn't until he found himself homeless and rummaging through garbage cans for food that he began to have a true change of heart. It was then that he earnestly called on the name of the Lord for deliverance. And it was then, prodigal son that he was, that God heard his cries and had mercy on him.

Now, twenty-two years later, his family had long forgiven him, but every now and then he caught himself momentarily wishing he could undo the hurt and pain he'd caused them.

After he'd been delivered and set free from his addiction, Tony discovered there were still consequences he would have to pay for the crimes of petty theft he'd committed and been convicted of.

"Along with restitution," the judge had said, "I'm ordering you to forty hours of community service. You may not have the money to pay back everyone right now, but you certainly have plenty of time to volunteer." He had slammed the gavel down on the pad, then stood up to leave. "Now get out of my courtroom and go make yourself useful," he'd said as he stepped down from the bench. "Make something out of yourself other than a thief or a hoodlum."

The comment had stuck with Tony. It could have been his own father talking to him, and it had been like a slap in the face.

The forty hours of community service had involved picking up debris and litter that had been scattered around the city. It was during this time that Tony's upbringing returned to him. He knew God had spared him from a far worse fate, and Tony realized he had not been spared just to complete his forty hours of service, and then mosey on about his business.

He had a story to tell and—if he stayed clean—a testimony. He realized his life could be an inspiration to other people going through the same thing he'd gone through, and after he had fulfilled all of the judge's requirements, he had enrolled in college. He obtained a degree in human services and had been working as a certified substance abuse counselor ever since.

He continued browsing through the list of jobs on the Web site.

"Find anything good yet?" Shari asked.

"Not yet." He pressed his wavy, cropped hair down onto the nape of his neck. "Still looking."

"Are you feeling better?" she asked.

"A little. I didn't eat anything out of the ordinary. I don't know why my stomach started hurting like that."

"I do," she said.

"Come on now," he glanced at her, "don't start that again."

Shari looked at her husband of twenty years. They were the same age, but the stress of losing half of his income was beginning to have an effect on him. Multiple strands of gray hair had begun to reveal themselves around the temple of his hairline and in his goatee. The darkness under his eyes was the same shade of brown as the freckles that decorated his fair skin, and it made him look older than his forty-five years.

She looked at her husband lovingly. The intense look of concentration on his face made her decide to postpone telling him about the utility disconnection notice they had received in the mail.

Chapter Eleven

Tia's heart was beating fiercely as she turned the corner with a screech. She slowed the car down as she steered it into the church parking lot and remained seated in the car, giving herself time to settle down.

A few minutes later, she entered the huge foyer of the First Temple Church and walked through the multicolored arched doorway that led to the sanctuary.

Bibles, coats, and hats took up much of the space on the wooden pews, and Tia continued down the carpeted aisle until she found a seat just a few rows from the pulpit.

"Today," Pastor Worthy said as the melodic tenor of his voice resonated throughout the small church, "I want to preach about the temptations of the flesh. Turn your Bibles to 2 Timothy, chapter 2, verse 26," he commanded.

Of all things to preach about, why this topic at this time? Tia thought as she sat down on a wooden pew in the middle row. She listened to the rustling sound of Bible pages turning simultaneously as the pastor spoke.

"I want to talk about captivity," the pastor said. And then he read verse 26.

"and that they will come to their senses and escape from the trap of the devil, who has taken them captive to do his will."

"Satan," the pastor shouted out, "has so many different snares that he uses to hold a soul captive. Bullets," he hollered. "Let's call them bullets. Now, the first bullet only grazes you by finding your weakness, and if you're not saved, let me tell you there are many." He paused to wipe the moisture from his forehead with the white cloth he always had with him.

"The second bullet," he continued, "is just a flesh wound, but it draws you in nonetheless by enticing you with whatever your weakness—or weaknesses—may be. Now, in the beginning it's pleasurable."

Tia tugged at the collar on her shirt. It was hot in the sanctuary—or was it just her?

"Uh-huh," the pastor continued. "Oh yeah. The enemy's going to see to that. But after awhile," he slammed his fist down onto the podium, "after awhile, you're going to find that it holds less and less pleasure!" He let out a little moan, and then he wiped his forehead again.

Tia caught the attention of one of the ushers and asked for a fan. Moments later, he returned with a small hand held fan. She gripped the thin wooden handle and began waving the round piece of paper connected to it back and forth in front of her face.

"You're gonna want to walk away from it," the pastor said, "but now your flesh—" he was interrupted by the congregation's stomping of feet and clapping of hands, "—your flesh, having been wounded, is too weak to do so!"

"This," he pointed his finger out into the congregation. Tia glanced around at the other members. Had he only been pointing at her? "This," he continued, "is the point when the third and final bullet gets embedded deep into your flesh." He swayed backward as he emphasized the word *deep*.

"And you are now being held captive by the enemy." He stopped to catch his breath. "He ends up enslaving you with the lustful desires of your own heart! And the Bible says, '. . . sin, when it is full-grown, gives birth to death.'"

The man sitting next to Tia jumped up from his seat and began clapping his hands as he yelled, "Preach!"

Various members of the congregation shouted out, "Yes, Lord!" "Amen!" and "Have mercy!"

Tia remained stoic and showed no outward signs of the turmoil going on within her.

Pastor Worthy concluded his sermon by asking, "Brothers and sisters, do you see how that old devil works? He's doing the same old thing, the same old way. This ain't nothing new!" His eyes roamed across the congregation. "Just look in your Bible," he said. "There are countless stories in there about individuals who got caught up by the lust of their flesh: Samson, David and Bathsheba, and more."

The pastor lowered his voice. "Remember what 1 Corinthians, Chapter 6, Verses 9 through 10 tells us about the consequences of unrepented sin." He began to read.

"Or do you not know that wrongdoers will not inherit the kingdom of God? Do not be deceived: Neither the sexually immoral nor idolaters nor adulterers nor men who have sex with men nor thieves nor the greedy nor drunkards nor slanderers nor swindlers will inherit the kingdom of God."

Tia stopped fanning.

"Now, folks," he said, "this is God's Word, not mine so don't get mad at me." He extended his arms out to the congregation. "If anyone is here tonight and you've fallen into one of those categories . . . or maybe you fell into another category that I didn't mention, but you want to know Jesus—you want a new life—you want to be changed . . ." He stepped down from the pulpit. "You don't want to do the things you used to do, say the things you used to say, act the way you used to act . . . Come to Jesus. Come now."

The choir started singing "Just As I Am." Tia remained seated as several men, women, and teenagers got up from their seat and made their way down to the front of the pulpit. Her eyes became watery. One more blink and the clear liquid would start rolling down her cheeks. She hadn't planned to commit adultery, but what was she supposed to do if her husband ignored her desires?

She clenched her teeth. Surely God didn't want her to live with such depravity—but then again, what had God said about adultery? She picked up the fan and began fanning herself again as the tears began rolling unevenly down her face. The strong voices of the choir softened as the service came to an end.

Tia wiped her eyes and prepared to leave. What had Pastor Worthy said about sin? He'd said it felt good, and Tia convinced herself that she deserved to feel good for a change. Right now, she felt like a woman. She felt alive. But with a twinge of guilt she had to admit that it had been another man, not God, who had resuscitated her.

She grabbed her Bible and stood up. Yes, Pastor Worthy had said sin felt good, but what he'd also said—and what Tia had tried to ignore—was that the end result of sin was death.

Serenity entered the house through the kitchen door, which allowed her to bypass the living room—and her father—who she thought would be passed out on the couch like he almost always was. She headed for her bedroom upstairs when he called her name.

"Serenity!" he yelled.

He startled her, and she stood still, trying to decide if she should go into the living room or run upstairs like she wanted to.

She heard his footsteps coming toward the kitchen and decided to meet him halfway.

He loomed over the entryway of the kitchen. "Where you been?" His question sounded more like an accusation.

"At Cookie's house," she said defensively.

"Your mama was looking for you. Ain't this church night?"

"I had to study." She looked up at him. His eyes were filled with what she thought was disapproval, and she was immediately sorry she had looked into them. He brushed past her and headed for the refrigerator.

Serenity went upstairs to her bedroom and sat by the window facing the fenced in backyard. She tried to visualize the landscaping below that had been made invisible by a sheet of crystallized snow. Fallen acorns from the ominous-looking oak tree formed a haphazard pattern on top of the frozen snow and the trees' branches hung low from the weight of the thick ice that encased them.

Bushes struggled to maintain an upright position under the weight of the icy burden, and a mound of snow covered the bench that sat in the center of the yard. Serenity noticed a display of small animal prints decorating the surface of the snow-covered bench.

Suddenly, several squirrels began ducking in and out of the many nooks and crannies of the timeworn trunk. As cold as it was, they didn't seem to be affected by the single-digit temperatures at all as they continued their fast-paced game of hide-and-seek. After a few minutes, all but one of the squirrels had disappeared.

The last squirrel continued darting in and out of one of the trunk's crevices until Serenity tapped on the window; then it crawled down to the bottom of the tree and stopped.

She thought about how she'd almost knocked over the lamp at Cookie's house, and the comment Cookie had made. Her mind pictured the look of disgust her mother gave her every time she knocked something over and it broke. Another sting. And lately, she'd noticed that same look on her father's face, even when she hadn't stumbled over anything, even when nothing had shattered to pieces.

Serenity realized she was squeezing the fashion magazine she'd gotten from Cookie in her hand. She turned from the window, smoothed out the wrinkled pages, and opened the magazine to the page that had captured her attention earlier.

She discovered that a modeling agency was looking for girls between the ages of thirteen and eighteen years old to model the upcoming fashions for spring. Local auditions were going to be held at the Brookridge Mall on the first Sunday in March.

Her heart began to race. That was only three weeks away. This could be her chance to prove everyone wrong, to silence the jokes that Cookie made, and erase the looks of disapproval from her parents' faces. She would do it. She would go down to the mall and audition.

Her only prayer was that her mother would not stand in her way. She looked out the window once more, and the last squirrel was nowhere to be found.

Chapter Twelve

Tia left the sanctuary quickly after Bible Study was over. Not only was she still agitated with Lorenzo, but she was upset with Serenity for not coming home in time for church.

The frozen snow on the ground crunched and flattened under the weight of her car. She was driving too fast as she approached the sharp corner ahead of her. She put her foot on the brakes, and her car spun halfway around, leaving her facing the opposite direction of traffic. She heard the honking of a car horn as the driver behind her slowly maneuvered his way around her vehicle.

After making sure there were no other cars approaching, Tia put the car in reverse and slowly turned the car back around, being careful not to apply too much pressure to the brakes. It took her almost thirty minutes to get home—longer than she had planned. She was relieved when she finally drove her car into the garage.

After turning off the engine, she picked up her Bible and ran her fingers over the clear rhinestones that decorated the pale pink cover. She sighed, knowing her relief would be short-lived and would be replaced with agitation once she went into the house.

She got out of the car and entered the house through the side door. She walked past Lorenzo who appeared to be sleeping on the couch as Catch came running up to her. She stopped to give the dog several quick pats on the back.

Suddenly, Lorenzo sat up on the couch. "How was church?" he asked.

You'd know how it was if you'd been there. "Fine," she said. "You should have come." He chuckled as he resumed his position on the couch.

Just then, Tia heard Serenity coming down the back stairs. Seconds later, they were face to face.

"Where have you been?" Tia asked sternly.

"I was at Cookie's house," Serenity answered.

"Didn't I tell you to be home in time for church?"

Serenity was silent.

"Do you hear me talking to you?"

"Yeah," she answered defiantly.

"And what were you doing at Cookie's house? Didn't you tell me you had to go to the library?"

Serenity lowered her head. "Yes."

"So you lied."

"No. I was gonna go, but we changed our mind. I did my research on Cookie's computer."

"If that's true," Tia said, "that still doesn't excuse you from not getting home in time for Bible Study. I'm sick of this mess!" she yelled. "Every time I turn around, it's one thing or another. You do that again," she said, pointing her finger at Serenity, "and you won't be going *anywhere* for the next month!" She moved in closer to Serenity. Her breathing came rapidly. "Do I make myself clear?"

"Yes," Serenity whispered.

"You lucky I don't whip your butt!" Tia said as she stormed upstairs to her bedroom.

Tia slammed the door behind her and sat on the edge of her bed. She stared at the slender bronze cross hanging on the wall in front of her. A pair of hands had been placed together in the center of the cross to represent prayer. A feeling of defeat crept into her soul.

Nothing was going right. Her husband had no desire for her in any capacity, her daughter had resorted to lying to her in order to get out of going to Bible Study, and she was still dealing with this ongoing battle, a struggle between her soul and her flesh. She didn't want to feel the way she felt about the other man, but it was hard not to when her husband didn't want anything to do with her physically or in any other way.

She closed her bedroom door and picked up her phone. She entered Scamp's number into her phone; then changed her mind and quickly disconnected the call. She rubbed her forehead as a scripture from the book of Ecclesiastes came to her mind:

"What has been will be again, what has been done will be done again; there is nothing new under the sun."

Nothing new. She sighed. *The only thing new was the person, time, and place.*

She opened her Bible to a random page and started reading. It was a verse from Romans, Chapter 6. *"For the wages of sin is death; . . ."* She stopped reading. Such a high price to pay for her discontentment.

She flipped through several pages and stopped in the book of 1 Corinthians, Chapter 10. She had highlighted verse 13:

"No temptation has overtaken you except what is common to mankind. And God is faithful; he will not let you be tempted beyond what you can bear. But when you are tempted, he will also provide a way out so that you can endure it."

Hadn't God delivered her countless times before?

More turning of the pages landed her on a verse in James, Chapter 4. *"Submit yourselves, then, to God. Resist the devil, and he will flee from you."*

She closed her Bible and looked up at the cross. It seemed as though every scripture she'd randomly chosen had a message pertaining specifically to what she was going through. Then there had been the message she'd heard at church earlier. She knew she needed to submit herself to God. He was the answer. Not another man. She closed her eyes and lowered her head.

"Father, forgive me of my sins," she whispered. "Purify my heart and renew my spirit." She clasped her hands together. "Give me the strength to resist ungodly temptations, Lord, especially the physical ones.

"Lord, if You will, take all sexual desires away from me . . . at least for a time. At least until You restore Lorenzo back to me," she prayed.

"Strengthen me, Father. Renew a right spirit in me and in Lorenzo. Restore him back to You and to me. Keep Serenity safe from all harm, Father. And please . . . touch her heart so that she might have a desire to know You, Lord."

She paused for a moment. "I need You, Lord." She cried out softly. "I need You. Let Your will be done in me. In the name of Jesus I pray. Amen."

She raised her head, wiped the tears from her eyes, and went downstairs to warm up the beef ribs Lorenzo had baked earlier.

It was Thursday morning as Tia entered the small nurse's lounge at the hospital.

"Looks like somebody had a rough night," Janelle, the third-shift nurse, said as she prepared to give Tia a full report on the sixteen patients she would be caring for.

"I just didn't sleep well," Tia said. And it was the truth. How could she sleep with all the turmoil going on in her house? She had tossed and turned all night, unsettled by the confrontations she'd had with Lorenzo and Serenity.

Janelle gave her an update on all of the patients she would be caring for except Francis, the patient in room 523 whom she'd just cared for yesterday.

"What about the patient in room 523?" Tia asked pouring herself a cup of coffee. "Franny, I mean Francis Woodard?"

"Oh, the nurse on duty after you left yesterday had to call a code on her," Janelle said nonchalantly. "She's been transferred to ICU."

"She was just admitted to our floor yesterday in stable condition," Tia said surprised.

"I know," her colleague agreed. "When I got here last night, they told me that the nursing assistant went in to get her vitals, and she saw her lying in bed with her eyes closed and one hand on top of the phone. The nursing assistant said she called her name several times, but she was unresponsive. So she got the nurse and they called it."

Tia took a sip of coffee. "Wow. That's two codes in one day."

"Yeah," Janelle said. "I heard about the patient across the hall."

"Uh-huh," Tia said. "It happened as soon as I started my shift. You know, they say these patients are stable enough to be moved up here, but it doesn't seem like it for some of them, does it?"

"No, it doesn't."

"So what was it with Ms. Woodard?" Tia asked. "A heart attack?"

"You guessed it."

Tia shook her head. "Her vitals were stable all day on my shift. Her lungs were a little congested, and her heartbeat was irregular, but that was nothing new according to her records."

"I know," Janelle agreed. "She came up that way. And it looked like she was getting better. But I guess she took a turn for the worse."

"That's too bad," Tia said, "She seemed a little sad too. When I was in her room, I asked her if she was ready to go home, and she didn't answer." Tia stared off into space remembering the conversation. "I thought that was a little strange. You know, most people can't wait to get back home."

"I know. Wasn't she married?"

"I don't think so." Tia stood up and clipped her papers to her clipboard.

"Well, she must not have any family at all because there weren't any emergency contact numbers in her records," Janelle said.

Tia walked toward the door. "I guess that's not too surprising," she remarked. "I remember her telling me that she had a son she hadn't seen in a while." She put her hand on the doorknob, then stopped. A fleeting memory of the length of time she'd been separated from her own mother came to her mind. "I hope she and her son reconcile before it's too late," she said softly as she opened the door and walked out.

Chapter Thirteen

It really didn't matter that it was Thursday. For Homer, all of his days—Monday to Friday—were the same. Every morning between 8:30 and 8:45 a.m., he arrived at his accounting job.

He limped down the hallway, passing a multitude of tight and sterile smiles similar to his before entering the 1,200 square foot office that he shared with nine other employees. To make matters worse, the supervisor insisted on keeping the door closed, forcing Homer to endure a stifling and perfumed-filled modern-day tomb.

"Good morning," Leslie, his coworker, said with a fake smile pasted on her face.

Homer barely moved his lips. "Morning," he said as he passed by.

He sat down at his desk and turned on his computer. Didn't she know he could see through that fake smile of hers? He saw right through it just like he'd been able to see through the smiles of the girls he'd gone to high school and college with. Back then, when he'd asked a girl out on a date, they would politely turn him down with a smile on their face just like hers.

He unlocked his desk drawer and pulled out a stack of papers he'd partially completed the night before. He thought about the rest of his coworkers and their tight expressions. It was difficult enough for him to open his mouth and say hello, and he wondered how they managed to do it. Not that he wanted them to. He would have been quite happy if they had remained silent. But they never did.

When Natalie, their supervisor arrived, the tight-lipped women transformed themselves into a group of hyenas, laughing at the silly story Natalie was telling them about her two-year-old son's attempt to put his right shoe on his left foot. This created such a wave of laughter that Homer, thinking about his own deformed left foot, almost got up and left the office.

The cackles dwindled down to snickers, and Homer looked up to see Natalie's amazon-like frame standing in front of his desk. Whatever comments she'd made after talking about her two-year-old's fiasco, he hadn't heard. But even if he had, he would not have laughed. He never laughed at anything she said.

He was not there to be entertained by Natalie. Besides, not only were the things she said humorless, some of them weren't lady-like either. But what could he expect? She was just like his mother who, in his opinion, was also not a lady, but a failing imitation of one. He stood up. With her shoes on, Natalie towered over Homer's six foot frame.

"Good morning, Homer," she said. Her silver hair tumbled gently across her face as she reached for a stack of papers on his desk. "Are these the statistics for me?" She began flipping through the papers, and then handed them back to him.

"Yes," Homer said, looking at the sheets. His chest rose up and down heavily as he noticed the faint red marks from her fingernail polish staining the corners of each sheet. He couldn't stand it when she did that. Wasn't it enough that the polish was on her nails? Did she have to put some of it on his papers as well?

"Natalie," he spoke her name as if it were a command. "Do you think you can stop leaving all these red marks from your fingernail polish on my papers?"

She stared at him for a few seconds before she spoke. "This *is* just a copy, right?"

"No. It's my original."

"Oh, well then you better start making copies," she said. "Then you won't have to worry about that." She turned and walked briskly away from his desk.

And you better watch how you speak to me, Homer thought as he stared at the back of her bouncing hair. Had she been like some of the girls he met online or almost twenty years younger, like his neighbor, she might have been his next quest. He wasn't in high school or college anymore. Homer had been studying women, and he'd learned how to play the game—deformed foot and all. As a matter of fact, if the women in his department knew that he was now a conqueror, *all* of them would watch how they spoke to him.

He heard someone snickering behind him. When he turned to look, everyone's head was down. He wasn't a fool. He knew they were just pretending to be writing or typing or doing anything other than what they had really been doing, which was listening to what the boss had just said to him.

He turned his attention back to the stained papers. He sat down and began vigorously rubbing at the red marks left behind from her fingernails. They remained just as he knew they would. He opened his drawer and pulled out a bottle of liquid paper. That was females for you, he thought, young and old—always playing games.

Just like the little fish he'd met online, pretending to be grown but who was really just a kid trying to play on both sides of the fence. He would be meeting her real soon, and he'd show her what being a grown-up was all about.

She was like a fish out of water and she didn't even know it. He'd show her.

He began applying tiny droplets of the white liquid fluid to every red mark he saw on his papers until there were no longer any stains visible to the human eye.

Chapter Fourteen

Shari kissed Tony good-bye, and then headed for her job at a nonprofit community resource agency. The Thursday morning commute had been backed up, and when she finally pulled her brown Pontiac into the parking lot of her job the time on the dashboard in her car read 8:05 a.m.

She was already five minutes late as she began her ritual of driving up and down the twelve rows of parking spaces on the lot. She was hoping to snatch a parking spot close enough to the building so she would not have to park in the parking structure and walk what felt like half a mile just to get to work.

She knew some employees coveted the parking structure because it protected their cars from the elements. Since it was only February, it was still pretty cold outside, and more snow could not be excluded from the coming days. But Shari didn't care about that. By the time she got off at four-thirty, daylight would be just about gone, and her preference was to not have to walk a mile in semi-darkness just to get to a clean car.

She found a parking space in the second row on the lot and shouted, "Thank you, Lord!" She grabbed her purse and her coffee mug, and got out of the older model vehicle. She walked through the front door of the maroon-colored brick building and showed her ID badge to the security guard on duty. Then she headed for the elevator that would take her to the second floor where her department was located.

Her job was to provide information and referrals for various types of resources to people in low-income communities, and the majority of her day was spent listening and problem solving in order to determine which referral numbers would best benefit the person calling.

She had accepted this position four years ago because it gave her the opportunity to do what she liked most—helping other people. And the bonus had been that she could get paid while doing it.

At the time, it seemed like the perfect job, the best of both worlds. But for the last year or so, it seemed as though she was getting the worst of what the world had to offer.

The demeanor of the people she provided services to was changing. They were getting meaner, their attitudes uglier. Often, she would get calls from clients who would become hostile if they could not get whatever resource information they needed. And the negative comments she received from them—the very ones she was trying to help—never ceased to amaze her.

She prayed to God for strength and inner peace every morning before she left her house. Sometimes she had to pray to Him several times during her shift, asking Him to guide her heart and, most importantly, her tongue.

Her shift was just about over when a woman called the agency looking for a food pantry. Shari had gotten a rash of last-minute calls for open food pantries and had checked the computer so many times that she had stopped bothering to check because she already knew there would be none still open.

"I'm sorry," Shari said to the woman on the other end of the phone, "all of the pantries are closed for the evening. They're usually only open for a few hours during the day. The latest site closed at one o'clock," she continued. "But I can give you information for one that'll be open tomorrow."

"I don't need one tomorrow!" the woman yelled into the telephone receiver. "I need one today!"

Shari closed her eyes. *Today is not the day.* She took a deep breath. "I understand that, ma'am, and I'm here to help you," she said in her softest voice. "You don't need to yell at me." But before she could open her eyes and give the woman an address to a meal site location where she could get a hot meal for the night, the woman started calling her every cuss word imaginable.

"Ma'am," Shari's heartbeat quickened, "as I stated, I'm trying to help you."

"You know what you can do with your help, don't you?" the woman yelled. "You can stick it up your—!"

Shari disconnected the call. "Lord, give me strength," she whispered to the silent receiver. The phone rang again. She inhaled deeply before answering. "First Stop Central. This is Shari. How can I help you?"

"Hey, girl." It was Tia on the other end.

Shari let out a sigh.

"Can you help me get a new husband?" Tia asked. "I am so frustrated with Lorenzo. Last night we—"

"Tia," Shari interrupted. "I'm at work. You know I don't like to talk about personal stuff on my work phone."

"Oh yeah, I forgot. Well, I'm on my break, but what are you doing when you get off?"

"Going home."

"Wanna meet me for coffee after work?" Tia asked.

Shari stopped shuffling the papers on her desk. She thought she heard a sense of urgency in Tia's voice. "Is everything okay, Tia?"

"Yep."

Shari hesitated. "The usual spot?" she asked.

"Uh-huh."

"Okay," Shari said. "I gotta go. My other line's ringing." She disconnected her call with Tia, and pressed the flashing square light on the telephone.

"First Stop Central. This is Shari. How can I help you?"

"Hello?" the harsh male voice on the other end of the line yelled.

"This is Shari. How can I help you?"

"Um, yeah. My lights got turned off. And I need to get them back on."

"Have you spoken to someone from the electric company?" Shari asked.

"No, I haven't."

"Well, you'll need to call them and see what kind of payment arrangements you can make to get your lights turned back on."

"Somebody told me I could call this number and y'all would be able to help me," the man said impatiently.

"I'm sorry, sir, but you have to first make a payment arrangement with the electric company, then once a payment has been made we may be able to assist you with future payments."

"Future payments?" The man's tone was escalating. "How does that help me? I need my lights on now!"

Shari hesitated, hoping the momentary silence would diffuse the situation. "I understand sir, but what I'm trying to tell you is—"

"No, you don't understand!" he interrupted her. "Are your lights turned off?"

Not yet, Shari thought, *and I pray to God they won't be.*

"Hello?"

"I'm here, sir," she answered. "And again, you'll have to contact the utility company first before we can help you."

There was a loud click on the other end of the line, and then silence. Shari looked at the analog clock on the wall in front of her. It was 4:25 p.m. That was her last call for the day. "Thank you, Lord," she whispered.

She switched her phone to answer with an automated voice message that informed callers the office was now closed and to call back at eight o'clock the next morning. She began tidying up her desk as she called Tony.

"Hey, babe," she said lightly. "How's it going?"

"Not bad," he said yawning. "I applied for a couple of jobs today."

"What kind?"

"One is for a full-time AODA counselor, but it's in Waukegan."

"Oooh." Shari flicked the top of the Bic pen she was holding up and down. "That's almost an hour's commute one way," she said.

"And that's if there's no traffic," Tony added.

"What's the other one you applied for?"

"Hold on," Tony said.

Shari heard the rustling sound of papers, and then Tony returned to the phone.

"The second one I applied for is in Maywood."

"Oh, that's not too bad."

"But," he added, "it's only part-time. So that means I would have to try to juggle both jobs."

"Well, with your experience, somebody should be calling you soon."

"I hope you're right, babe."

"I am," Shari said assuredly. "Just keep the faith. It's just a matter a time."

"I know."

"Well, I just wanted to let you know I'll be a little late getting home. Tia wants me to meet her for coffee after work."

"Okay," he said. "But don't get anything to eat. I cooked dinner."

"Oooh," Shari squealed. "What did you cook?"

"My special pot roast."

"Well, all right then," she said, smiling. "That's what I'm talking about!"

Tony laughed. "Don't be too late, okay?"

"I won't be."

Shari hung up the phone. Her thoughts returned to the last two clients who had called in. In her forty-five years of living, she had never encountered a situation of not having enough food to eat, praise God. But she realized not having electricity or heat in her home was a very real possibility for her and Tony if they did not get the bill paid or make arrangements to pay it before the moratorium ended on April 15th.

The closer it got to the end of the moratorium the more calls she anticipated receiving from people wanting assistance with paying their utility bill. Once the moratorium actually ended and the disconnection process began, the nature of the calls would shift to folks wanting to know how they could get their utilities turned back on.

Even though Shari had received a disconnection notice in the mail yesterday, she prayed that her family would not find themselves in the same situation as many of her clients would be in—sitting in a cold, dark house come the middle of April.

Chapter Fifteen

Shari walked into the cozy coffeehouse at the end of the strip mall. Its bold green letters on the outside of the building were a stark contrast to the warm interior decorated with mahogany tables, soft lighting, and a small fireplace in the corner. During warmer weather, she and Tia would often sip their flavored coffee outside at one of the metal tables under the green awnings.

Tia tapped her shoulder just as the door swung closed behind her. "Hey, girl," she said.

"Hey," Shari turned quickly. "So what's up?" she asked, prepared for her role as the sounding board Tia needed her to be.

Tia led them to a small table with two cushioned chairs. "Thanks for meeting me," she said as she took off her coat. "What kind of coffee do you want?"

Shari studied the menu hanging on the wall. "I think I'll have a caramel frap," she said preparing to walk to the counter with Tia.

"No, stay there," Tia motioned to her to sit down. "This is my treat."

"Ooh," Shari wiggled in her seat. "Thank you."

Shari had come to know Tia after she and Tony had moved into their home last spring. Their house was situated on the other side of the cul-de-sac, two houses down from Tia and Lorenzo. Not only were both of their daughters thirteen years old, but they also attended the same junior high school and rode the same school bus.

The families realized they shared another commonality when they saw each other in church one Sunday morning. Shari and Tia began to share casual conversations with each other, and they eventually formed a friendship.

Tia returned and handed Shari a covered plastic cup filled with a mixture of coffee, caramel syrup, milk and ice, all topped off with whipped cream bursting from the round opening in the center of the top.

"Thanks," Shari said.

"You're welcome," Tia said as she left the table and returned a second time with a tall white paper cup and a white paper bag.

"What's in the bag?"

"A scone. Want some?" She held the bag open for Shari to reach into.

"Uh-uh." Shari held her plastic container up. "I'm good." She took a sip from the long green straw in the container. "Hmm, these are so good." She looked at Tia's cup. "What did you get?"

"A chai latte," she said, looking at her strangely.

"Why are you looking at me like that?"

"You just said, I'm good." She opened several small packets of sugar and added it to her spiced tea before taking a sip. "That's what Lorenzo said last night when I asked him to come to church with me. He said, 'I'm good.'" She sat up straight. "Anyway, I don't know how you can order a cold drink when it's still cold outside."

"I don't know how you can add all that sugar to a cup of tea. And ordering a cold coffee is no different from ordering a cold soda when you go to a restaurant."

Tia held her cup in midair. "Good point," she said.

"So what's up?" Shari asked again.

"I don't know," Tia said breaking off a bite-size piece of the scone. "There's this man," she started off slowly. "And, well, it's kind of hard to describe. I mean, it's his voice. You know, it just kind of makes me feel prickly all over." She waved her hand holding the piece of scone midway in the air. "You know what I mean?"

Shari's forehead creased as she narrowed her eyes. "Uh, no, I don't know," she said. She pointed to the bag with the scone still in it. "Give me a piece of that."

"I thought you didn't want any."

She thought about Tony's pot roast waiting for her at home. "Just give me a little piece," she said. "And shouldn't your husband be the one making you feel all prickly?"

Tia handed her the scone. "You'd think so, wouldn't you?"

"Yes, I would. But you answered my question with a question. Don't think I didn't notice that."

"I know. But there's just something about this man. He's older . . . and his eyes," Tia spoke like a teenage girl, "his eyes are so mesmerizing. I mean, they're really pretty and kind of a hazel color, and when he's looking at you it's like he's almost hypnotizing you. Whew!" She stopped to fan herself. "Add that to his voice, and girl, you're in trouble."

"No," Shari said. "*You're* in trouble. What does the Word say about that?" She stared hard at Tia.

"I know what the Word says," she confessed. "As a matter of fact, lust was what Pastor Worthy spoke on last night."

"That's always a good topic," Shari said. "I wish I could have been there. The one night I miss, he speaks on something good."

"His messages are always good," Tia said.

"You know what I mean," Shari said, pressing her lips together.

"How come you weren't there anyway?"

"I had to work late. And Tony wasn't feeling good. But, when I got home, Serenity was upstairs with Cookie so I thought you didn't go either."

"Yeah, Serenity told me she had to go to the library to do some research for a paper, but she knew she was supposed to be home in time to go to Bible Study." Tia tore off a piece of scone and began chewing it furiously. "If I had known she was at your house I would have grabbed her little behind on my way out!"

"Well, I don't think they went to the library. I'm pretty sure they were at my house all day."

"I know," Tia said. "I dealt with Serenity when I got home last night."

"So the message was good, huh?" Shari wanted to redirect the conversation.

"Yeah, and it was such a coincidence too," Tia said. "I felt like he was talking directly to me."

"That's not a coincidence. That was God sending you a message, and right on time like He always is." Shari paused. "So, who is this man? And how old is he?"

Tia looked down at the lid of her cup. "He's older than me," she whispered.

Shari barely heard her. "What?"

Tia leaned forward. "I said he's older than me."

"How much older?" Shari asked.

Tia repositioned herself on the chair. "I don't . . ." she said. "He's in his fifties."

"Fifties? And where did you meet him?"

"At the grocery store," Tia answered. But that was only partially true. She had seen the man on several occasions, but they'd never struck up a conversation until he'd approached her in the grocery store back in January and had introduced himself.

"So," Shari said, clearing her throat. "Let me get this straight. You, a married woman, met a man at the grocery store who's literally old enough to be your father . . ."

"He's not that much older than me," Tia interrupted. "I'm only thirty-two."

"He's old enough to be your father. Girl, what's wrong with you?"

Tia sighed heavily. "Me and Lorenzo are having issues," she said. "I need to talk to somebody."

"What kind of issues?"

"You know," Tia stared at her hard.

Shari stopped chewing on the piece of scone in her mouth. "Y'all not having sex?"

Tia quickly looked around the half-empty restaurant. "Can you say it any louder?"

"Sorry," she whispered.

"Now you want to whisper." Tia sipped slowly from her paper cup. "He's been sleeping on the couch for a long time," she said softly.

"Why?"

"I don't know." She nibbled at the tiny piece of scone in her hand. "He's changed. He's taking a lot of pills, and he's always talking about how his back is hurting." Her voice cracked. "But I don't believe that."

Shari took a sip from the straw in her cup. She kept her eyes on Tia, expecting a teardrop to fall at any minute. "Then, what do you think it is?"

Tia's voice hardened. "I don't know what to think," she said dry-eyed. "But I know I'm tired of it."

"You haven't slept with this other man, have you?"

Tia looked into her cup. "What would you say if I said yes?"

"I'd say you've made a big mistake," Shari said with a serious look on her face. "Have you?"

Tia raised her head and looked into Shari's eyes. They were full of scrutiny. She straightened her back. "Of course not," she said. "I just wanted to know what you'd say if I said I had."

"Then what do you plan to do about Lorenzo?"

"I don't know."

"Well, running to another man is not the answer," Shari said in a motherly tone. "Don't let a pair of hazel eyes and a deep voice fool you." She gave her head a quick nod and thumped the table with her finger. "'Cause even the devil can masquerade as an angel of light."

"You think I don't know that?" Tia said turning back her head to get the last drop of sweet tea from her cup.

"Do you?" Shari asked. "Because I can't tell," she said.

Chapter Sixteen

The downstairs was empty when Serenity came home from school. She made a sandwich for herself, grabbed a bottle of water, and went into the den. She turned on the computer and signed into her usual chat room.

She scrolled down the list of screen names hoping to find Saucer's name. She was almost at the bottom of the list when a comment from him appeared in a private box on the screen.

    iluvhotgurlz13: hey
    Serenity2cute_13: hey
    iluvhotgurlz13: wen u gonna send me dat pic?
    Serenity2cute_13: i am
    iluvhotgurlz13: wen?

Serenity put her index finger in her mouth and began biting her nail. She took her finger out of her mouth and began typing.

    Serenity2cute_13: u can c me at the mall
    iluvhotgurlz13: lol, but how am I gonna know it's u?
    Serenity2cute_13: ima wear a pink Hello Kitty hat so you'll know it's me
    iluvhotgurlz13: so u sayin' you ain't got no pic u can send me?
    Serenity2cute_13: yup

No new messages appeared in the box. After a few minutes, Serenity started typing again.

Serenity2cute_13: u still there?

A few seconds passed before a message from Saucer appeared in the box.

iluvhotgurlz13: u gonna meet me on Sunday?
Serenity2cute_13: don't kno. I have 2 practice for my audition
iluvhotgurlz13: 4 wat?
Serenity2cute_13: a modeling show
iluvhotgurlz13: u like 2 take pics?
Serenity2cute_13: yup
iluvhotgurlz13: lol, i like to take pics 2. Can i send u a pic rite now?

Serenity's heart started racing.

Serenity2cute_13: ok

Saucer sent her a picture of an athletic-looking, chocolate brown, shirtless chest and torso. The head of the body was missing from the picture.

Serenity2cute_13: ur cute, lol
iluvhotgurlz13: I bet u r 2
Serenity2cute_13: where's ur head?
iluvhotgurlz13: i have one

Serenity smiled.

iluvhotgurlz13: wanna see it?

She was about to type *yes*, instead she jumped at the sudden sound of Lorenzo's voice behind her.

"What are you doing?" he asked as he walked into the den.

She turned off the monitor. "Nothing," she said.

"Nothing?" He pressed the button on the computer screen and turned the monitor back on. He leaned over her and read the last few lines of the conversation she'd been having with Saucer:

"i have one"
"wanna see it?"

It? He placed one hand on the desk to balance himself and scrolled up a few lines until he saw the picture of the naked torso and chest. Deep lines spread across his forehead, causing him to resemble a bull dog. "What the . . ."

"Daddy, I didn't ask him to send that," Serenity said quickly.

"But you didn't tell him not to either, did you?" Lorenzo looked at her with a dull stare. "Get up."

She got up from the chair and crossed her arms while she watched her father exit out of the chat room, and then shut down the computer. "I don't know what you think you're doing," he said with a slurred voice, "but don't let me catch you doing it again."

She shifted her weight to one foot. "I wasn't doing anything," she said.

He turned around. "What do you mean you weren't doing anything?" He pointed to the computer. "Looking at naked bodies is not doing anything?"

"I wasn't looking at naked bodies," she said staring up at the ceiling.

Lorenzo sat on the edge of the desk and looked at her. "What do you call it?"

"It was a naked chest, and I wasn't looking at it."

He stared hard at her. "Are you trying to get smart with me?"

Serenity looked at her father's distorted face.

"Answer me," he said.

She returned her gaze to the desk lamp. "No," she answered.

Lorenzo stood up. "Like I said, whatever you think you're doing, don't let me catch you doing it again."

"You won't," Serenity said. She left the den and ran upstairs. She meant what she said. He wouldn't catch her again because she would be more careful next time.

Serenity waited until her father had closed the front door behind him. She didn't know where he was going, she was just glad he had left. She went into the living room and browsed through the television guide until she found the television series, *America's Top Model*. Dang! She stomped her foot. She had just missed the first fifteen minutes of the show.

She continued watching until each of the contestants was told to walk toward the judges. Serenity sat completely still as she watched the way each model moved. This was the part she had been waiting for. She studied their posture—shoulders back, hips forward—as they all walked with confidence.

After the show ended, she grabbed her iPod, put in her earplugs, and turned up the volume to a fast-paced beat. She placed a book on top of her head, then pushed her shoulders back, and tried to thrust her hips forward. With one foot in front of the other, she took her first step.

She practiced placing her heel down first instead of her entire foot the way she'd just seen the models on television doing. Then she walked with long strides up and down the length of the braided wool runner in the hallway. She looked straight-ahead with her chin up and tried to keep her head and shoulders still. The book on her head kept sliding to one side, and she constantly reached up to push it back in place.

Her foot continued to trip on the edge of the runner each time she got to the end of her walk. She sighed. *Stupid rug!* At the end of each walk she paused for a moment, turned, and then finished walking in the opposite direction. She pretended that the front door she was looking at was the faces of the judges, and Serenity made sure her head was the last thing she turned as she walked away.

After she auditioned in March, people were going to look at her differently. No longer would they see her as a clumsy, long-legged girl. She smiled. People would recognize her as one of those pretty and elegant models walking on runways all over the world! And there'd be no tripping over things, no more sighs from her mother— only hugs and praises. Serenity moved the rug out of the way and continued practicing.

Chapter Seventeen

It was almost 5:45 p.m. when Shari left the coffeehouse. She got in her car and trailed behind Tia on her way home. She had sensed that something might be wrong with Tia and Lorenzo's relationship a while back.

One afternoon she and Tia had been outside talking when Lorenzo had pulled up and had gotten out of his car. He'd barely spoken to Tia and had ignored Shari altogether.

"Can't you say hi?" Tia had asked him while she tilted her head to her right where Shari sto od.

"Oh, hi," he'd said like a child who had been reprimanded. He continued walking to the house, and Shari remembered thinking how odd his behavior had been. Then there had been the time when Tia had invited Shari over for a cup of coffee. She and Tia had been sitting at the kitchen table when Lorenzo had come home and had proceeded to walk past both of them without speaking as he went upstairs. Once again, Tia had to remind him to speak.

Now Tia had told her about some other man she was infatuated with, and Shari prayed to God that's all it was—although that was bad enough. When Shari had asked her if she was sleeping with the man, she hadn't been convinced by Tia's answer. It hadn't been her answer as much as it had been the *way* she'd answered. All Shari could do was pray that it had not gotten physical.

The traffic light turned yellow, and Shari stopped as Tia picked up speed and drove through the intersection. She watched Tia's SUV turn into the entrance of their cul-de-sac. Seconds later, the light turned green, and Shari crossed the intersection and made a left turn into the cul-de-sac just as a pizza delivery car was exiting. She saw the red taillights from Tia's SUV as her garage door slowly lowered itself to the ground. Shari smiled as she drove past her neighbor's house on the right side of the street. She'd caught a glimpse through the large picture window of a teenage boy dancing with a slice of pizza in his hand. She turned left into her driveway just as the porch light on the stucco house directly next to hers came on.

Since she and Tony had moved into their house almost a year ago, she'd had little opportunity to get to know her next-door neighbors. She saw the woman of the house frequently in passing, but her neighbor seldom offered anything more than a stoic hello. Most of the time, she didn't acknowledge Shari's presence at all, and Shari thought she appeared to be quite unhappy.

Before it had gotten ridiculously cold, Tony had occasionally stood at the metal fence that separated the two driveways and engaged in small talk with the husband. At one point, her neighbor had even helped Tony secure the hanging bumper on their car with two bungee cords until they could afford to get it repaired at the body shop.

She turned off her car and got out. Just as she made it to the front door, it suddenly opened and Tony stood smiling at her as the aroma of beef, onions, and peppers drifted up her nostrils.

"Hey," she said, looking up at him.

He closed the door behind her and lowered his head to receive her kiss. "Hey back," he said.

"It's freezing out there," she said. Then she inhaled. "But it's sure smelling good in here."

"You didn't eat, did you?" he asked as he helped her take off her coat.

Shari thought about the little piece of scone she'd had. "No," she said, "unless you consider a coffee and a bite-size piece of scone eating."

"I don't," he said. "So how's Tia doing?"

"It's not how she's doing but *what* she's doing. Either way, it's not good."

Tony frowned, creating a furrow between his eyebrows. "What do you mean?"

"Well," Shari said, taking off her boots, "I guess she and Lorenzo are having problems."

"What kind of problems?"

"Tia said he's been sleeping on the couch and he's been taking a lot of pills."

"What kind of pills?" Tony asked with a serious look on his face.

"I'm not sure. I think Tia said they were for his back."

Tony sighed. "That doesn't sound good."

"No, it doesn't," Shari agreed with her husband. "Not at all. And there's more."

Tony waited silently for her to continue.

"The girl has gotten herself involved with another man," Shari finally said.

"Oh no," Tony replied shaking his head. "How involved is she?"

"I don't know," Shari said.

Tony walked back to the kitchen shaking his head as Cookie came skipping down the stairs.

"Hey, Ma," she said cheerfully.

"Hey, sweetie," Shari said. "How was your day?"

"Fine," she answered as she headed toward the kitchen.

Shari followed behind her. "Do you have any home-work?"

"Yep," she answered before breathing in deeply. "Mmm, Daddy, it smells good in here. What are you cooking?"

"My special pot roast," he said smiling.

Shari opened the oven door. "This was so thoughtful of you, Tony," she said, half turning to look at him.

Tony hugged her from behind. "Well, it was the least I could do since I was home today." He began rocking her back and forth. "Of course, I'd rather be working."

"I know, sweetheart. You'll get something full-time soon."

"Ugh," Cookie said, rolling her eyes, "get a room!"

"Uh, excuse me," Shari said. "How about *you* get a room?" Shari tapped her on the shoulder. "*Your* room," she stressed, "and make sure you get that homework done right after you eat."

"How do you know I didn't do it already?"

"Did you?"

Cookie smirked.

"That's what I thought."

"Okay, okay. Right after dinner."

Shari looked at Tony and rolled her eyes.

Tony nodded. "Let's eat, everybody."

Shari made a plate for Cookie while Tony fixed a plate for himself and Shari. They sat down at the kitchen table and held hands as Tony led the prayer, thanking God for yet another meal.

He watched with pride as his family enjoyed a hearty serving of the pot roast complete with onions, carrots, and potatoes. He knew that if Shari knew how low their funds were getting, she would have admonished him for buying such an expensive cut of beef. She would have told him to buy a few pounds of ground beef instead. "That would make a nice meatloaf," she would argue, "and you can still add gravy to it."

But Tony didn't want to be restricted to buying ground beef only. Just because he'd hit a financial setback didn't mean his family couldn't enjoy a nice meal. He was in the valley right now, but he knew he'd be back on the mountain top in due time. In God's time. He recalled a verse from Isaiah 43:2: *"When you walk through the fire, you will not be burned . . ."*

Right now, he was walking through the fire, but all he had to do was walk steady. All he had to do was keep the faith. And he was determined to do so because he'd been through worse things than this.

Chapter Eighteen

Tia reflected on the conversation she'd had with Shari a few hours earlier in the coffee shop. As much as she liked Shari, there was no way she could tell her that the other man she had gotten herself involved with was her next-door neighbor.

As she drove into the cul-de-sac, she could see that the downstairs portion of her house was lit up light a Christmas tree. She entered the house through the garage to find the downstairs completely empty.

She marched to the bottom of the staircase. "Serenity!" she yelled. She didn't get an answer and called her name again. When her second call was met with silence, Tia went upstairs to make sure Serenity was home. Her bedroom door was slightly open, and Tia walked in.

"Didn't you hear me calling you?" Tia asked angrily.

Serenity removed an earplug from one of her ears. "Huh?"

"I was calling you. Why are all the lights on downstairs and nobody's down there?"

"I don't know."

"What do you mean, you do know?"

"They were on when I came home."

"Was your daddy here when you got home?"

"Yep," Serenity said as she put the earplugs back in her ears.

"Take those things out," Tia said. "I'm talking to you."

There was still a small amount of residual tension from the day before that loomed between them. Serenity removed the earplugs and turned down the volume on her purple iPod. She stared at the large Hello Kitty poster nailed on the wall across from her bed.

"How was your day today?" Tia asked.

"It was all right."

"Anything interesting happen?"

"Nope."

Tia stood staring at her for a few seconds. "Okay," she said and turned to leave the bedroom.

"Oh, wait," Serenity said, jumping off her bed. She grabbed the fashion magazine from her nightstand, nearly tripping over her own feet in the process.

Tia looked up at the ceiling and sighed. *Would Serenity ever stop being so clumsy?*

"There's gonna be a fashion show at the Brookridge Mall, and they're holding auditions for models in March. Can I go?"

"To the show?"

"No. To the audition."

Tia stared at her in disbelief. "The audition?"

"Yeah," Serenity said defiantly.

Tia held out her hand. "Let me see that magazine."

"It's on page 32," Serenity said, handing the magazine to her mother.

Tia remained standing as she looked at the page Serenity had dog-eared. She flipped through several pages before and after the article. "You think you can really walk up and down that stage as . . ." Tia caught herself.

"I can do it," Serenity said quickly.

Tia handed the magazine back to her. "I don't know," she said. "After yesterday, I'm gonna have to think about it. You got any homework?"

"I'm getting ready to start it now. What's for dinner?"

Tia rubbed her right temple. *Since your trifling daddy didn't cook nothing I guess I'll have to.* "Chicken and rice," she said as she left the room and went downstairs to start dinner.

While Tia was pouring the rice into the pot of boiling water, her cell phone began ringing. She let it ring several times before finally deciding to answer it.

"Hello, Scamp," she said quietly. The guilty pleasure she'd indulged in with him a few nights earlier had continued to eat away at her conscience. And she'd been rejecting his calls all day.

"Hello," the deep voice said on the other end.

She moved the phone to her other ear. "How are you?"

"A better question," he said, "is how are you?" He clicked on a picture of a female on the dating Web site he was viewing.

"I could be better," she sighed.

He clicked on the many different poses the woman had posted online. "I'm sorry to hear that," he said.

An uncomfortable silence settled between them.

"How about we meet somewhere?" he said as he viewed the online woman in a bikini. His voice was husky. "I'll give you another one of my massages."

She didn't answer. His offer of intimacy at a time when all she needed was emotional support irritated her. She could see where this thing—whatever is was—was headed, and the same insignificance she'd felt with Lorenzo who cared nothing about her physical needs, she began to feel with Scamp who was not interested in her emotional state of mind.

"Still there?" Scamp asked.

The sound of his voice was no longer mesmerizing to her. In an instant, it had become an unpleasant reminder of the mistake she'd made getting involved with him. She'd convinced herself that she had every right to harbor feelings for another man because of her husband's neglect. She'd adopted the mantra—what one man won't do, another one will. But deep down inside, she knew that was only her flesh speaking. It was not the way of the Savior.

It had become clear that her lover did not care about her. He wasn't interested in why she wished she could be better. He was only interested in one thing from her, and it was the one thing she would have freely given only to her husband. But for almost two years he'd wanted nothing to do with her, and even on those rare occasions when they did engage in intimacies, it had been obvious to her still that he was not very interested.

Even so, she couldn't justify her act of adultery by blaming her husband's lack of interest in her, and the fact that she kept trying to was confirmation that it—she—was wrong.

It was just like her grandmother used to say, "If you got to keep convincing yourself that whatever you're doing is right, then you best believe it's wrong. Don't be blinded by your own sight, girl." And what had Shari said to her in the coffee shop? *"Even the devil can masquerade as an angel of light . . ."* Tia knew what she had to do, and she had to do it quickly.

"I have to go," she said. She didn't wait for him to say good-bye before she disconnected the call. She went through her phonebook until she found his number. She pressed the option button, then the edit button and typed "Do not answer" in the space where his name would have gone.

She changed her mind and pulled up his number again, hesitating for only a second before deleting his number from her phone altogether.

Chapter Nineteen

Homer clicked on the category of Females seeking Males, and began browsing through the ads, clicking only on the ones that included pictures. He let a few minutes pass before he called Tia again. He'd put her number on speed dial and continually hung up and pressed the same number pad each time her phone went directly to her voice mail.

The creaking of the hardwood floor startled Homer. He closed his laptop and turned to see his wife Sandra standing behind him.

"Who was that on the phone?" She stood rigidly with her arms hanging loosely by her side.

"No one," he snapped.

"Was that also no one's pictures you were looking at on the computer?"

He got up from his desk. "What do you want, Sandra?"

She stared at him for a long time before she spoke. "I want out, Homer."

"You want out?" He stood dumbfounded, waiting for her to answer.

"Yes," she said.

"What is it now?" he hollered. "You said I was unemotional so I tried to be more open. You said you didn't feel loved so I tried that!"

She held up her hand to stop him. "You tried that? What is *that?*"

"You know what I'm talking about," he glared at her. "All the things you keep telling me you need," he said mockingly.

She looked at him sadly. "You can't even say the word, can you?"

"I don't have to!" he yelled. "I go to work. I pay the bills. You don't have to do nothing but sit on your—"

"That's not enough," she yelled. "Don't you get it? It's not just about you working and paying the bills, Homer!"

"It's never enough!" he said breathing rapidly. "You said I need to lighten up. Okay. I tried that." But he was lying. How could he tell her that he did not know how to lighten up? How could he tell her that when he tried to laugh freely like other people did, it only made him feel awkward and out of place?

"When?" she asked. "When in the two years of our marriage have you ever tried to lighten up?"

"It doesn't matter," he said wiping away the buildup of saliva that had begun to form in the corners of his mouth. "It's never enough for you, and I'm not going to stand here and try to defend myself."

"Of course, it doesn't matter," she said. "And that's part of the problem," she pointed to his laptop, "along with that."

"You know what?" Homer said, his excitement escalating. "I can't keep up with all your requests!" He waved his arms in the air. "There's too many of them. And if you want to know the truth about it, I'm getting pretty tired of trying to!" He swallowed hard. "You're just like my mother!" he screamed. "And I couldn't please her either!"

"What are you talking about?" She frowned. She knew Homer had been raised by his grandmother, but how did that make her just like his mother?

She was exhausted. "I'm out of here," she finally said.

"Yes," he agreed, "you are."

He followed her to the front hallway where two suit-
cases sat already packed. He searched her eyes for the
finality of her words. She looked back at him with eyes
that were cold and empty.

"I'll be back for the rest of my things," she said, and
then she opened the door and walked out.

Homer grit his teeth as he felt the pain rising from
the pit of his stomach. He pushed and shoved until he
had forced it back into its internal hiding place, a burial
ground for his other emotional pains that he'd never
found a cure for.

He leaned against the door. He didn't know what
Sandra was talking about. So what if he wasn't able to
tell her that he loved her. And never mind if he wasn't
as emotional as she wanted him to be. None of that was
going to pay the mortgage on their ranch-style home. It
wouldn't put food on the table or clothes on their backs.
He'd paid all the bills, and she had not had to work in
the two years that they'd been married. Hadn't that been
enough?

To Homer, love was overrated. The only exception
he made was for his grandmother who had loved him
unconditionally. Even during his high school and college
years, there had been no love relationships for Homer.
There had been the useless visits from his mother when
he'd been younger, and she'd always ended them by
saying she loved him. But he'd never felt or seen her love.
She'd never demonstrated it.

It had only been after his grandmother had died that
Homer had met Sandra. She had been fifteen years
younger than he was, and had been one of the very
few women at his job that he'd found himself attracted
to. She'd been working as a cashier in the employee
cafeteria, and after his grandmother's death, Homer had
begun to frequent the cafeteria more often just to see her.

It had been her youthfulness that had allowed him to initiate a friendship with her that, after three years, led to marriage.

After they were married, he insisted she stop working, telling her his income was enough for both of them. At first, Sandra seemed quite complacent, but as time went on, he noticed that even she, who had claimed to love him, had begun to want or need something from him that he couldn't give.

She *was* just like his mother in the sense that he had never been able to please her either. Not since the day he was born. Homer had always felt that his mother had left him because of his foot. Why else would she have abandoned him? And now his wife had left him too. The reasons Sandra had given him for leaving had nothing to do with his foot, and she'd never made an issue of it throughout their marriage . . . still, Homer wondered. A sharp spasm of pain rippled across his stomach as he decided in his heart this would be his first—and last— marriage. He bent over and waited for the pain to pass.

The cold air lingered in the hallway. But there was a greater chill growing inside of Homer as he added his wife to the long list of women who had never loved him. His sad affirmation only made him feel colder. And the spasm of pain spread across his stomach again.

Chapter Twenty

It was a Saturday afternoon, and Lorenzo was still sprawled out on the couch when Tia and Serenity returned from the grocery store. He raised his head from the armrest when he heard the front door open.

Serenity stopped to give the dog a quick rub on the back, and then headed to the kitchen to make a sandwich.

"Hurry up," Tia said to Serenity. The two of them were going to visit Tia's mother, Ida, and her grandmother, Mavis. "It's already after one o'clock, and I'll be ready after I change my clothes."

"Hey," Lorenzo said. "Y'all can't speak?"

"Hi," Serenity said as she continued to the kitchen.

"Hey," Tia said dryly.

Tia went upstairs and exchanged the sweatpants and tee shirt she had on for a pair of bootleg jeans and a cowl-neck cable sweater. She came back downstairs and looked in the kitchen. Serenity was sitting at the round glass table eating the last half of a sandwich. "You ready?" Tia asked.

"Yep," Serenity said. She picked up her glass still partially filled with milk and her empty plate. She put the plate in the sink and poured the half glass of milk down the drain.

"Serenity!" Tia yelled. "Why did you waste all that milk?"

Serenity looked at her mother with a blank expression on her face. "I didn't want it."

"Well then, you shouldn't have poured it. We don't have food to waste like that."

Lorenzo came shuffling into the kitchen. "No sense crying over spilled milk," he said sarcastically.

"That's not funny," Tia said.

"I didn't mean for it to be," he said as he brushed past her arm.

"You know what?" Tia stared at his back for a few seconds before she continued. "It'd be nice if you came with me and Serenity to visit my family for a change."

"Oh no," he waved his hand in the air as he stood in front of the open refrigerator door. "I'll pass on that."

Serenity walked out of the kitchen as Tia tried to maintain a calm demeanor. "Why, Lorenzo?"

"Don't start, Tia," he warned her. "You know why."

"I know what you say," she continued, ignoring the tone in his voice. "And I know you used to always come with us."

"And you also know why I don't anymore, don't you?" he insinuated.

She looked at him hunched over in front of the refrigerator. He still hadn't turned around to face her.

"Don't you?" he repeated himself. The tone of his voice grew harsh.

"Your back?" she said putting her hands on her hips. "For *two years?*" She shook her head and walked out of the kitchen. "Same old excuse," she mumbled.

"What did you say?" he asked loudly as he followed behind her.

"I said it's the same old excuse!"

"How many times do I have to tell you?" he said. His agitation was escalating. "It's too uncomfortable to sit in one spot for an hour and a half!"

"But you can sit in front of the TV for hours at a time, right?" Tia's voice was laced with hostility.

"Yeah, but I'm in a recliner," he yelled. "That's a big difference!"

"You weren't in a recliner a few minutes ago when we came in!"

"Stop yelling!" Serenity intervened.

"Serenity," Lorenzo said, breathing heavily, "this is between grown folks."

"Okay, but can you stop yelling at Mama?"

"What about me?" His sleepy eyes suddenly grew wide. "You didn't hear her yelling at me?"

Serenity stared at him coldly.

"Oh, I guess not," he said. "You too busy talking to boys on the computer. You don't know what you talking about, little girl. You need to stay in your place."

She kept her gaze fixed on his pinpoint pupils. "I might not know what I'm talking about," she said as he turned and shuffled back to the living room, "but I know an addict when I see one."

Lorenzo turned around quickly.

"Serenity, be quiet!" Tia said.

"Is that what you're telling her?" Lorenzo asked.

"Go get in the car," Tia said to Serenity.

Serenity walked defiantly past both of them to the garage.

"I didn't tell her anything," Tia said to Lorenzo.

"Then what made her say that, Tia?"

"She's not stupid. Half the time you're gone. And even when you're here . . . you're gone," she said pointing to her forehead. "All you do is lie on that couch. Then you get up and stagger to the kitchen or the bathroom, and you think she can't put two and two together?"

He dropped down on the couch with a thud. "Y'all have a good trip," he said without looking at her.

She slammed the door behind her without responding.

***

Tia was still fuming as she merged onto I-94 West toward Milwaukee. Serenity sat beside her preoccupied with her iPod. Although her daughter had placed both earplugs in her ears, the distorted sound of music still filtered through.

Tia tapped Serenity firmly on her thigh. "Turn that down," she said.

Even though it took approximately an hour and a half to get to Milwaukee, Tia was thankful that she was still able to visit her mother and grandmother once a month.

When they'd first started taking the drive, Tia would point out to Serenity the cows and occasional horses they passed. The animals stood grazing in the various fields off the highway without a care in the world.

In two years, things had changed. The endless miles of land had been eradicated by new developers eager to make their presence known, and new subdivisions had been constructed one or two miles apart from each other. The few farmhouses that remained looked out of place among the upscale houses for sale, and the visibility of cows and horses had decreased significantly.

Tia tapped Serenity's thigh again and pointed to her ears. She waited while her daughter removed the earplugs from her ears.

"Why did you say that?" Tia asked her.

"Say what?"

"That your daddy is an addict."

"Because."

"Because what?"

Serenity looked down into her lap. "Because he acts like one," she said.

"And how would you know how an addict acts, Serenity?"

"Well, let's see." She raised her head and looked up toward the car ceiling. "He's always sleeping on the couch, and sometimes when he talks it's all mumbled."

Tia sighed. "Just don't call him that again, understand?"

Serenity turned to look at her. "Why do you stay with him?"

"I'm trying to give him time, Serenity."

"Time for what?"

"I don't want to talk about that now." Tia exhaled deeply. "And what did he mean about you talking to boys on the computer?"

Serenity looked away then. "I don't know," she said.

"Oh, he just made that up?" Tia cut her eyes sideways at Serenity.

"Yeah," she said. "I was just talking to my friend. I wasn't talking to no boys."

"Well, you make sure you keep it that way," Tia said.

Serenity put the earplugs back in her ears. She thought about how her father had told her to stay in her place. *What place was that?* She turned the volume up on her iPod and began nodding her head back and forth as the music played loudly.

Tia passed a highway marker that showed eighteen miles before they would be in Milwaukee. They rode in silence for a few more miles before Serenity turned off her iPod and turned to face her mother.

"Don't you ever feel funny being around Grandma and Great-grandma?" she asked.

Tia kept her eyes on the road. "Why would I feel funny?"

"You know, because of everything that happened when you were younger."

Tia had only recently told Serenity about her past, leaving nothing out except for her promiscuous ways. She'd told Serenity about Ida, and how she'd been sent to prison for the death of her son, Tia's brother. Then, she'd told her about the short time she'd spent in foster care, and how she eventually ended up being raised by her grandmother.

Tia glanced over at Serenity. "The past is the past," she said. "Everything bad doesn't have to stay bad, and we certainly don't need to carry those memories around with us. We can try to learn from them, but then we need to let them go." She adjusted the cruise control on the steering wheel. "If we don't, it makes a heavy load," she said.

"So you never feel funny?"

"Not anymore because the key is to be willing and able to forgive somebody who's done you wrong." She stared straight-ahead. "If you can't forgive," she said, "you're gonna have a hard time."

"Are we almost there?" Serenity asked.

"Serenity, we've made this trip a hundred times. You should know by now when we're almost there."

"I don't be paying attention," she said and turned her iPod back on, this time lowering the volume so the music wasn't quite as loud as it had been.

Tia passed another highway marker. "A few more miles and we'll be pulling up in front of Grandma's flower shop," she said to Serenity whose only response was the continued nodding of her head.

Tia thought about how Ida had initially encouraged her to go into the floral business years ago when Ida had still been in prison. Although Tia had completed all of the online floral design coursework required at the Milwaukee School of Floral Design, when she'd given birth to Serenity everything had changed.

The night she became a mother was also the night she'd decided to leave Lorenzo. He'd almost missed the birth of their child, and his controlling and abusive ways had taken a toll on her. But then he'd begun to cry and had asked God to forgive him. And right there in her hospital room, he'd gotten down on his knees and repented. Not only had he renewed his relationship with Jesus, but he'd asked for her forgiveness as well so she'd made the decision to stay.

After Serenity's first birthday, Tia had decided to enroll in a traditional college and study nursing. Ironically, it was her mother who ended up enrolling and successfully completing the eight-week course at the School of Floral Design, and after working for a florist for several years, Ida had opened her own small flower shop, naming it Flowers To Go. Tia could still remember how elated Ida had been on opening day.

"Ain't God good?" Ida had proclaimed.

"Yes, He is," Tia agreed. She had been so proud of her mother. She had come a long way.

"You know when I started going to those Bible studies in prison," Ida had said to Tia, "I learned that God's plan for me didn't include a life of misery, hatred, and unforgiveness."

Tia had quietly listened to her mother's testimony.

"God opened my eyes," Ida had said. "He made me realize that I was a sinner in need of His forgiveness. I learned that through His grace and mercy, I could actually be set free from all my emotional pain. Everything," she said, and she'd placed her hand on the left side of her chest, "that was holding me down and keeping me a hostage.

"You know, Tia, I came to Jesus just as I was," she'd continued. "I answered His call of salvation. I accepted Jesus Christ as my Savior, and I was baptized in His name."

Tia remembered her mother's eyes growing misty as she'd continued her testimony.

"I asked God to forgive me," she'd said, "and He did. And then He turned around and gave me the strength to forgive others!"

Tia smiled.

"No, honey, that broken spirit of mine wasn't healed by my own strength." Ida had shaken her head feverishly. *"Uh-uh. I been healed by the power of God. And you know what's funny?"* she had asked Tia.

Tia remembered answering no.

"God set me free long before I was released from prison."

Tia recalled the gleam in Ida's eyes on the day she opened the flower shop.

"Won't He do it?" Ida had asked smiling.

Tia had looked at her mother—a living testimony. *"Yes, He will,"* she said.

Chapter Twenty-one

After the healing and reconciliation process had taken place between Tia, Ida, and Mavis thirteen years ago, Tia made a vow that she would not allow another gulf of emotional distance to form a barrier between the three of them again. That was the reason for her regular visits. She wanted to keep the bond between them close and make sure that Serenity had an ongoing relationship with both of them as well.

She parked her SUV in front of the lannon stone building, and she and Serenity got out of the car. A small silver bell attached to the top of the door jingled as they entered.

"Hey," Ida said coming from behind the counter. Her smile was almost as wide as her outstretched arms.

"Hey, Momma," Tia said, embracing her slender frame. "How are you doing?"

"I'm fine," she said. She turned to Serenity and gave her a full hug, and then stepped back to look at her granddaughter. "And how is my big girl doing?"

"I'm fine, Grandma," Serenity answered, smiling.

"Girl, every time I see you it looks like you've gotten taller."

"I think she has," Tia said. "You see she's taller than me now."

Ida waved her hand. "Hush," she said to Tia. "Every-body's taller than you."

Serenity giggled.

"Stand up straight," Tia said to Serenity.

Serenity stopped smiling.

Tia looked around the room. "Where's Grandma?"

"She just went downstairs to get some more supplies," Ida said.

"I'm gonna audition for a fashion show in March," Serenity blurted out to her grandmother.

Ida looked at Tia. "Oh yeah?"

"Yeah, I might let her," Tia said.

"Might?" Serenity's eyes grew wide. "You said you would!"

"I'm still thinking," Tia said looking at her sideways. "And don't you start pouting or I'll make up my mind now, and you won't like the answer you get."

Ida gave Serenity another hug. "So what high school are you going to next year, honey?"

"Mommy's making me go to Divine Savior," Serenity said unhappily.

"Why do you say it like that? You don't want to go to that school?"

Serenity shifted her weight. "Not really."

"Why not?"

"Because it's an all-girls school," Tia said.

"Yeah," Serenity spoke up. "Nothing to look at but girls all day."

"That's right," Tia said. "The less distractions, the better."

Ida agreed. "Listen to me, girl," she said gently lifting Serenity's chin up. "I'm about to be fifty years old so I know what I'm talking about. Been there, done that. You need to make something out of your life first. You gonna have plenty of time for boys."

Serenity remained silent but the discontented look on her face revealed her dissatisfaction with her mother's decision.

"Come on," Ida said, waving them toward the back room. "I got something for both of you." Tia and Serenity followed her past a colorful array of potted plants, flowers, and hanging baskets all creatively displayed throughout the store.

They entered the back room where there were more flowers resting on a workbench, waiting to be grouped together in bunches and secured with an assortment of brightly colored ribbons. Ida reached beneath one of the workbenches and pulled out two bouquets of pink, white, purple, and yellow carnations wrapped in colorful papier-mâché. She gave one to Tia and the other one to Serenity.

"Aww, these are so pretty, Grandma," Serenity said as she slowly twirled the bouquet around. "Thank you."

"You're welcome," she said smiling, with her hands clasped together.

Tia inhaled the soft aroma from the flowers. "Umm, and they smell good too. Thank you, Mama."

"I call this my bouquet of happiness," Ida said. "Being surrounded by all these pretty flowers makes me happy." She looked at Serenity and smiled. "Make sure you keep you some happy," she said. "Because I'm telling you, a sad soul can kill you, child. You remember that."

"Amen," Tia said.

"Preach!" the familiar voice of an older woman shouted out.

Everyone turned to see Mavis walking toward them smiling.

"Hey, Granny," Serenity said smiling.

"Hey, sweetie," Mavis said squeezing her tight. "Seeing you always lifts my spirits."

Then it was Tia's turn. "Hey, Grandma," she said hugging her long and hard. "How are you doing?"

"Well, I'm worse than some, better than most," she said with a smile.

Tia gave her a solemn look.

"I'm just getting old," Mavis reassured her. "That's a natural course of life. You're a nurse. You should know that!"

"I know, Grandma," Tia sighed. "I'm just concerned about you."

Tia remembered her grandmother's reply after she'd told her how much she admired her for taking care of Henry.

"Ain't nothing to admire," Mavis had said. "I ain't doing nothing that God ain't already done for me. He forgave me for all my sins, and I know," she had hit the table with the top of her index finger, "that if I want to get to heaven, I got to forgive Henry and everybody else." She'd nodded her head. "And that's what I plan to do. End of story."

"Don't worry," Ida said interrupting Tia's thoughts. "She's in good hands."

After Henry's death, Ida had moved back into the house to keep a closer eye on her mother. Mavis had eventually decided to put the house up for sale, and once it sold, she and Ida thought it would be a good idea to invest some of the money from the sale into a flower shop for Ida.

They found an eye-catching two-story lannon stone building; the lower unit already housed a flower shop, and the upper unit had been renovated into a spacious apartment with a living room, dining room, galley kitchen, three bedrooms, and a small bathroom. It was practically move-in ready. After Ida had added her own personal touch to the flower shop, they were able to move in and pick up where the previous owner had left off.

Investing in the flower shop had proved to be a good decision. Not only was Ida her own boss, but her business provided a modest income for herself and Mavis. She liked living above her shop. Although coexisting with her mother sometimes got on her nerves, it was a comfortable living arrangement, and since Mavis was getting up there in age, Ida did not want her living alone.

"When are we gonna eat?" Serenity asked. "I'm hungry."

Ida chuckled. "Just hold on, little lady." She walked over to the window and turned the OPEN sign over so that the word CLOSED now faced the street. Then she locked the door and turned on the alarm. "Y'all made it just in time," she said, looking over her shoulder.

"Come on," Mavis said, heading for the stairs that led up to their apartment. "Let's eat."

Chapter Twenty-two

Tia and Serenity entered the upper unit above the flower shop and were welcomed by the inviting aroma of baked chicken with mashed potatoes and gravy, corn bread, and green beans.

"Umm," Tia said. "It's smelling good in here."

No one knew it, but the aroma of Mavis' home-cooked meals held a special sentiment for Tia. It had been during a meal similar to this one years ago when she had lived with Mavis that she remembered noticing what would be the beginning to a change in her demeanor. Her grandmother had seemed a little bit softer around the edges on that day, and Tia remembered liking the change, yet being apprehensive and confused at the same time.

Not only was Tia hoping that this monthly tradition of visiting the two matriarchs in her family would create a legacy for Serenity, but preserving the few good memories she had of Ida and Mavis allowed her to create good memories now, right here in the present. Not only were they welcomed by the aroma of Mavis' and Ida's hospitality, but the warm décor of the apartment itself beckoned them in each time they came to visit.

The octagon-shaped living room, which was at the front of the apartment, had a floor-to-ceiling window on each of the three walls, allowing an abundance of natural light to fill the room and make its way into the connecting dining room as well. The arched entryway combined with the crown molding in the dining room finalized the touches of warmth and grace.

Mavis opened the built-in china cabinet and took out four plates. "Go on and sit down," she said. "Everything's ready."

"Let me go wash my hands," Tia said while Serenity quickly sat down at the rectangular dining-room table.

"Serenity," Tia called from the bathroom, "did you wash your hands?"

She pouted as she pushed the chair back from the table and headed for the bathroom.

Ida started laughing. "Lord, that child is really hungry."

"Uh-huh," Mavis said. "Let me make her plate first."

After everyone was seated with their food, Mavis said grace.

"Lord, we thank you for this food we're about to eat, and we pray that you bless each and every morsel. In Jesus' name, amen."

"So where's that husband of yours?" Mavis asked as she put a piece of chicken in her mouth. "How's he doing?"

Tia glanced at Serenity whose eyes were focused on the food on her plate.

"Yeah," Ida said. "He never comes to visit anymore."

"His back is still bothering him," Tia said. "The doctor said he can't sit in one spot for more than thirty minutes at a time," she lied.

Now Serenity was looking at her. Tia glared at her hard.

Ida looked at Serenity, then at Tia. "That doesn't sound good," she said.

Tia felt like she was being scrutinized.

"Maybe he should see another doctor," Mavis said.

"What he needs to do is stop taking all those pills," Serenity blurted out.

Tia stopped chewing.

Ida and Mavis looked at each other, then at Tia. "What pills?" Ida asked.

Tia glared intently at Serenity. "Are you done?"

Serenity looked at her plate. "You mean with eating?"

"Yes," Tia said tightly. "With eating."

"Uh-uh," she said. "Can I have some more chicken?"

"Here," Ida said getting up from the table, "bring me your plate." She put a leg and a thigh on Serenity's plate. "You want some gravy?" she asked.

Serenity nodded her head. "Just a little," she said. "Thank you."

"You're welcome," Ida said. "You can eat that in the living room but take some napkins and eat over this towel. I don't want no gravy stains on my couch."

Serenity went into the living room, and after a few minutes, they heard the television set come on.

Ida sat back down at the table. "So what is she talking about?" she asked Tia.

Tia took a sip of iced tea from her glass and wiped her mouth.

"What's going on?" Mavis asked.

"It's just his back," Tia said. "Well, he says it's his back."

"And what?" Ida asked. "He's taking a lot of pain medication?"

Tia moved her green beans around in her plate. "Yes," she said.

"Does he realize how dangerous that is?" Mavis asked.

"I tried to tell him," Tia said still stirring the green beans around.

"Well, did he listen?" Ida asked. "I mean you *are* a nurse."

Tia sighed. "That's what I said. But no, he didn't listen."

"Well, I can tell you right now," Mavis said in that way that would always be hers, that way that confirmed a little piece of the old Mavis still remained, "if y'all end up getting a divorce, you better make sure that man pays."

"Aw, Mama," Ida said, "ain't nobody getting a divorce. And keep your voice down. Serenity might hear you."

Mavis threw her napkin down on the table. "That's just ridiculous," she said. She picked it back up to wipe her mouth. "What is he trying to do? Kill himself?"

After dinner and all the way home, Serenity tried to be on her best behavior. She really wanted to attend the audition in March.

"Please, Ma," she begged as they entered the house.

"I don't know, Serenity," Tia said taking off her coat. "What day is it on?"

"It's on the first Sunday in March at eleven o'clock," Serenity said with anticipation in her voice.

Tia frowned. "That means we'd have to miss Sunday services."

"We could go to the 8:00 service," Serenity said eagerly.

Tia looked at her and arched her eyebrows. "You must really want to go, don't you?"

Serenity nodded her head quickly.

Lorenzo spoke up from his usual spot on the sofa. "Just take her," he said harshly without diverting his attention from the television set.

Serenity looked at him, bewildered by his approval, especially since she'd called him an addict right before they'd left for Milwaukee that afternoon. Maybe he'd spoken up because he was tired of hearing her whine or maybe he actually wanted her to go—she couldn't decide. She looked at her mother. "Please," she whispered.

"Well," Tia said after she shot an angry look at Lorenzo, "we'll have to go to the 8:00 service."

"Yay!" Serenity yelled.

Lorenzo turned the volume up on the television set. "Can y'all quiet it down?"

Tia ignored his request as she pulled her cell phone out of her purse. "Don't be too quick to yell 'yay'," she said.

"I also have to work on that day." She walked into the kitchen. "Let me see if I can switch shifts with somebody."

A few minutes later Tia ended her call. She turned around and jumped, startled to find Serenity standing right behind her. "Okay," she said, "I got somebody to switch shifts with me." She looked toward the living room where Lorenzo still sat on the couch. "Now, you can yell 'yay'."

"Yay!" Serenity yelled.

Chapter Twenty-three

Homer roamed through the empty rooms of his house holding his cell phone to his ear. Franny was on the other end updating him about her condition. He didn't really care, but he listened anyway.

"They tell me I had a heart attack," Franny said, "but I'm stable now."

Homer sighed heavily and rolled his eyes.

"I was on a medical floor," she continued, "and then they shipped me right on back to where I was before all this happened; the same room and everything."

Homer remained silent. He knew what she was leading up to, and his mind fluctuated between whether he should let her stay with him when she asked.

"I'm being discharged today." Her statement lingered in the air like unsettled particles of dust. Homer stopped pacing the floor.

Franny didn't want to ask him again, but it was too cold to sleep in her car. Her only other option was to stay in a shelter, but that would have to be her last option. She put aside her pride once more.

"I know you said you didn't have the room," she said slowly, "but it would only be for two months. I'm still on that waiting list."

Even though Homer believed Franny had forfeited her relationship with him by reason of default, he changed his mind and decided to let her stay with him.

"Well," he said slowly, "since Sandra's not here . . ."

"Oh? Is she on vacation?" Franny asked.

"No," Homer said quickly. "She left."

"Is she coming back?" Franny asked quietly.

"I don't think so," he said coldly.

"I'm sorry to hear that, Homer."

"So you said two months, right?" he asked, ignoring her condolences.

"Two months," she reassured him.

He hesitated before answering. "All right," he said slowly.

"Thank you," Franny said, appreciative of what she thought was her son's change of heart.

But Homer's decision had nothing to do with his heart. He had his own agenda, and this time, things were going to go his way. Once he brought his mother home, he was going to make her admit to the real reason why she'd abandoned him. He wasn't going to allow her to leave him again with unanswered questions.

"What time are you being discharged?"

"They tell me I'll be able to leave anytime between one and two o'clock," she said.

"I'll be there around one thirty."

"Okay," Franny said but Homer had already hung up the phone.

Several hours later, Homer pulled his car into one of the patient pickup spots in front of the hospital. He turned on his flashers and got out of the car. It had been two years since he'd last seen his mother. He walked through the sliding doors and stopped at the information desk. A young woman who appeared to be in her early twenties addressed him. "Can I help you?" she said.

Homer stared at her. Her youthful voice and vibrant appearance distracted him.

"Can I help you?" she asked again.

He blinked. "What room is my mother in?"

The receptionist looked at Homer as if he were crazy. "Who is your mother?"

"Oh, I'm sorry," Homer chuckled. "Francis Woodard."

The receptionist looked at the computer as she moved the mouse slightly on the pad before clicking it several times. "Room 523," she said without smiling.

As Homer rode the elevator up to the fifth floor, he wondered how it would feel to see his mother again.

He walked down the long corridor and found the door to room 523 ajar. He entered without knocking, and saw Franny sitting on the side of the bed listening to the nurse finalize her discharge instructions.

She had aged considerably since he'd last seen her, and she was almost unrecognizable to him. Her hair was now completely gray and stopped just at the base of her neck. The passing of time had altered his perception of how she would look, and her short and frail appearance was completely opposite of the image he'd had in his mind.

Franny saw him enter the room and tried to smile, but the hostile look in his eyes stopped her. She returned her focus to the nurse who continued going over the discharge instructions with her.

Homer fixed his eyes on the nurse's back and tilted his head to the side. There was something familiar about her stance and the sound of her voice.

"Do you have any questions, Ms. Woodard?" the nurse asked.

"No, ma'am, I don't," Franny said softly. She looked past her shoulder and pointed to Homer. "My son's here now to pick me up."

The nurse turned to say hello. Her mouth opened, but the words came to a halt somewhere between her vocal cords and her tongue.

Homer struggled to greet her. "Hel-lo, Tia."

Tia regained her composure. "Hello," she said stiffly.

"Oh, you two know each other?" Franny asked.

"No," Homer said quickly. He pointed to her name tag. "Her name's right there."

"Oh," Franny let out a weak laugh, "that's right. I forgot about that."

"Are you ready?" Homer asked impatiently. "I have my flashers on."

Tia looked at Franny. "I'll send an assistant in to take you downstairs." She glanced at Homer as she walked past him. "I'm all done here," she said as she left the room.

Chapter Twenty-four

Homer pulled the zipper of his coat up as far as it would go as he dropped the garbage bag into the bin behind his house. He stopped to look at a squirrel that seemed to have made his home in his backyard. February was almost over, but there were still icy mixtures of snow that randomly covered the grass and created shiny borders along the edges of the walkway.

He kicked at a section of semifrozen gravel and discovered a handful of stones buried underneath the icy blanket. He picked up the rocks and tossed them back and forth in his hands as he thought about the way Tia had treated him—not just at the hospital but the last time he'd talked to her on the phone, the same night Sandra had left him several weeks ago.

He'd been trying to reach her ever since their last telephone conversation when she'd abruptly hung up on him, and she hadn't returned any of his calls. He pulled out his phone and dialed her number again. It rang several times before transferring over to the automated voice instructing him to leave a message at the sound of the beep.

"Hi, Tia," Homer said in a deep sultry voice. "Call me when you get this message. I'd like to see you."

He disconnected the call and shoved his phone back into his pocket. The wind was blowing furiously as he took a few steps toward the squirrel. Homer remembered when he'd met Tia at the grocery store that day in January. The meeting had not been accidental. He'd been curious about his neighbor and her daughter for months. He liked the youthfulness both of them displayed, and he had been watching them come and go on a regular basis. It had been a Saturday afternoon, and Homer had been looking at Tia's house from his basement window when he saw her garage door go up.

The urge to follow her had hit him instantly, and he remembered running upstairs, grabbing his coat and car keys and getting into his car. He'd followed her from a distance, and when she'd pulled into the parking lot of a large supermarket just a few miles down the road, Homer had pulled in too.

He'd been careful to keep some distance between the two of them, and he'd parked his car several rows down from the row she'd parked in. Then he'd sat in his car and waited until Tia had entered the grocery store.

She hadn't been easy to find. The store had been crowded with shoppers buying groceries to replenish their kitchen cabinets and pantry shelves. Homer had roamed up and down each aisle, placing random items in his shopping cart until he'd turned the corner and spotted her. She was standing over a bushel of apples in the produce section, and he'd gathered his composure and pushed his shopping cart in her direction.

He remembered the startled look on Tia's face when he'd introduced himself. He hadn't meant to startle her; he'd just wanted to get to know her and he'd wanted her to know him too. He'd wanted her to know that he gave a good massage . . . before she had a chance to notice his limp.

Once he'd told her about his special skill, it was *her* curiosity that had piqued. And that had been exactly what he'd hoped would happen. Homer had meant what he'd said when he'd told Tia that if she needed anything, he was her man. She'd taken him up on his offer once. Now she was ignoring him.

The squirrel took a few steps back just as Homer threw one of the rocks in its direction. It scurried to the right, barely saving the end of its unkempt tail from the impact.

Homer sighed. He felt like he would never escape his unlovable fate. The wind died down, and the next two rocks Homer threw at the squirrel produced a game of dodge ball. Then, he made a fake lunge toward the squirrel, and it stood up on its hind legs, looking at him with fanatical eyes.

Just then, he heard the hinges on the back door creak. He glanced over his shoulder. "Go back in the house, Franny," he said sternly.

He heard the back door creak again as the squirrel stretched its neck up high as if a newfound sense of courage and dignity had been instilled into its blood.

Egged on by a feeling of hopelessness, Homer threw the fourth rock, and it caught the squirrel on the left side of its chest. The squirrel dropped back to the ground and rested on all four limbs.

Homer took a few steps forward, but the squirrel did not run away. It just kept its distance, watching him. He pulled a small red apple out of his coat pocket and stretched out his hand toward the squirrel.

"Here, squirrelly, squirrel," he whispered, "come and get your apple."

The squirrel inched forward, hesitated, and then moved a few feet closer. Homer's other hand held the last and biggest rock. He raised his hand with the rock in it over his head. He was trying to figure out the distance and precise amount of force it would take to put this creature out of its misery. The squirrel continued to inch closer to the hand that held the apple, then suddenly darted in the opposite direction.

Smart squirrel, Homer thought as he limped back to the house. He stopped just before opening the back door, and wondered how big the rocks would have to be for a person.

Chapter Twenty-five

It had only been one day since Franny had moved into Homer's house. She knew it would take time for her feelings of awkwardness to decrease. But she hoped the dark vibe she encountered when she first walked through the foyer of his home would not remain. It threatened to suffocate her, and many times she felt as though she could not breathe properly. Then there was the incident with the squirrel that had created a dreadful feeling within her.

Even though she'd closed the back door after Homer instructed her to, Franny had continued to watch him from the kitchen window. It had been disheartening to see him throw rocks at the squirrel; that had been cruel enough. But when the last rock he'd thrown had actually hit the squirrel, Franny let out a small moan as if she, herself, had been hit.

When she saw him lift his hand with the rock in it over his head, she'd turned away from the window. Surely, he wasn't trying to kill the squirrel! She covered her mouth with her hand. *Why would Homer do such a thing?*

After dinner, Franny began washing the dishes. Homer had not allowed her to cook but had delegated her to cleaning up the kitchen instead. She put away the leftovers from a meal that she and Homer had eaten in separate rooms; he'd eaten his meal in the living room in front of the television set, she'd eaten hers in the kitchen.

She stood scrubbing the last metal pan as she entertained herself with thoughts of paradise, *her* paradise, which she imagined to be an environment that was faultless and unsullied . . . nothing like the unforgiving atmosphere she now found herself living in. She dried the pan and put it away, then went into the dimly lit living room to watch television.

She sat down on the leather sectional, then got back up. "Homer," she said walking over to the closed blinds, "why do you keep it so dark in here?"

"Don't open them," he said sternly. "The light hurts my eyes. Besides, when you let the light in, it reflects off the TV, and I can't see the picture clearly."

Franny walked over to the small Tiffany lamp sitting on the end table next to the sectional. She bent down slightly and pulled the chain. A small amount of light mingled with the semidarkness. She sat down and sighed as she began watching a man on the television screen.

He was sitting behind a desk with a small stack of papers in front of him and a computer situated behind the papers. "How far would you like to go?" he asked the woman on the other side of the desk.

The woman shrugged her shoulders and said, "At least 2,000 miles or so."

"That's not far enough," Franny mumbled as she began thumbing through the pages of an outdated *Seventeen* magazine. "She should go farther."

"You mean like you did?" Homer asked.

Franny stiffened.

"I waited," he said.

She turned toward him. "I tried to explain to you years ago, Homer," she said. "But you wouldn't or couldn't hear me."

"I can hear you now," he said. "Try again."

"Can you?" She looked at him with tired eyes.

"Try again," he repeated.

Franny removed her glasses. "I was seventeen, Homer," she said. "I was young and, of course, very naïve." Even though Franny hoped she would be able to make amends between herself and her estranged son, she was discouraged by the possibility that it would not happen if he continued to remind her of her mistake every day for the next two months.

"I thought my mother could take care of you much better than I could," she continued. "She had the experience and she wanted you."

"So you left me with her and ran off to another city, right?" he said harshly.

"I didn't just leave you, Homer," she said rubbing the bridge of her nose. "I left you with family, with someone who loved you."

"You think that makes a difference?"

She looked at him. "Actually, I do," she said. "It was better than leaving you with a stranger."

"Why'd you have to leave me at all?" His voice was hard and cold.

"Your grandmother was going to take me to court if I didn't make her your legal guardian. That showed me how much she wanted you, so I signed the papers. I'm sorry, Homer."

"If you would have been there for me, she wouldn't have had to go that far."

Franny looked at him with sad eyes. "Is that what she told you?"

"It doesn't matter," he said lowering his head.

"Homer. I've asked God to forgive me, and He has. Now, I'm asking you to forgive me."

Homer remained silent.

"What do you know about Jesus, Homer?"

He jerked his head up and stared at her from across the room. "Really?" he said. "You're asking me what I know about Jesus?" A look of bewilderment spread across his face. "What does that have to do with anything?"

"It has a lot to do with everything," Franny said. "Now, and when you die."

"I already know about God," he said returning his eyes to the television set.

"But I didn't ask you that," she said gently. "I asked you what you knew about Jesus."

Homer crossed his leg and wiggled his deformed left foot.

Franny's eyes traveled to the deformity that was hidden by the cotton socks Homer had on.

He stopped wiggling his foot. "I know a little something about Jesus," he said. "And the part I know is that He didn't abandon anybody. But that's cool." He uncrossed his leg. "Everything's cool."

"No, Homer, it's not cool," Franny said. "It's never been cool. And I understand why you're angry." She wanted to move closer to him, to hug him or even touch him which she had not done in two years. Instead, she remained seated. "Homer," she said gently, "I can never apologize enough for leaving you. I'm sorry, and I'd like to have a relationship with you for whatever length of time I have left on this earth."

He looked at her and a stab of guilt pierced his conscience. He snickered in an effort to convince himself that her sparkless eyes were due to her old age and not his unpleasant demeanor directed toward her. She was just getting what she deserved. It was karma.

"You want a relationship now?" he said. "After fifty-one years? It's kind of late, don't you think?"

"Yes," she agreed, "it's kind of late. But it doesn't have to be *too* late. I'm willing to try if you are. It might be the death of me. But I'm going to try if it's the last thing I do."

He stared at her hard. "Can a leopard change its spots?"

She stared back at him. "Well," she said slowly, "since God made the leopard, anything is possible."

Chapter Twenty-six

It was three thirty in the morning when Franny got up quietly and tiptoed to the kitchen to get a glass of water. An increasing feeling of uneasiness had come over her ever since she'd seen Homer throwing rocks at that squirrel.

She began to wonder if she'd made a mistake by moving in with her estranged son. She tried not to remind herself that she still had 59 days to go before an apartment would be available for her.

As she passed Homer's closed bedroom door, she noticed a faint light flowing from underneath the opening. The dark spirit that encompassed every room of the house grew even darker, and she hurried on to the kitchen.

On her way back, she heard soft irregular tapping sounds coming from behind his door. *What is he doing in there at this time of the morning?* She stopped to listen; she heard three taps, a burst of taps in rapid succession, and then one final tap.

Suddenly, the light went out, and Franny hurried down the hall to her room. The water in her glass rocked back and forth like a pendulum leaving liquid teardrops on the hallway floor. She closed her door and sat down on the bed.

"Franny!" Homer yelled knocking hard on her door.

She jumped, and more water escaped from the glass to her nightgown. Her hand shook as she placed the glass on the nightstand. Ever since the squirrel, she didn't know what Homer might be capable of.

"Franny!" His voice sounded like thunder. "I know you're awake. You spilt water all over the floor."

Her chest heaved up and down as she opened the door. His menacing figure blocked the doorway, and his hazel eyes frightened her as he stood looking at her.

"Well?" he said.

She opened her mouth to speak but nothing came out.

"Water." He pointed to the hallway floor. "Mop." He spoke to her as if she were a child—no—less than that—as if she were an idiot. "Now," he barked over his shoulder as he walked away.

Franny held on to the doorknob with one hand and the wall with the other hand until her trembling subsided. When she heard Homer's bedroom door slam shut, she got the mop from the utility closet and quickly swabbed away the wet spots on the floor. She made sure to return the mop to its exact resting position in the closet when she had finished.

She went back to her bedroom and changed into a dry gown. Her heart was still beating rapidly as she got down on her knees to pray.

"Heavenly Father," she started, "forgive me for my sins as I forgive those who sin against me. I tried to make amends, Lord, but my son is full of anger. Touch his heart, Father. Prepare him to receive Jesus Christ as His savior, and let his soul be healed. Thank you, Father. In Jesus' name I pray, amen."

She rose slowly and got into bed. She turned onto her side and pulled the cover up tight around her shoulders. Her body had become weakened by disease, and her heart was heavy from loneliness and pain. The thought of living under Homer's roof for another six weeks had now become unbearable to her.

Three hours later, a familiar heaviness returned to the center of her chest. As it traveled to her left arm with greater intensity, sixty-eight years of living passed before her in a flash. She remembered part of a prayer she'd been taught as a child . . . *If I should die before I wake, I pray, dear Lord, my soul do take.* A chill passed through her as she sighed heavily. And then she saw the paradise she'd been dreaming of.

Chapter Twenty-seven

It was early Sunday morning when the ambulance pulled into the cul-de-sac. Its siren was silent. Homer walked calmly to the front door and let the paramedics in. He led them to the room where Franny lay still, eyes closed with the covers still pulled up around her neck. The glass of water she'd gotten in the middle of the night remained untouched.

"What happened?" the paramedic asked.

"I got up around eight o'clock this morning," Homer said nonchalantly. "I called her name and she didn't answer. I went to check on her," he stretched his arm out toward the bed where she lay, "and there she was."

The paramedic looked at him strangely. "Was she on any medications or did she have any illnesses?"

"She had a heart condition."

The paramedic opened the folder he was carrying, pulled out a pen, and began writing down the answers to his questions. "What kind?"

"I'm not sure," Homer said. "But she just had a heart attack recently."

"Was she on any type of medication?"

"I don't know."

The paramedic stopped writing and looked up at Homer. "She just had a heart attack and you don't know if she was on any medications?"

Homer looked directly into the paramedic's eyes. "No, I don't."

"And you said she's your mother?"

Homer looked down at the blanket his mother had wrapped herself in. "That's right," he said.

The paramedic turned and raised his eyebrows as he looked at his partner. "Let's get her transported," he said.

After they left, Homer went into the kitchen to make himself a cup of coffee. As he removed a scoop of coffee grounds from the container, he heard Franny's words from their last conversation echo in his head: *"It might be the death of me,"* she'd said. *"But I'm going to try if it's the last thing I do."*

A lump began to form in his throat. How dare she die before he had a chance to tell her how he felt? He dropped the scoop and the coffee grounds scattered across the counter. It wasn't enough that she had abandoned him as a child; now, she'd gone and did it again, only this time, it was permanent!

He threw the open can of coffee against the wall, then balanced himself against the kitchen counter. After a few minutes, his heavy breathing began to subside but the rage inside of him had not.

The contempt he'd felt for his mother returned. He brushed the coffee grounds off the counter and snatched a broom out of the kitchen closet. After he'd swept the crumbs into a neat pile, he carefully scooped them into the dustpan and dumped them into the wastebasket.

He stood thinking about what kind of funeral his mother would have. He realized he had no idea who her friends were, or if she even had any, for that matter. He stared at the dark mass of coffee grounds huddled together at the bottom of the white plastic bag. He inhaled deeply and decided he would just have her cremated.

Homer rotated his shoulders and turned his neck from side to side, then he walked out of the kitchen. He went into his bedroom and turned on his laptop. There was no time to feel sad about her death, and he didn't have any tears to shed. As a matter of fact, he hadn't shed any tears in a long time—not since he'd been a little boy.

Chapter Twenty-eight

The beginning of March arrived unnoticed and uncelebrated by most people. It might just as well have been the month of February because of the unrelenting cold temperatures. The only reason Serenity took note of the month was because it was the first Sunday in March—and audition day had finally arrived.

As she walked into the Brookridge Mall with Tia, Serenity was convinced that she was the perfect candidate for the audition. They rode the elevator to the basement level, and after being checked in, Serenity entered the small auditorium. She stood in line with the other candidates, listening to the coordinator as she told everyone what rules to follow for the audition that was to begin in a few minutes.

There would be a three-minute practice walk down the makeshift runway situated in the middle of the room, and everyone should smile, not be nervous, and just have fun.

Fun? Serenity wasn't there to have fun! She was there to prove everyone wrong about her. And if—no—*when*, she was chosen, it meant that she was going to be a part of the first fashion show that the Brookridge Mall had ever had! It also meant no more jokes from Cookie.

This could just be the beginning, Serenity thought. Once she was chosen and whisked away to New York, or Paris even—where the *real* models lived—maybe that look on her parents' face would go away for good!

The large industrial fan circulated the stagnant air around the small room, which contained several empty metal chairs pushed against the bare walls, the makeshift runway, a full-length mirror, and a rectangular table for the judges.

Serenity listened to the racket of voices all talking at once. There were at least a hundred people waiting to audition, and her five foot ten inch frame towered over almost everyone else, including several boys who had come out to audition as well.

She was next in line to audition. She felt her shoulders beginning to hunch and her spine beginning to curve. She arched her back and straightened up. The sharp ache that followed reminded her to stand up straight like Tia was always telling her to do.

She looked over toward her mother who sat stoically in one of the metal folding chairs. The young girl sitting next to Tia watched the events unfold. She smiled at the girl standing behind Serenity and gave her a thumbs-up sign. Serenity thought about Cookie and wished she could have come along to be her support, but her parents would not alter their church schedule.

Finally, it was Serenity's turn. She walked up the three wooden stairs that led to the stage. She pushed her shoulders back and thrust her hips forward. She had studied the way the models walked on *America's Top Model*, and she had been practicing. She placed her left foot in front of her right one and inhaled deeply. She was ready to take the first step.

"Crazy In Love" by Beyoncé started to play, and Serenity hit the runway stomping, one long beautiful stride after the other. Left, right, left, right. She kept her steps steady and in unison with the music, strutting up and down the aisle.

The only problem was the heels on her shoes. They were too high, and they made her feet hurt, but these were the kind of shoes she'd seen on the feet of the models on television. After a considerable amount of pleading and begging for the shoes, her mother had relented and had purchased them for her. Serenity tried to maintain some sort of elegance within her stride. She let her long legs lead her in a smooth and flowing motion. Nice and easy. *Yes. Now she had it!*

When she got to the end of the runway, she stopped and looked each judge directly in the eye just like she'd seen the models do on TV. She released the judges' gaze seconds before her jaws released the flawless smile she had attached to her face.

She made her pivot, and it was then that the ridiculously oversized heel on her left shoe decided it could not handle such an elaborate turn. The shoe, along with her ankle, leaned inward and she stumbled sideways off the elevated platform. Some of the contestants rushed to her aid, and in a haze Serenity saw her mother shaking her head. The girl sitting next to her covered her mouth.

As she scrambled to her feet, she caught a glimpse of herself in the mirror. The pretty white lace had been ripped away from the hem of her black chiffon dress, the red velvet bow in her hair now swung back and forth in front of her face, and the heel that had caused all the trouble to begin with was now completely broken off.

Serenity looked at her mother, who was still shaking her head, that familiar look of disgust plastered all over her face. She felt like crying, but there wasn't time. She removed the other shoe from her foot and got back on the runway, walking barefoot all the way to the end.

Chapter Twenty-nine

Serenity was not chosen to be one of the models. Now she had time to cry as she and Tia drove home in silence.

Tia sighed. "Don't feel bad," she said as she pulled up to the curb in front of their house. "You'll be picked next time."

"No, I won't," she said between sniffles.

Tia got out of the car quickly and rushed up the walkway. "I've got to change clothes and get to work," she said.

"Ma . . . ," Serenity followed after her.

"It's almost two o'clock," Tia said hurrying past a sleeping Lorenzo on the couch. "Messing around with you and that audition's gonna make me late."

Serenity stood in the middle of the foyer watching her father sleep.

A few minutes later, Tia came skipping back down the stairs and whizzed past her. "I left twenty dollars on the counter," she said. "You can order a pizza for dinner if your daddy don't cook nothing."

Before Serenity could reply, Tia had shut the door.

Serenity went over to the couch and shook Lorenzo's shoulder. "Daddy," she said. "Daddy, wake up!"

Lorenzo raised his hand to his face and opened his eyes briefly. "What?"

"Daddy, I didn't . . ."

He rubbed his nose, and turned to his other side.

". . . make it," Serenity said to his back.

She stood over him listening to him snore. Today had been the worst day ever, she thought. The one thing she'd hoped wouldn't happen during her audition had happened. She tiptoed into the den and turned on the computer. She immediately went to the chat room and signed in. Moments later a message from Saucer appeared.

iluvhotgurlz13: wat happened?
Serenity2cute_13: wen?
iluvhotgurlz13: last time we talked
Serenity2cute_13: my dad came in
iluvhotgurlz13: oh snap
Serenity2cute_13: i kno
iluvhotgurlz13: where u at?
Serenity2cute_13: home
iluvhotgurlz13: where ur pops at?

Serenity tilted her head to the side and listened intently until she heard the reassuring sound of Lorenzo snorting as he inhaled.

Serenity2cute_13: sleep
iluvhotgurlz13: still wanna meet?
Serenity2cute_13: where?
iluvhotgurlz13: in front of that restaurant i told u about
Serenity2cute_13: which one?
iluvhotgurlz13: neds

Serenity looked over her shoulder.

Serenity2cute_13: neds?
iluvhotgurlz13: yup
Serenity2cute_13: when?

iluvhotgurlz13: 2:30
Serenity2cute_13: ok, g2g
iluvhotgurlz13: don't be late
Serenity2cute_13: i won't

Serenity signed out of the chat room and shut down the computer.

She went into the kitchen and called Cookie.

"Hey," Cookie said with enthusiasm, "did you make it?"

"No, I didn't," Serenity said solemnly.

"Aww, I'm sorry. But maybe next year, huh?"

"Yeah, maybe," Serenity said. "But guess what I'm about to do."

"What?"

"I'm going to meet Saucer."

Cookie gasped. "For real?" she whispered.

"For real," Serenity said.

"Where? At the mall?"

"No, at that old restaurant."

"Neds?"

"Yep," she said defiantly.

"Ooh," Cookie squealed. "Are you scared?"

"Umm, not really," Serenity lied. Her heart was beating fast, and she tried to control the nervousness in her voice. "You wanna come with me?"

"I can't. We're going back to church."

"Well, I'll tell you what happens."

"You better."

"I will," Serenity said.

She hung up the phone, disappointed that Cookie could not come with her. She began to have second thoughts about going downtown alone to meet Saucer. What if he wasn't who he said he was?

She went upstairs and grabbed her favorite Hello Kitty hat, stopping to look at herself in her bedroom mirror.

What if Saucer didn't like the way she looked? She stood still, staring at her reflection in the mirror. Her dream of becoming a model had just been crushed. Nothing could be worse than that.

She went back downstairs and picked up the twenty-dollar bill her mother had left on the counter. Then she left to meet the boy she'd met online.

Chapter Thirty

Tony turned on his daughter's computer to check her browser history. He was dismayed when he discovered how many times she'd visited the same chat site over the course of several weeks.

"Shari," he called, "can you come up here, please? And bring Cookie with you," he added.

Shari came upstairs with Cookie following behind her. They entered Cookie's bedroom where Tony stood continuing to browse through the history. He turned when they entered the room.

"What is this?" he asked pointing to the computer screen.

"What is what?" Shari asked.

"I'm actually talking to Cookie," Tony said. He stared at her. "Well?"

Cookie stood with her mouth open.

Shari moved closer to the computer and frowned. "Are all of these chat rooms?"

"Yeah." Tony said angrily. "Is this what you've been doing on the computer?"

"Daddy, no," Cookie whimpered. "I mean, we only got on there once."

"Once?" He started counting the URL locations in the history box. "One, two, three . . ."

"It's the same one, Daddy."

"I don't care if it is," he said. "We specifically told you what the rules were for having a computer in your room, didn't we?"

"Yes," Cookie said looking at the floor.

"What are the rules, Cookie?" Shari asked as she stood next to Tony with her arms folded.

"No chat rooms," Cookie said softly.

"And why?" Shari asked, tapping her foot.

"Because they're not safe."

"What kind of people visit chat rooms, Cookie?"

Cookie looked confused.

"What kind?" Shari repeated.

Cookie shrugged. "I don't know."

"Exactly," Tony intervened as he began to exit out of the browsing history window. "You don't know. You don't know who you're talking to, and too many times we hear about grown men pretending to be boys luring young girls away from home."

"And who is *we*?" Shari asked.

"Huh?"

Shari was losing patience. "Cookie, stop standing there acting like you don't understand English! You said, 'we only got on there once' so I'm asking you, who is *we*?"

"Me and Serenity," she said.

Tony shut down the computer and began disconnecting the mouse and keyboard from the monitor. Then he disassembled the rest of the computer. "Since you've shown us that you can't follow the rules, you won't be using this computer anymore," he said as he unplugged it from the wall.

"I'm sorry," she said softly.

"You should be," Shari said, still standing in front of Cookie with her arms crossed. "Trust is a very important part of a person's character, and you've just shown us that we can't trust you."

"I'm sorry," she said again tearfully.

"Stop being sorry," Shari said. "Be more responsible. You know better!"

"But I wasn't talking to nobody on there. Serenity was."

"What do you mean, Serenity was? Who was she talking to?" Shari asked.

"A boy she met."

"What was this boy's name?"

"Saucer."

The frown on Shari's face deepened. "What?"

"We called him Saucer."

"Was that his real name?"

"I don't know. That's what we called him."

"Lord, have mercy," Shari said.

"And what did this boy and Serenity talk about?" Tony asked sternly.

"He wanted to meet her."

Shari looked at Tony.

"Meet her where?" Tony asked.

"At the mall but she said she couldn't."

"Thank God," Shari said.

"But she said she was gonna meet him in front of the restaurant today," Cookie added.

Tony looked at her in amazement. "What restaurant?"

"He just said some parking lot where a pizza restaurant used to be across the street from the mall."

"I'm going to call Tia," Shari said. She pulled out her phone and waited while the phone rang on the other end. "She's not answering," she said to Tony and disconnected the call. She gave the phone to Cookie. "Call Serenity and see if she's home," she said.

Cookie called Serenity's house number and listened to it ring several times before going to voice mail. "She's not answering."

Shari looked at Tony. "What should we do?"

"Let's go," he said. "Maybe we can find her."

Chapter Thirty-one

Homer smiled as he parked his tan two-door Cavalier across the street from the empty parking lot and waited for his little fish to show up. His car glistened under the February sun as he kept the engine running.

He marveled at how easy it had been to get her to meet him. The younger girls were so gullible, and that's what Homer liked best. But he liked them a little older too—they were just as gullible. Most of them required little to no coercing if a man knew what he was doing.

He smiled at his own cunningness. He was smart enough not to park his car directly on the deserted parking lot, but he'd chosen this particular area because it sat adjacent to a heavily trafficked street. He hadn't wanted to scare her off by suggesting they meet in a secluded location. This way, she would think she was safe. She wouldn't even realize that she was a fish out of water, already caught.

But then they never realized what they had gotten themselves into until it was too late . . . at least on their end. Sometimes, the teen girls—expecting to see a teenage boy—would be frightened when they saw him . . . a grown man. Many would try to run away, but they were never successful. They were no match for his strong grip, and he'd pull them into the car, and then drive them to a secluded location.

It was during these times that almost all of them would suddenly remember some vague responsibility they had to attend to at home. Homer thought it was funny how none of them ever came up with a different excuse to get away from him, and each time he ignored their pleas.

It was a game of bartering that Homer engaged in with the girls, and he never became violent with any of them. He might have been somewhat firm and aggressive getting them into his car but never violent. Not even with the girls who were unwilling to cooperate. With them, he offered a deal, a trade-off of sorts. "You do this for me," he'd say, "and I'll take you home."

Well, he hadn't meant their actual home. Once they stopped crying and did what he wanted them to do, he'd take them back to the pickup location and drop them off. He didn't know how they got home, and he didn't care. That was not part of the bargain.

The occasional women he'd met through online chat rooms were different. Most of them had been quite agreeable to meeting him at various motels, and there had been no need for him to barter and trade for favors.

Once he'd gotten married to Sandra, Homer had slowed down—no, he'd practically stopped—his search for women and young girls on the Internet. But then Sandra began to reveal her dissatisfaction with him, and he'd had no idea of how to become the man she said she needed him to be.

Little by little, Homer returned to his online obsession where neither his persona nor his existence required an explanation. But it didn't stop there. As his wife's dissatisfaction grew, Homer's fixation with his neighbor and her daughter began to intensify.

He surveyed the parking lot from behind the dark sunglasses he had on. The weeds sprouting up through the many cracks in the pavement were an indication of how long the restaurant in the center of the city had been closed.

The building had housed several different establishments over a period of five decades; from a mom-and-pop diner when he was a child to countless fast-food burger joints that migrated into various soul food restaurants to its last reinvention which was now defunct. Now, the mortar and brick building stood abandoned, and had been for quite some time, its windows boarded up.

Homer ran his fingers through the few strands of hair remaining on the top of his head. He looked up at the sign perched on top of the building's roof. It was a faded remnant of what used to be.

His attention was drawn to the city bus pulling up to its stop. Three teenage boys got off, and then the bus drove away. He looked at his watch and sighed. It was 2:20 p.m. Ten minutes passed before Homer saw the white top of the city bus approaching with its flashing LED letters. At the same time, his laptop lying on the passenger seat next to him beeped, indicating he had an e-mail message. He clicked on the mail link, and saw it was a delayed message from his fresh catch. Apparently, she'd uploaded a picture of herself after all.

"Hi" she wrote, "Here's my pic."

He clicked on the attachment and waited for the picture to download. He saw the light brown hair and recognized the cherry coloring on the tips of the bangs. *Well, well, well.* He chuckled. *So that's who the little fish is.*

His humor was short-lived when he looked up and noticed a brown Pontiac trailing two cars behind the city bus. His heartbeat increased as he looked at the front bumper held down with bungee cords. *Surely there's more than one brown Pontiac with a loose front bumper in this city . . .*

The computer stalled right at the bottom of her bangs, and his hands grew sweaty as he rolled his finger around the mouse pad, desperate to confirm her face. The screeching brakes of the bus startled him, and he looked up again. His heart was beating wildly as he searched for the Pontiac which had gotten caught by the red traffic light at the intersection.

The bus came to a stop, and Homer saw Serenity get off. Only her brown bangs that were dyed red on the ends were visible underneath her Hello Kitty hat. He slouched down in his seat and watched as she looked up and down the street, and then suddenly removed her Hello Kitty hat.

He continued watching her as she merged into the crowd of other people who had gotten off the bus, and quickly walked in the opposite direction of where his car was parked. Homer remained in his slouched position until Serenity—and the brown Pontiac—had disappeared.

He slowly returned to an upright position, wondering if it was just a coincidence that Tony and Shari happened to be driving down that particular street at 2:30 in the afternoon. He pulled out his cell phone. He'd missed the little fish this time, but what one won't do another one will, he thought.

He pressed *67 before dialing Tia's number.

"Hello?" she answered with a hint of caution.

Homer got straight to the point. "Why haven't you returned my calls?" he asked.

"Homer, this is not the time," she said. "I'm on my way to work."

He ignored the irritation in her voice. "Are you so busy that you can't take five minutes out of your day and pick up the phone?"

"Yes," she said as she sat in her car in the hospital's parking structure.

"Can I see you tonight?" he asked. "I can give you one of my massages to relax you."

Tia sighed heavily. "No, you can't see me tonight, Homer. Or any other night. I'm going to need you to stop calling me."

"Oh, okay," he said as his words spewed from his mouth with a moderate amount of speed. "Let me make it easy for you, then. I won't call you anymore, and you don't have to worry about calling me any—"

"I haven't," she interrupted.

"That's right," he said. "But you could have at least returned my calls. When were you going to anyway?"

Tia switched the phone to her other ear. "Homer, I told you what happened was a mistake." She took a deep breath. "I'm going to need you to stop calling me, now. I mean it."

"That's not what I asked you," he said dryly.

"But that's what I'm telling you." She began to feel uncomfortable. "I'm going to let you go, now."

Homer laughed sarcastically. "You already have, haven't you?" He cleared his throat. "If you don't want me, all you have to do is let me know."

Tia looked at her phone in astonishment. She didn't have time for this. Hadn't she made it clear that he would have to stop calling her? She knew what he wanted, the *only* thing he wanted, and her conscience would not allow her to cheat on her husband a second time. "I don't want you," she said firmly.

"The problem is," he said with a mixture of anger and urgency in his voice, "I still want you."

For just a few seconds Tia felt sorry for him. She knew what it felt like to want someone who didn't want you. But she was a married woman, and she'd had no business dealing with him—a married man—in the first place. Why hadn't she considered his wife and how she would have felt had she known her husband was cheating on her?

"This should have never happened," Tia said. "I have to go." And she disconnected the call before he had a chance to reply.

Chapter Thirty-two

Lorenzo sat on the couch floating in and out of consciousness. The tiny Ziploc bag lay empty on the floor at his feet.

"Suicide is not the answer," the elderly woman on the local Christian channel said. *"God, through Jesus Christ, made a way for you to surrender your heavy load. All of your burdens. Not some of your burdens,"* she emphasized as she stretched her arms out wide. *"All of them to Jesus."*

Lorenzo kept listening.

"Jesus," she continued, *"said, 'Come to me, all you who are weary and burdened, and I will give you rest . . .'"*

Lorenzo's thoughts were muddled, but his heart could still feel the heavy weight of his pain, the burden that had first come to visit him shortly after the incident happened when he was eleven years old.

Although he'd been too young to give it a name, he knew it had left him with an unpleasant feeling, one that he could not clearly communicate to anyone. The pain had left him for a while but later returned, and then made regular visits throughout his teen years. When he became an adult, the pain took up permanent residency in his soul.

"Do you believe that Jesus Christ is the Son of God" the woman asked, *"and that He died on the cross for your sins?"* She pointed her finger at the camera, and through his blurred vision, Lorenzo thought she was pointing directly at him.

"We're all sinners in need of forgiveness and change," she continued. *"Can you admit that you're a sinner? Are you in need of change?"* Her voice got stronger. *"Do you want to be forgiven?*

"Accept the Lord Jesus Christ as your savior." She was almost yelling. *"Surrender yourself to Him,"* she said. *"Ask Jesus to come into your life and take control of your heart. Ask Him,"* she pleaded, and her voice became soft again. *"He will if you ask Him to."*

Soft music began playing in the background, and Lorenzo thought it was the sweetest sound he had ever heard.

The woman lowered her voice. "Ask Jesus to come into your heart," she whispered. *"Let Him take over and give you the rest and the peace you can't find anywhere else. It doesn't matter what you've been through. It doesn't matter what your pain is. He can heal you. Surrender to Him and be healed. Surrender to Jesus and be set free!"*

Lorenzo's level of consciousness was fading. "Help me, Jesus!" he cried out.

"And remember," the elderly lady added with optimism, *"John 8:36 says, 'So if the Son sets you free, you will be free indeed.' Amen!"*

"Amen," Lorenzo mumbled.

"This is God's promise to you personally," she said, *"and God cannot lie. But,"* she stared directly into the camera, *"Satan can."*

She encouraged everyone who had been watching or listening to the program to pick up the phone and dial the 1-800 phone number that she gave. She also pointed out that the number was visible on the bottom of the television screen.

She said volunteers were waiting to talk and pray with people who were hurting, lost, and confused—people just like Lorenzo. In fact, Lorenzo thought he heard her say his name specifically, and he smiled.

He opened his eyes to look at the television screen. He tried to read the phone number, but all he saw was one short, blurry line. He reached for his phone and accidentally knocked it to the floor.

"Call now," he heard her saying. "Jesus is waiting." She read off the phone number again. Her voice sounded closer, louder, as it rose above the music playing in the background. He thought he heard a phone ringing. "Call now," she said, "before it's too late."

He bent down to pick up his phone.

"Jesus is the answer," she continued. "The only cure. He can do for you what that alcohol won't do, that needle can't do, and those pills you take will never do."

Lorenzo stood up quickly. How did she know he had taken all those pills? The room began spinning as he tried to focus on the numbers still showing on the television screen. He reached for the back of the couch in an effort to balance himself but fell sideways instead. His head bounced like an underinflated basketball as it made impact with the hardwood floor. Then he was still.

Chapter Thirty-three

It wasn't until Serenity had made it around the corner that she slowed down. Disappointed that she hadn't met Saucer, she wondered why Cookie's next-door neighbor had been sitting in his car across the street from the empty parking lot.

Now, she walked slowly home from the bus stop. She kept her head down as she carefully maneuvered her steps between the intermittent patches of ice on the sidewalk. Why was she such a failure? She couldn't even walk down a simple path without tripping over her own feet.

And no one seemed to care—not just about the failed audition but about her. She stepped over the cracks in the sidewalk. Her mother was too busy, and her father was too high. She thought Saucer had cared but even he hadn't shown up.

She reached in her pocket and pulled out her key as she walked up the pathway to her house. As soon as she opened the door, Catch came running up to her, but this time he didn't wait for her to rub and pat his back. He paced around in a circle, then ran back and forth from the hallway to the living room.

"Hey, Catch," Serenity said taking off her Hello Kitty hat. "What's wrong?" She followed him into the living room and immediately saw Lorenzo lying sideways on the floor.

She bent down and gently shook his shoulder. "Daddy?"

He didn't answer.

"Daddy!" She pushed his shoulder harder, causing his entire body to shake.

There was still no answer.

Her eyes searched quickly for the house phone sitting on the corner table in the hallway. She picked it up and called the hospital where her mother worked. When the operator answered, she asked to be connected the fifth floor.

"Victory Memorial, 5 West subacute unit. This is Stephanie. How can I help you?"

"I need to speak to my mom," Serenity blurted out.

"And who is your mom?"

"Tia Sparks!"

Moments later Tia was on the phone.

"Ma!" Serenity screamed. "There's something wrong with Daddy. He's lying on the floor, and I can't wake him up!"

"Wait," Tia spoke firmly. "Serenity, calm down. What do you mean you can't wake him up?"

"He's on the floor, and he won't wake up!"

"Is he breathing?"

It was silent.

"Serenity!"

She was crying now. "I can't tell!"

"Call 9-1-1. No, wait. I'll call them. You call Tony and Shari and tell them what happened!"

"Okay."

Tia hung up the phone and dialed 9-1-1.

"9-1-1," the operator answered. "What is your emergency?"

"I'm calling from Victory Memorial Hospital. My daughter just called and told me my husband is unconscious on the floor at our home. The address is . . ."

"What is your name, ma'am?"

"Tia Sparks."

"And your husband's name?"

"Lorenzo."

"What's the address?"

"5325 Cooper Circle."

"I'm sending someone now, ma'am."

"Can you have them bring him to Victory Memorial?"

"Yes, ma'am."

"Thank you." Tia's hands were shaking as she hung up the phone.

"What's going on?" her colleague asked. She'd been standing close by and had heard Tia on the telephone.

"My husband is hurt. They're bringing him here. Can you cover for me? I'm gonna have to leave when he gets here."

"Sure."

Tia quickly went over her patients with the other nurse. She was thankful that everyone was stable and that there were no elaborate procedures needing to be done on any of them.

"Thank you so much," Tia said as she swiped her badge through the time clock and ran to the elevator.

"No problem," the nurse said. "You go and check on your husband."

Tia's cell phone rang while she stood waiting for the metal elevator doors to open. It was Shari. "Hi, Shari. I'm on my way down to the ER now."

"The ER?" Shari repeated. "For what?"

"Didn't Serenity tell you?"

Shari hesitated. "I haven't talked to Serenity. We're not at home. But I've been trying to call you for about twenty minutes. What happened?"

"Lorenzo fell. Let me call you back," Tia said and quickly disconnected the call.

She dialed the number to her house. It rang five times before going to voice mail. "Serenity, where are you?" she yelled. "Pick up the phone!"

house almost falling
:e spread across the
he rang the doorbell
ouse. The ambulance
cided to turn around
and Shari—Homer's
ng on his door.
Hi, Serenity," he said

athing rapidly. Thick
· mouth as she talked.
hey're not home. My
ning."

He looked down toward her house, and then scanned the cul-de-sac. "Come in and calm down," he said feigning concern. "It's freezing out here." He touched her shoulder and stepped to the side. "I can take you to the hospital."

Serenity looked into his hazel eyes, then past the halfway open door. The foyer behind him was dark and uninviting, and something about the way he touched her shoulder made her feel uncomfortable.

"I have to get back to the house," she said backing down the steps.

"Wait," he reached out and grabbed her arm and pulled her into the foyer just as the shrill sound of the ambulance neared the cul-de-sac.

Serenity struggled to get away, but Homer's grip was too tight. He pulled her farther into the foyer, and then slammed the front door closed.

***

Tony saw the concerned look on Shari's face as she ended her call with Tia. "What's going on?" he asked.

"Lorenzo fell."

"Is he hurt?"

Shari sighed. "Apparently so. Tia called the ambulance."

"How did she know he fell?"

"I'm not sure. She must have talked to Serenity because she thought Serenity was with us."

Tony looked at her silently.

Shari gave him a knowing look. After hearing about Lorenzo's fall and the ambulance being called, Shari couldn't bring herself to tell Tia about Serenity. She didn't have the heart to tell her that the reason they weren't at home was because they were out looking for her daughter who had made plans to meet a total stranger. Shari decided she would tell her once things settled down.

Now, having been unsuccessful in their search for Serenity, Tony and Shari were just turning into the cul-de-sac when they saw the ambulance in front of Tia's house. Tony pulled up next to the ambulance.

"What happened?" he asked.

"Looks like a fall," one of the paramedics said as his partner helped him load Lorenzo into the back of the ambulance.

"Is his daughter here?" Shari asked.

"No one was home when we got here," the paramedic said. He headed for the driver's side of the vehicle. "The door was open when we arrived."

"Where is she?" Shari said looking at Tony.

Tony rubbed his chin. "We'll find her," he said as the ambulance left the cul-de-sac with its siren blaring. "I'm sure she's okay." He tried to sound optimistic. He turned to look at Cookie in the backseat. "Where did they say they were going after they met?"

Cookie's eyes grew big as Tony looked at her. "I don't know," she said. Her posture remained rigid. "He just said something about a pizza restaurant that closed."

"And why didn't you say something, Cookie?" Shari admonished her again. "You know better than that!"

Cookie's eyes became watery. "I don't know."

"Well, because you don't know, *we* don't know where she's at or what might be happening," Shari said angrily. She looked at Tony. "I told you we should have put a block on that computer."

"I put a timer on it," he said with a slightly irritated tone. "That should have been enough."

"I'm sorry," Cookie said, crying heavily.

Shari rolled her eyes.

"Sorry doesn't cut it," Tony said. "Not only are you on a punishment for the next month, but you can forget about using that computer again."

"Lord, please let her be safe," Shari whispered.

Chapter Thirty-five

Homer kept his arm around Serenity's small waist as he carried her toward the basement door.

"Stop!" Serenity yelled. "Let me go!" She frantically turned her body back and forth as she beat on Homer's chest.

Homer tightened his grip. "Stop moving!" he said.

"No! Let me go!" Serenity cried. She began beating on his chest, but she was no match for his more than three hundred pounds.

"Stop hitting me!" Homer said. He reached over with his other hand and held both of her arms down.

He took her down into the basement and held her down in an old torn leather chair as he removed her coat.

"Why are you so frightened?" he asked as he began unrolling the ball of twine he'd purchased earlier. "You wanted to meet me, right?"

Serenity looked up at him with surprise. "You're *Saucer?*"

He pulled her arms behind the chair and secured her wrists with the twine. Homer wrapped the string around her wrists several times, and then tied a knot.

Serenity sat still as tears began to spill from her eyes.

Homer pulled off the elastic band that was holding her hair together in a ponytail. Her hair fell down and stopped at the base of her neck.

"Now we've met," he said as he ran his fingers through the strands of her hair all the way down to the red tips.

He walked away and sat down on a bench across from her. Every now and then he twisted the wedding band he still wore on his left ring finger as his hazel eyes traveled the length of Serenity's legs stretching out from the seat of the chair. He stood up and walked back over to her.

Serenity tried to catch her breath.

"You have pretty legs, you know that?" he said as he stroked the side of each of her legs.

She jumped at his touch. "It's cold down here," she said in an unsteady voice. "Can I have my coat back?"

Homer scrutinized her under the 100 watt light bulb she sat beneath. Even with fear etched all over her face, she still bore a striking resemblance to her mother. He grabbed her coat from the bench and placed it across her lap.

"Can I go now?" She blinked, and the tears rolled down her cheeks.

"Can you go now?" He looked surprised. "We're just getting started."

"Please," Serenity struggled from side to side.

A distant look appeared in his eyes. "I told her I still wanted her," he said. "But she hung up on me. Now she won't answer my calls." He snickered. "I guess you'll have to do, little fish."

"I need to go home!" she screamed. "Let me go! The police will come!"

"No, they won't," Homer said smugly. He poked her forehead with his finger. "Because they don't know where you are."

Serenity blinked quickly. "Yes, they do. My friend knows your name. She'll tell them!"

"My friend knows your name." He mocked her. "Don't be so naïve, little girl. Saucer is not my name." He pulled a small key out of his pocket and began tossing it back and forth. "If you're going to play with fire you better learn how not to get burned."

"Please," she begged. "I won't tell anybody. I promise." She started crying again. "Just let me go home!"

He looked at her and thought about Tia. "That will depend on your mother. But really, she should have returned my calls."

"What . . . What are you talking about?" Serenity cried. "What does my mother have to do with this?"

"You'll find out soon enough, little fish."

"Please," she pleaded again, "let me go. I promise I won't tell."

"Oh, you'll tell," he snarled. "You don't care about me either." He stopped tossing the key. "You're just like your mother."

Serenity stiffened as confusion spread across her face.

Homer thought about the pain he had suffered because of Tia's rejection. It was completely unwarranted, and he was tired of it. It had been that way all his life: his mother, the girls in school, his wife, and now her. He rubbed his forehead. He needed to show Sandra—no, he meant Tia. Yes, he needed to show Tia that this time it was going to be his way. And his way was to not let the relationship end until and *if* he said so.

"I'm sorry," he said to Serenity. He pulled the string above her head to turn off the light bulb. "But it's your mother's fault."

"Wait!" she cried. "Mr. Woodard!"

Homer ignored Serenity's cry as he limped up the basement stairs. He closed the door behind him and locked it. All this time, he had unknowingly been chatting with Tia's daughter. He felt it had been an act of fate that she had turned up on his doorstep after their failed meeting earlier. Now, he had her in his basement.

Homer felt proud of what he had accomplished. Soon, he would pull out his phone, press the familiar number on the key pad and wait until Tia answered his call. Maybe this time she'd be more interested in what he had to say.

***

Serenity watched the pull string from the light bulb above her head swing back and forth. "Please, God," she prayed, "please let me get out."

She anxiously looked around the unfinished basement and noticed a medium-size square window just above the washing machine on the other side of the room. She began to cry as she started wiggling her slender wrists back and forth in an attempt to loosen the string.

The sun was beginning to set. Soon, it would be completely dark in the basement. "Please, God," she whispered over and over as she focused all her energy on being freed. Sometime later, she abruptly stopped crying when she noticed the string slowly but surely beginning to loosen.

Chapter Thirty-six

Tia had a gut feeling that Lorenzo had taken too many pills. Even though their marriage was in serious trouble, she prayed he would be okay. She went over to the nurse's station in the emergency room. It was late in the afternoon and almost every chair in the waiting room had been taken. Some of the patients sat solemnly, waiting to be called. Others were less subdued, in obvious pain and agitated. She caught a glimpse of the burly security guard standing close by just in case his assistance was needed.

"Excuse me," she said to the attendant behind the counter, "have they brought in a Lorenzo Sparks yet?"

As the attendant typed information into the computer, the faint sound of an ambulance grew closer. "Maybe that's him now," Tia said. She waited nervously while they drove into the bay and brought in a patient covered up on a gurney.

She recognized Lorenzo's head sticking out from the covers, his Afro smashed down on one side. His eyes were closed, and he was wearing an oxygen mask. An IV was running fluids through a vein in his right hand.

The paramedics wheeled him toward Tia as she ran to meet them. "This is my husband," she said. "How is he?"

"We've got him stable." The paramedic looked at Tia's nursing uniform. "His pupils are pinpoint, and his vitals and respirations are pretty low. What kind of medication is he on?"

"Too many," she said wearily. "He's been taking a muscle relaxer, a pain reliever, and a sleep aid."

"Were the pain reliever and sleep aid over-the-counter or prescribed?"

"Prescribed," she said. "All prescribed."

The emergency room nurse came over to where they were standing. "You can put him in room 1-B," she said.

Tia followed the paramedics as they took Lorenzo to his room and transferred him to the bed. A lab technician came in to get a few blood samples. And then a nurse came in to check his vital signs again.

"How is he?" Tia asked wringing her hands.

"His vitals are stable, but the doctor ordered a gastric lavage," the nurse said.

"You mean you're going to pump his stomach?"

"That's right." she said, preparing Lorenzo to be moved. "Why don't you wait in the waiting room. The doctor will update you as soon as he can."

Tia returned to the waiting room and sat down heavily on one of the oversized cushioned chairs. She stared at the newspaper on the coffee table with its pages old and worn. Although her love for Lorenzo had been through some rough times, it was still mixed in with her DNA, and as much as she wanted to, she could not remove it even though he was unwilling to receive it. The only thing she could do was relegate it to a place in her heart where it remained wrapped up in an emotional cocoon.

She rested her head on the back of the chair. She wanted to be happy. She told herself she could be as long as the crack inside of her didn't spread any wider; as long as that internal gulf kept submerging her resentments, she would be happy.

But the gulf was close to overflowing, and the personal coaching she'd been giving herself off and on for the past two years did little to ease her tension. It had spread down the back of her neck like the malignancy that had spread through the cavities of her marriage, leaving little deposits of unforgiveness within the intricate merger.

She looked up at the ceiling. Lorenzo's unemotional attitude may have pushed her toward another man, but in the end, she'd made the choice to do what she'd done. She knew their problems went deeper than just the physical. Their lack of intimacy was just a symptom of something bigger. She just didn't know what. And because she didn't know, she had no idea how to fix the problem.

She closed her eyes. How foolish she'd been to think the answer to her marital problems was in the arms of another man. Her desire to be with Homer had not been based on a physical need. What she had truly craved was an emotional connection, and she thought that was what Homer was offering her. She'd latched on to it even though she knew she was committing an act of sin by stepping outside of her marriage—emotionally or physically.

She thought about the day Homer had walked up to her in the grocery store two months earlier. She remembered how flustered she'd become when he'd told her that he gave good massages.

"Oh," she'd stuttered. "Are . . . are . . . you a masseur?"

"I can be," he'd said laughing. "Actually, I'm an accountant."

Tia could still see the penetrating look he'd given her.

"But that also requires the use of my fingers," he'd said with a serious look on his face.

She remembered looking at him and not finding anything particularly attractive about him other than the color of his eyes and the sound of his voice. But she'd been grasping at straws, and those two features had been enough.

"How about we exchange phone numbers," he'd said pulling out his phone. "You never know when you just might be in need."

She'd looked at him. "In need of what?"

"What have we been talking about?" he asked.

She remembered the slight smile on his face. "Oh, the massage," she'd said feeling a little embarrassed.

"Right."

He'd continued to stare at her until she'd had to look away . . . but not before she'd given him her phone number and had accepted his. And by the time she'd made it home from the grocery store, Homer's number was lighting up on her cell phone.

She'd told Shari that it was Homer's deep voice and mesmerizing eyes that had drawn her in. But it actually went beyond that. The real truth was that the only man she'd ever wanted to pay attention to her the way Homer had was her husband. But Lorenzo had wanted nothing to do with her. And the sad part was that she still didn't know why.

Although she had betrayed Lorenzo only once, the fire that had burned in her birthed from lust and desire now condemned her, and she could not come to terms with what she had done. She wished she could remove every piece of her skin that she had allowed Homer to touch.

With her eyes still closed, she lowered her head. *Make me over, Lord*, she prayed. *Please, just make me over.*

An hour went by before the emergency room doctor came out to talk to Tia. "Well," he spoke softly, "the toxicology screening came back positive for opiates and benzodiazepines. And he's got a minor concussion from the fall. As you know, we had him undergo a gastric lavage, and we're going to keep him here overnight for observation. But you can go in and see him now before we transfer him to a room."

"Thank you," she said as she stood up. She was glad she had never worked with this particular doctor or any of the staff on that floor. It would have been such an embarrassment.

"You're welcome," he said as he walked away. "Oh," he stopped and walked back toward her. "He wouldn't tell me who's been prescribing all that medication for him but you might want to get him to stop seeing whoever it is."

"I've tried," she said.

He looked at her with gentle eyes. "I'm not a therapist but getting him into rehab would probably be a good idea."

Tia nodded. She waited until the doctor had disappeared around the corner before rising slowly from the chair.

She went back to the holding unit in the emergency room and walked over to Lorenzo's bed. He continued staring at the ceiling and did not speak. She reached over to give him a gentle hug, careful not to disrupt the IV tubing that ran from the machine to the top of his hand. His body stiffened like a corpse under her embrace and she quickly released her hold.

"Who found me?" he asked as he continued to stare at the ceiling.

"Serenity," she said, staring straight-ahead. "What happened?"

"What does it look like happened? I fell."

"That's not what the doctor said."

"What?" Lorenzo looked at her with a blank look in his eyes. "Are you telling me that I didn't fall?"

"No, you fell," she said. "But what caused you to fall?"

Lorenzo returned his gaze to the ceiling.

The IV pump began beeping at regular intervals. Tia looked at the hanging bag of solution and saw that it was almost gone. Like the bag, she was running on empty, and she didn't know how much longer she would be able to handle Lorenzo's unemotional state. She looked back at him. "What's wrong, Lorenzo?" She placed her hand on the bed rail. "What's really wrong?"

He remained silent as he choked back the tears he knew would come as soon as he opened his mouth.

She touched his shoulder gently. "Tell me."

He looked at her and rolled his eyes.

She stood next to his bedside feeling completely useless.

Just then, the nurse came in, and Tia picked up her purse to leave.

"The bag is almost empty," she said to the nurse as she walked angrily out of the room.

Chapter Thirty-seven

Tia sat in her car in the hospital parking structure. She started the engine and let the car warm up, then lowered her head onto the steering wheel. What was wrong with Lorenzo? Why did he hate her so?

The past thirteen years of their marriage hadn't been easy. She'd had to get used to Lorenzo's episodes of gloominess, and the hardest part had been never knowing when they were going to occur or even why they occurred. Still, their years together hadn't been all bad. There had been some good times too, some beautiful times, and she had held on to them.

She remembered the drives she and Lorenzo would take to Milwaukee when Serenity had been younger. Sometimes they'd drive the whole way back without speaking. And Tia would be amazed at the connection that flowed between them in the silence.

At the end of those drives, Lorenzo would park the car in the garage and say, "That was a nice drive."

And Tia would respond. "Yes, it was beautiful."

She remembered the silly jokes she told that made him giggle, and how just him smiling would make her smile. And she remembered how they would study the Bible together, often searching for answers to questions that one or the other had.

As time went by, Tia began to notice a decrease in the number of intimate times she and Lorenzo shared. And when there was an occasion, it seemed as if he was just going through the motions.

It was during Serenity's eleventh year that Tia noticed a distinct change in Lorenzo. The severity of his sullen moods increased, and he became distant and emotionally unavailable. Trying to talk to him about his behavior had been useless. He would either deny that anything was wrong or he'd give her short, snappy answers in an attempt to shut her up.

Droplets of moisture fell from her eyes and landed on the bottom of the steering wheel. What had happened? She couldn't do this much longer. It was too much. Even now, lying in a hospital bed, he still had nothing nice to say to her.

"Father, help me," she cried. Her shoulders heaved up and down rapidly. "It's too much. It's just too much!" She shook her head from side to side. "How much do you want me to bear, Lord? I can't do this." She folded her arms and began rocking back and forth. "Give me strength," she whispered as her tears subsided. "Give me strength."

The air flowing from the car vents began to feel warm as Tia slowly pulled out of the parking structure. She looked at the digital clock on the dashboard. It was almost 8:00 p.m. It had been a long day, and the nausea rising in the center of her stomach reminded her that she hadn't had anything to eat since she'd left for church that morning, and then headed straight to Serenity's audition.

She drove the several miles home quickly. When she pulled into her garage, the only thing on her mind was eating something and going to sleep. She didn't have the energy—mentally or physically—for anything else. She left the garage door up while she called Shari. The phone rang once before Shari answered.

"Hey, how's Lorenzo?" Shari asked.

"The doctor said he'll be all right," Tia said coldly. "He took too many pills."

Shari let out a sigh of relief. "Thank God he'll be all right."

"Yeah, *this* time," Tia said angrily. "What if Serenity hadn't found him? I should go and throw away every pill I find. How's Serenity?"

Shari looked at the phone, then at Tony.

"You're going to have to tell her," he said.

Shari inhaled deeply.

"Tia," she said, "when we pulled up in front of your house, the ambulance was just leaving." Shari hesitated. "And Serenity wasn't there."

"Where was she?"

"We don't know."

Tony nudged Shari's shoulder. "You have to tell her," he said.

Tia could hear Tony in the background. "Tell me what?" she asked. "What is Tony talking about?"

"Well," Shari said. She spoke slowly and with a tranquil tone; it was the same tone she used at work when a frustrated or agitated client called her looking for help. "Earlier today, Tony and I found a bunch of chat sites on the computer that Serenity and Cookie had been visiting."

Tia's mind went back to the day before when she and Serenity were going to visit her mother and Lorenzo had accused Serenity of talking to boys on the computer.

"Was Serenity talking to a boy?" Tia asked.

"Yeah, but it's more than that."

"What else, Shari?"

Shari could hear the tenseness in Tia's voice. Her mouth had suddenly become extremely dry. "Well," she said swallowing hard, "Cookie said Serenity made plans to meet the boy."

"She did *what?*"

"Now try to stay calm, Tia. You already have one situation on your hands."

"When was this supposed to happen?" Tia's voice was hard and edgy.

"Today. That's why we weren't home. When I couldn't reach you or Serenity, Tony thought we should go try to, you know, intercept the meeting."

"And you didn't find her?" The pitch of her voice rose.

"No, we didn't."

"Oh my God," Tia moaned. Just when she thought God had heard her prayer and had given her an extra dose of strength, here was another battle. Was this the reason God had strengthened her? Not so she could make it through what she was already going through but to bring her through what was about to come. "I can't do this. Not now, Lord!"

"We'll be right over," Shari said and hung up the phone.

❖

Chapter Thirty-eight

Moments later, Shari, Tony, and Cookie were sitting in Tia's living room. She was about to call the police when her cell phone rang.

Shari picked up Tia's phone and answered it. "Hello?"

"I have something to tell you," Homer said.

"Who is this?" Shari asked as Tia looked up quickly.

Homer hesitated before answering. "Who is *this?*"

Tia heard the familiar low pitch of the voice echoing from the phone. She grabbed the phone from Shari. "I thought I asked you not to call me anymore," she said impatiently.

"Okay if that's how you want it. It's about your daughter but never mind. Good-bye." Homer smiled. This time he had hung up on her.

A feeling of dread swept through Tia's veins. "My daughter? Hello?" she yelled frantically. "Hello?"

"Who was that?" Shari asked.

"Homer," Tia said as she tried to call him back. He had blocked his number before calling her so she began frantically searching for his number in her contacts list, forgetting that she had completely deleted him from her phone book.

"Homer?" Shari's forehead creased. She looked at Tony. "Who's Homer?"

Tony raised his eyebrows. "Our next-door neighbor," he said.

Just then Tia's phone rang again.

"Where's my daughter?" she screamed into the phone.

"When can I see you?" Homer asked calmly.

"What are you talking about?" she yelled. "If you know something about my daughter, you better tell me right now or I'm calling the police!"

"Meet me at the motel and I'll tell you."

"I'm not meeting you anywhere. I'm calling the police!"

"Call them," he said. "But I don't know anything about your daughter."

"Then why did you mention her name?" Tia asked as she choked back the emotions that threatened to send her into a fit of hysteria.

"Did I?" Homer asked. Then the line went dead.

Shari sat through the whole interaction with her mouth hanging open. Finally, she spoke. "Tia, what's going?"

"He knows something about Serenity," she said. Her hands were shaking so bad she could barely hold the phone steady while she called 9-1-1.

"Why would he have anything to do with Serenity?" Shari asked.

"Operator," Tia said staring hard at Shari, "I need the police." She turned her back to Shari and Tony and continued. "My daughter hasn't come home, and I think my neighbor might be involved."

Shari's eyes grew wide. Her mouth opened again, but this time no words came out. Now she understood what was going on. She looked at her daughter who sat listening to it all. "Cookie," she said, "go in the other room. I'll be in there in a minute."

As Cookie walked out of the living room, she noticed Serenity's Hello Kitty hat sitting on the desk in the hallway. She picked it up and returned to the living room. "Ma," she said holding the hat.

"What did your mother tell you to do, Cookie?" Tony said sternly.

"But it's her hat," Cookie said holding it up. "She said she was going to wear this hat when she went to meet him."

Tony grabbed the hat from Cookie.

Tia was still on the telephone. "And why do you think your neighbor is involved, ma'am?" the 9-1-1 dispatcher asked.

"Because he just called me and said he had something to tell me about my daughter. But he hung up when I said I wouldn't meet him."

"Wait. So your neighbor asked you to meet him somewhere?"

"Yes! Yes! Why are you asking all these questions? Can you just send someone over to check his house?"

"Well, ma'am, we have to get as much information as we can. Has he ever threatened your daughter before?"

"No," Tia said as she began weeping. "No. I told him I didn't want him to call me anymore, and that's when he told me he knew something about my daughter."

"Okay, ma'am. What is your neighbor's name and address?"

After Tia had given Homer's name and address to the 9-1-1 operator, she was told a squad car would be dispatched to his address as well as hers. She hung up the phone, and Shari touched her shoulder.

"Tia, is that the man you've been—"

"I don't want to hear it," she said jerking her shoulder away from Shari's touch. "Not now, Shari. I already know I've made a mistake. And I'm telling you, now is not the time for you to remind me of that."

"I wasn't going to," Shari said. "What can we do?"

"You can *not* judge me," Tia said rocking back and forth. "That's what both of you can do!"

"We're not here to judge you," Tony said. "Like you said, this is not the time." He held up the Hello Kitty hat.

"Cookie just gave me Serenity's hat. She said Serenity was going to wear it when she met the boy."

Tia grabbed the hat. "Well, then, why is it here?" There was a faint sound of hope in her voice. "Does that mean she didn't go?"

"I don't know," Tony sighed.

"Either she went and didn't wear the hat," Shari said. "Or she didn't go at all."

"Then where is she?" Tia cried out.

Tony placed his wife's hand in his own, and then extended his other hand toward Tia. "Let's pray," he said.

Shari held Tia's hand firmly in her own as they lowered their heads and Tony began to pray.

"Father, in the name of Jesus we come to You."

"Yes, Lord," Shari whispered.

"Have mercy, Lord. Let Your grace be with Serenity right now, Father, and keep her safe from *all* harm wherever she is. Give Tia strength, Lord," Tony squeezed her hand harder, "strength to make it through this situation. You said we can do all things through Christ which strengthens us, Lord. And because you said it, we believe it."

"Yes, Lord," Tia said through her tears, "I believe."

"So let it be done," Tony continued. "In the name of Jesus we pray, amen."

"Amen," Shari and Tia whispered in agreement.

Shari raised her hand and wiped the tears away from Tia's face. "Remember, God is in control," she said.

"I know," Tia sniffed. "But where is Serenity?"

Chapter Thirty-nine

Twenty minutes later, two female police officers arrived at Tia's house. She opened the door and immediately pointed to where Homer lived before noticing a squad car was already parked in front of his house.

"Ma'am, you called about your missing daughter?" one of the officers asked.

"Yes, yes," Tia said continuing to point toward Homer's house. "He knows something."

"How long has she been missing?" the officer asked.

"Well, I dropped her back off at home," Tia said wringing her hands, "and then I went to work. That was around two o'clock. She called me at work a few hours later to tell me her father had fallen and nobody's seen her since."

"We were out looking for her," Tony said, "but obviously we didn't find her."

"And how are you two related to Mrs. Sparks?"

"We're her friends," Shari said, "and we also live in the last house next to Homer's."

"Did either of you see anything suspicious going on over there?"

"Well, it's like my husband told you," Shari said, "we were out looking for Serenity."

"But we did find her hat here at home," Tony added.

The officer looked at the hat. "What's the significance of the hat?"

"My daughter said she was supposed to wear this hat when she went to meet a boy she met online."

The officer addressed her next question to Tia. "I thought you said your neighbor might have something to do with your daughter's disappearance."

"That's what he implied," she said with a worried look on her face.

"But it's possible your daughter might have gone to meet someone else?"

Tia placed both of her hands on the side of her head. She shook her head violently from side to side. "I don't know. I don't know."

"What time did you get home, ma'am?" the police officer asked Tia.

"A little after eight o'clock," she answered.

"So pretty much no one's seen your daughter or heard from her in about six hours. Would you say that's about right?"

"Yes," Tia answered. "Yes."

"What was she wearing?"

Tia thought back to the rush she'd been in to get to work. "I don't know." She became distraught again. "I can't remember."

"Didn't you take her to that audition after church?" Shari asked.

"That's right," Tia perked up. "I did. And she had on a black chiffon dress with a white lace trim." Suddenly, her shoulders slumped. "But I doubt she kept that on because it got torn when she fell."

"She fell?" Shari asked.

Tia remembered the exact moment when Serenity had tumbled off the makeshift runway. She remembered the look of total devastation on Serenity's face as she'd gotten back up and hobbled to the other end. As hard as she'd tried not to, Tia could also remember the look of dissatisfaction she'd worn on her face as she'd watched Serenity fall. "Yes," Tia said sadly. "She fell."

"She must have been pretty upset about that, huh?" the police officer asked as she continued taking notes.

"She was," Tia said, feeling convicted by the fact that she'd done little to console Serenity before she'd rushed out of the house to get to work.

"Do you think she might have run away?"

Tia looked at the officer. "Of course not," she said enraged by the question. "I just told the lady on the phone that my neighbor called saying he knew something about my daughter! Why would I think she ran away?"

"Try to stay calm, Tia," Shari said, patting her knee. "They're just trying to get all the information they need."

"All the information they need," Tia said, her anxiety escalating, "is right down the street."

"And that's why we have two officers talking to Mr. Woodard right now," the police officer replied.

Chapter Forty

Serenity finally managed to free her wrists from the string Homer had tied them with. She quickly ran toward the washing machine below the window that was partially covered with newspaper. She climbed on top of the appliance and tried to raise the window. It didn't budge.

She pushed it a second time and nothing happened. She saw that the lock to secure the window was missing, and just as she was about to try to push the window up for a third time, she looked down at the newspaper covering half of it and stopped.

The date on the newspaper was from a year ago, and there was a picture of a young girl on the front of it. Serenity stared hard at the picture. The girl had been in one of her classes last year, and Serenity remembered when she had suddenly stopped showing up at school.

According to the news, her classmate had been missing for several days, and then had mysteriously shown up at the front door of her house. She never returned to school after that, and Serenity never saw or heard anything else about her. To this day, she still didn't know what had happened to her.

Although there was no heat in the basement, the palms of Serenity's hands grew moist and a layer of sweat began to form underneath her shirt. Why did he have this piece of newspaper on the window? She began pushing up on the window for the third time, but it remained unmovable. Just then, she heard the doorbell ring and she stiffened.

Homer walked to the front door and looked through the peephole. He saw two male police officers standing on the other side of his door. He stood watching them as they rang the doorbell several times, and then began knocking loudly on the door. Finally, he decided to answer.

"Who is it?" he yelled from the other side of the door.

"Police officers."

Homer opened the door slowly.

"Are you Homer Woodard?" one of the officers asked.

"I am."

"We received a complaint from your neighbor, Tia Sparks, that you might have something to do with her missing daughter."

Homer grunted. "Missing daughter? Don't nobody want her daughter."

The two police officers looked at each other. "Do you mind if we look through your house, sir?"

Homer had to maintain his composure. If ever there was a time for him not to show any emotion, this was it. He stepped to the side and bent over slightly. "Welcome," he said as he waved them in with his left arm.

One of the officers searched the main floor while the other one asked to look in the basement.

"I can't get that door open," Homer said as he fingered the key in his pocket. "It hasn't been opened in years. I think it's been glued shut or cemented or something," he said with ease.

The police officer looked at him. "How long have you lived here?"

"Almost three years," Homer replied.

"And you're telling me you've never been in your basement or tried to open this door?"

Homer wiped the sweat from his top lip. "Well, I tried to open it," he lied, "but it just won't open."

"So," the officer said frowning, "you just left it like that?"

"That's correct." Homer let out a nervous chuckle. "Is that a crime?"

"No, it's not a crime," the officer said, pulling on the doorknob. "It's just not believable." He waved his partner over to him, then looked at Homer. "We're going to need to open this door," he said.

The second police officer went to the squad car to retrieve a crowbar.

Homer's calm demeanor was quickly replaced by a growing level of apprehension. Once they opened that door and went downstairs that would be it. "What right do you have to mess up my property?" he blurted out.

"Well, if you would just open the door we wouldn't have to do this, now, would we?"

"I told you, I can't," Homer said moving closer to the door.

The police officer put one hand on his gun holster and pointed to the sofa with his other hand. "Sit down," he said sternly.

Homer sat down slowly as he watched the second police officer return and begin prying the basement door open with the crowbar. His eyes darted around the room as he gripped the edges of the sofa. The door hinges creaked under the pressure of being pried apart, and with each cracking sound Homer flinched, expecting to hear Serenity cry out at any moment.

Serenity heard the muffled voices and the sound of someone trying to open the basement door. Fearful of Homer's return, she wiped her moist hands on the fabric of her pants and gave the window another push upward as hard as she could.

At the same time, the basement door cracked lightly and a sliver of light came racing down the stairs. She began pushing wildly on the window and felt the top ledge hit something. She ran her hand across the front of the window ledge and felt a nail partially sticking out. She quickly pulled it out and pushed on the window again. This time, it slid up, and she eased her slender body out through the opening. She ran wildly toward her house, screaming hysterically as she got closer.

The police officer stopped trying to pry the door open when he heard what sounded like a young girl screaming. His partner ran outside to investigate while he remained indoors with Homer.

Homer stood up instantly when he heard Serenity scream.

"Sit back down!" the police officer ordered.

A wave of heat spread through Homer's body. He remained standing as he wiped away the chain of moisture that had formed on top of his balding head.

"I said sit down!" the officer repeated with more assertiveness. He began walking toward Homer.

Homer's respirations increased, and his pupils began to dilate. His impulses quickened as he charged at the police officer.

A struggling match began, and ended with Homer grabbing the officer's gun and running out the back door of his house.

"Stop!" the officer yelled as he chased Homer through the backyard, and then out of the cul-de-sac. He called for backup on his radio as he continued his foot pursuit of Homer.

Homer had no intentions of using the gun he'd taken from the officer, and he was sorry he'd taken it. He threw it onto a snow-covered lawn as he continued to run. The icy patches on the sidewalk along with his foot deformity would not allow him to run any faster.

The second officer had joined in the chase and was quickly getting closer to Homer. Out of breath and outnumbered, Homer stopped and fell to his knees.

The second officer drew his weapon. "Don't move!" he yelled. "Put your hands in the air!"

Homer raised both arms as he labored to catch his breath. Both of the officers approached him with caution. They placed the handcuffs on him as several squad cars came to a screeching halt directly in front of the sidewalk.

"Let's go," one of the officers said as he helped Homer stand up.

Homer began shivering as the flashing lights from the squad cars danced around his head.

Chapter Forty-one

Tia stood up when she heard Serenity screaming. "Serenity!" she cried out as she ran out the front door. She ran down the walkway to meet her child who fell full speed into her arms. Tia was crying as she put her arms around her. "Are you okay?"

Serenity trembled as she tried to catch her breath between sobs. She shook her head rapidly.

"Ma'am," one of the female police officers interrupted, "we need to get some information from your daughter. Let's go inside."

Tia held on to Serenity and guided her into the house.

Serenity looked around the living room, suddenly remembering how she'd found her father on the floor. "How's Daddy?" she asked sadly.

"He'll be fine," Tia said. She grabbed Serenity's shoulders and looked at her. Her hair was tossed about and the red tips of her bangs were pointed in various directions. "But are you all right?"

Serenity shrugged.

"What did he do to you?" Tia's grip around Serenity's shoulders tightened. "Tell me!"

"Nothing!" Serenity shouted. "He didn't do nothing!"

"Okay, young lady," the police officer said gently, "just tell me what happened."

"I don't know," Serenity whined. "I came home and found my dad on the floor. My mom told me to go to Cookie's house but nobody was home. So, I went to his house . . ."

"Mr. Woodard?" the police officer asked.

Serenity nodded. "He told me to come in and he would take me to the hospital, but it was dark in there," she stopped to catch her breath, "and then he pulled me in."

"And then what happened?"

"He made me go downstairs to the basement," she said as she wiped the tears from her eyes. "And he tied me to a chair."

"Lord have mercy," Tia whispered.

"And then what happened?" the police officer probed gently.

"He started talking about crazy stuff, then he turned off the light and went upstairs."

"What kind of crazy stuff was he talking about?"

Serenity cut her eyes at her mother. "I don't know," she said rubbing her forehead. "I can't remember."

"Serenity, it's important that you try to remember as much as you can," the officer said staring hard at her.

"I . . . some stuff . . . he was talking about a woman, and . . . I can't remember," she said and started crying again.

"Okay, Serenity. We're almost done. Just a couple more questions." The police officer flipped a sheet of paper over on her notepad.

"Now where were you coming home from when you found your dad on the floor?"

Serenity looked at Cookie. "Nowhere."

"Nowhere?"

"Yeah," she sniffled.

"Serenity, stop lying," Tia said harshly. "We already know you planned to meet some boy you met on the computer. Now where were you coming from?"

Serenity glanced over at Cookie who stood helplessly in one corner of the room. "I told you, nowhere," she whined. "I didn't meet him. He didn't show up."

"But you did go to meet him, right?" the officer asked.

Serenity nodded.

"Then you went somewhere. Just because he didn't show up doesn't change the fact that you still went somewhere, right?"

"I guess."

Tia sighed and began rubbing the side of her forehead. She was thankful her daughter was all right because she knew the outcome could have been much worse. Homer was 100 percent wrong for what he had done, but there was still the issue of Serenity putting herself in danger by going off to meet someone she didn't know.

The police officers began to wrap up their investigation. "We'll be in touch shortly," one of them said. "We're going to need an official statement from her."

Tia nodded her head. "That's fine."

The other officer gave her a card. "In the meantime, call if you have any questions or if your daughter comes up with any more information . . ."

"I will," she said.

"We're going to go too," Shari said.

Tia gave Shari a hug. She looked at Tony. "Thanks," she said.

"Try to get some rest," Tony told her as he escorted Cookie out after she said good-bye to Serenity.

Tia watched from her door as the three of them walked back toward their house. She closed the door and turned around when she heard Serenity going upstairs. "Wait," she said. "Come back down here. I need to talk to you."

Serenity went into the living room and sat down.

"So what's going on with you going to meet some boy you met online?"

Serenity lowered her head and began picking at one of her fingernails.

"Answer me!"

"I don't know," she said.

"What do you mean, you don't know?" Tia began pacing back and forth. "Do you know how dangerous it is to go and meet a boy you met online? Do you even know if he *is* a boy, and not some man waiting to do God knows what to you?" She stopped and stood directly over Serenity. "How do you know he wasn't someone like that monster," she pointed in the direction of Homer's house, "that you just escaped from?"

Serenity kept her head down. She didn't tell her mother that the boy online *was* Homer. Instead, she continued nibbling away the last bit of nail on her baby finger.

"Serenity!" Tia shouted. "I'm talking to you. What's wrong with you?"

Serenity's shoulders began to shake violently. "You tell me," she said in between sobs. "You always act like I get on your nerves!"

A look of astonishment covered Tia's face. "Serenity, that's not true. What are you—?"

"It *is* true," she blurted out crying heavily. "I saw how you looked at me when I fell. You acted like you didn't even care!"

Tia sat down on the coffee table in front of her. She softened her tone. "Serenity, I do care. Why do you think I'm so mad now?"

She sniffled. "I don't know."

"Listen. You can't be meeting boys you talk to online. You can't do things like that. It's just too dangerous. Bottom line."

"He said we were going to the mall," Serenity said softly. "And he was gonna buy me something pretty. But he lied."

Tia leaned in close to Serenity. "What do you mean he lied? I thought you said you didn't meet him."

Serenity kept her head down. "I didn't."

Tia sighed. "Look at me," she said. Her voice grew stern again. "I don't care what he said he was going to do. You can't trust people you meet online."

"And *you* shouldn't trust people you meet next door," Serenity said staring hard at her.

"What did you say?"

"That's why he did what he did, you know."

Tia felt her conscience stir. "What are you talking about?"

"He said you wouldn't talk to him."

Tia was speechless for a few seconds. She struggled with whether to tell her daughter that her connection to Homer had extended beyond him just being her neighbor. She shook her head violently. *What good would that do?* She decided to tell her only what she needed to know.

"He's right," Tia said. "I'm not talking to him."

Serenity continued staring at her. "Then how did he get your phone number?"

"I met him in the grocery store one day." Tia looked down at her hands. "We talked briefly, and then we exchanged phone numbers."

"Why?" Serenity's tone was accusing.

Tia looked up. She began shaking her head again. "I don't know why I did that, Serenity. But it was wrong. And that's why I'm not talking to him." Suddenly, Tia became defensive. "I'm talking to *you*," she said. "And I want it understood that you are not to go meeting anyone you don't know." She hesitated. "And there'll be no more knocking on someone's door just because they're your neighbor. You can't trust your neighbors either," she said with a finality to her voice.

"You should know," Serenity said angrily.

"Look," Tia said, "I know what you—"

"No, you don't!" Serenity blurted out. "You don't know anything! You're never around. And when you are you're always mad."

Tia's back became rigid. The memory of her mother never having been there for her, and the years she spent living with her angry grandmother came flooding back to her. The last thing she wanted was for history to repeat itself. She had worked too hard to reconcile with her mother and grandmother, and she did not want to see what had happened to her happen to Serenity.

Tia looked into Serenity's eyes and saw herself when she was just a few years older than her daughter, running from man to man trying to find love. "You don't need some boy to buy you something pretty," she said lifting her daughter's chin. "Don't you know you got enough pretty for yourself?"

She reached over to give Serenity a hug, but she was stopped midway when Serenity raised her arm to wipe her face with the sleeve of her hoodie.

Tia stood up. "You better get ready for bed," she said wearily. "It's been a long day."

Serenity followed behind her mother as she turned off the living-room light and trudged slowly up the stairs. "You really think I'm pretty?" she asked solemnly.

Tia stopped and turned around. She thought about her own mother and grandmother again, and she couldn't recall a single time that either of them had ever told her she was pretty. "Yes," she said looking directly into Serenity's eyes, "I do."

The two of them continued upstairs as the wind outside began to die down.

Chapter Forty-two

A few hours later, the shrill sound of Tia's cell phone jolted her awake. It was one of the female police officers who had been at the house earlier.

"Mrs. Sparks," the officer said, "I'm sorry to wake you, but I wanted to let you know that your neighbor, Mr. Woodard, ran away from the police officers earlier—"

Tia quickly sat up in bed. "What do you mean, ran away?" She fumbled for the light switch on the lamp next to her bed.

"After your daughter managed to escape from the basement, a struggle ensued and Mr. Woodard took the officer's gun and ran out of the house."

"Oh my God," Tia said, now fully awake.

"—But as I was going to say," the officer added quickly, "he was apprehended and we have him in custody."

Tia let out a sigh of relief. "Thank you," she said. "Thank you for letting me know."

"You're welcome. We'll be in touch."

After tossing and turning for the remainder of the night, Tia got out of the bed. She tiptoed down the hall to Serenity's bedroom and peeked through the halfway open door. Serenity lay on her side with her legs curled up. Her breathing was soft and even.

The sun was midway in the sky and caused a stream of light to enter the room through the slits in the window blind. Tiny specs of dust floated effortlessly in the air, and then settled on Serenity's Hello Kitty hat lying on the floor beneath the window.

Tia stood there watching her sleep. The peaceful name she'd given her daughter at birth had not transferred over into her life as she'd hoped it would. Something was not serene with her daughter. *But how could it be when she had a father hooked on painkillers and a mother . . .?* Tia leaned her head against the doorway.

At one point everything had been peaceful and calm with Serenity. But that had been a long time ago, when she'd been a child and her whole world had revolved around Tia and Lorenzo . . . when they'd both been decent parents. Now, Serenity was a teenager trying to deal with all the things that came with being a teenager. And just when she needed them most, neither of them had paid much attention to her. They were both guilty of being distracted by their own issues.

Tia inhaled deeply. What kind of mother was she being to Serenity? Had she been so consumed with her own problems that she'd put her daughter at the bottom of her list of priorities? She closed the door softly and went downstairs.

While she was in the kitchen making a cup of coffee, she heard the front door open. She walked out of the kitchen and was surprised to see Lorenzo coming in. He still wore the green hospital identification band around his wrist and a small Band-Aid covered the top of his hand where the IV needle had been.

"Why didn't you call me?" she said. "I would have come and picked you up."

"I didn't know you were staying home," he said in his usual dull voice.

Tia glared at him. He was still the same. Not even a near overdose had changed that cold demeanor he insisted on holding to. "We had a little bit of a scare yesterday with Serenity," she said as she stirred her coffee.

"What do you mean a scare? What happened?"

"Well, not only did she go off to meet some boy she met online, but one of the neighbors pulled her into his house and locked her in his basement."

"What?" Lorenzo's emotional state was awakened. "What neighbor?"

Tia looked down into her cup of coffee. "The man next door to Shari and her husband," she said.

Lorenzo waved his hands in the air. "Is she all right?"

"She's all right physically. She said he didn't do anything to her except tie her to a chair. And thank God he didn't tie it tight enough, so she was able to get out of it."

Tia took a sip of coffee from the cup she was holding.

The frown on Lorenzo's forehead deepened. "Are you going to tell me what happened?"

"I just did," Tia said.

He balanced himself against the kitchen counter with one hand. "Tell me the circumstances, Tia."

Tia took in a deep breath before she began. "When Serenity came home yesterday and found you on the floor," she paused to let her words sink in, "she called me at work. I called 9-1-1, and then I told Serenity to go to Shari's house. She said nobody was there so she went next door to the neighbors, and that's how he ended up pulling her into his house."

"Continue," Lorenzo said.

Tia saw the fury in his eyes. That was the one emotion he had no problem displaying.

"I called the police," she said, "and while they were over there talking to him, Serenity managed to untie herself and crawl out the basement window."

Lorenzo stormed to the hall closet. "Where's my bat?"

"He's not there," she told him.

"They arrested him?"

"Yes. One of the police officers called to tell me he tried to run away after Serenity escaped, but they caught him."

The awkward silence between them returned.

"I'm sure she's still a little shook up," Tia said as she carried her cup of coffee upstairs to her room. "You might want to check on her . . ." she hesitated, "if you have time."

"If I have time?" he said walking toward the stairs. "What is *that* supposed to mean?"

"Just what I said." She stopped and turned midway around. "What part of that don't you understand?"

"Oh, I understand," he said standing at the foot of the stairs. "But what are you trying to say?"

"I'm not *trying* to say anything." She turned her full body around to face him. "I thought I said it. Make time for your daughter. Maybe if you paid more attention to her, she might not be on the computer looking for boys to meet!"

Serenity flung her bedroom door open. "I wasn't looking for boys!" she cried out, and then slammed her door shut.

Lorenzo ignored her outburst. "*You're* one to talk," he said pointing his finger toward her. "How much time do you spend with her? Yeah, you take her to visit your mother and grandmother once a month, but what else do you do with her? All you do is go to work and church."

"There was a time when you went to church too," Tia replied. She turned and continued upstairs. "Maybe it's time you remembered that."

Lorenzo remained standing at the bottom of the stairs as he watched Tia storm away. He heard the bedroom door slam shut, and his mind began to pull him toward his old familiar escape route. He turned toward the front door.

Thirty minutes and two pills later, and he would not have to deal with what was going on in this house. Then he remembered the shame he'd felt lying in the hospital bed being told that his daughter had found him sprawled out in a drug-induced unconsciousness. He shook his head. *Why hadn't God just let me die?*

He put one hand on the stair banister while he kept staring at the door. He thought about the pamphlet and the referral for treatment he'd accepted at the hospital before he'd been discharged. He walked back to the hallway and picked up the pamphlet.

It was a faith-based treatment center that offered a one-year recovery and deliverance program for men and women. Several testimonies were printed on the cover from those who, through the power of Jesus Christ, had been set free from their addiction.

Lorenzo knew something needed to change—he knew *he* needed to change. That's why he had accepted the information, and an appointment had already been scheduled for him.

"Lord, give me strength," he whispered as he turned around and slowly headed upstairs to Serenity's bedroom. He knocked softly on her door, and then opened it slowly. She was lying on her bed with her earplugs in her ears. "Hey," he said.

She looked at him and did not speak.

He wiped his moist hands on the side of his blue jeans, then signaled with his fingers for her to remove the earplugs.

She reluctantly took one of them out of her ear.

"I want to talk to you," he said.

"I already told you," she said defiantly, "I wasn't looking for boys."

"That's not what I want to talk to you about," Lorenzo said as he sat down on the edge of her bed. "At least not now. Right now, I want to know how you're feeling about everything."

Serenity hunched her shoulders, and then let them relax.

Lorenzo stared at the pink Hello Kitty poster on her wall. The mouthless feline stared back at him. "What does that mean, Serenity?"

"Nothing," she said.

He continued to sit on the edge of the bed.

It's your fault, Serenity thought as she put the earplug back in her ear.

A few seconds passed before he spoke. "Listen," he said, "I'm sorry about what happened, and I'm glad you're okay." Then he stood up and walked out of her bedroom.

She rolled her eyes. *It's still your fault,* she thought. Then she turned on her iPod.

Chapter Forty-three

One week after being discharged from the hospital, Lorenzo walked into the Christian-based outpatient treatment center. After checking in at the receptionist desk, he pulled two chairs close together and distributed his weight evenly between the two. A piece of brown thread hung loosely from one of the seat cushions he sat on, and he nervously began twisting and untwisting the thread around his finger. He surveyed the lobby as he waited to be assessed by one of the AODA counselors.

A painting of a lilac against a white backdrop hung on the gray wall behind the receptionist. The recessed lighting in the ceiling, along with the wall-mounted water fountain, created a welcoming, serene effect.

Lorenzo gazed at the gentle stream of water trickling down from the fountain as his mind began to replay everything that had happened to him prior to the fall. He remembered the woman on the television screen telling him that suicide was not the answer. He could still hear her whispered invitation to ask Jesus into his heart, and he remembered calling out to Him for help.

But the thing that really stayed with him was what she'd said about Jesus being able to do for him what those pills he'd been taking couldn't do. That was the last thing he remembered before everything went dark.

When he'd woken up he was in a hospital bed. His head ached, and there'd been a tube down his throat and an IV needle stuck in his arm. When Tia had come to see him, he couldn't even bear to look at her.

He remembered her embrace and how badly he'd wanted to just dissolve into her arms, but he'd been unable to diminish his angry façade. It had become his defense mechanism, and he'd needed it then more than ever to hide the shame he'd felt. Why had he let himself get to this point?

The next day the hospital social worker came to talk to him. She'd brought several pamphlets pertaining to alcohol and drug treatment centers with her. After introducing herself and asking him a few questions, she'd given Lorenzo a short questionnaire to fill out. Based on his answers, she'd asked him if he'd like a referral to one of the treatment facilities, and he'd said yes.

The door opened and a fair-skinned man with dark freckles scattered across his face appeared. "Lorenzo," he called out as he scanned the small group of people in the lobby.

Lorenzo recognized the face, but it was too late now. There was nothing he could do. He stood up, smoothed out his shirt, and walked toward the man. "Hey, Tony," he said to his neighbor at the end of the cul-de-sac.

"Hey, man," Tony said to Lorenzo after he closed the door to his office. "I understand if this feels a little uncomfortable to you, but I want to let you know three things: First, I want you to know that I'm glad your daughter is okay."

"Thank you," Lorenzo said.

"Second, I won't be your counselor. I'm just doing the intake. All right?"

Lorenzo nodded his head.

"Third, there's something called HIPAA privacy rules. I'm going to have you read over it and sign it in a few minutes. But what it means is that your privacy is pro-tected. Everything that goes on here remains strictly confidential. None of us can discuss you, your business," he pointed his long finger at him, "or anything else that pertains to you outside of this facility or with anybody who's not directly involved in your care."

Lorenzo ran his fingers along the kinky curls of hair on the side of his face. "Does that include my wife?"

Tony nodded. "That includes your wife. We won't discuss your situation with her at all unless you sign a release form giving us permission to do so."

Lorenzo was relieved. He was not ready to divulge everything to Tia, and although Tony seemed like a decent person, Lorenzo wasn't sure if he'd be comfortable sharing his personal business with a member of the church he used to attend. Not to mention that he was his neighbor and both their wives were friends. It was all too close for comfort.

"Yeah," Tony said, interrupting Lorenzo's thoughts. "I don't want anything to get in the way of your deliverance, man." He looked at him. "Nothing," he repeated.

"Thanks, man," Lorenzo said. He rubbed his beard again, then put his finger on his chin and frowned. "I notice you used the word *deliverance* instead of *recovery*."

Tony smiled. *The door has just been opened.* This was the part of his job he loved the most. "That's right, man," he said, "because that's what it boils down to. At the end of the day, do you want to complete your treatment and keep on telling everybody you're in recovery? Or do you want to be delivered, healed," he placed his hand over his heart, "permanently set free?"

Tony smiled again and Lorenzo noticed how vibrant his appearance had become since he'd started talking about being set free and delivered.

"There's a difference between the two," Tony said. "And I can tell you right off the bat," he spread out his arms and held up his hands. "I'm a witness because I've been delivered."

Lorenzo remained silent as he continued to study Tony's glowing face.

"Praise the Lord," Tony said still smiling.

After the intake assessment was completed, Tony went over a few final pieces of information before Lorenzo left his office.

"Once you've seen the doctor, our clinical team will use the information from our assessment to create a care plan for you. There'll be a treatment plan that addresses your particular addiction. We'll have you set some goals for getting clean and staying clean," he smiled, "aka delivered. And, of course, we'll have to address your lifestyle and what led you down this path to begin with."

Lorenzo rubbed his forehead. His anxiety was returning. "Sounds like a lot of work."

"It is. But nothing worth having is easy," Tony said reassuringly. "And just so you understand, I'm saying we, but *I* won't be a part of the team. I just want to make sure you understand that."

"I understand," Lorenzo said.

"And also understand that I may not be your counselor, but I do support you because I know what you're going through."

"Thanks, I appreciate it," Lorenzo said looking at the floor. "Let me ask you something."

"Sure."

"You said something about a difference between recovery and deliverance."

Tony nodded his head slowly.

"What did you mean by that?"

"I mean what the Word means," he said. "The Bible says, when Jesus sets you free, you're free indeed! Ain't no going back unless you choose to. And some people do. The Bible talks about that too."

Tony opened his drawer and pulled out a miniature orange leather Bible. He flipped through its pages. "Here it is," he said. "Proverbs 26, verse 11, *'As a dog returns to its vomit,'*" Tony read, *"'so fools repeat their folly.'"* He turned the Bible around and pointed to the scripture so Lorenzo could see it for himself.

"That's deep," Lorenzo said.

"It is," Tony agreed. "We'll talk some more if you want to." He got up to take Lorenzo back out to the lobby. "Off the record," he added.

"Cool," Lorenzo said.

"You'll be seeing the doctor for a health screening next," Tony explained as he escorted Lorenzo through the door.

Lorenzo took a seat once more. He tried to ignore the anxiety he was feeling. He wanted to believe that he could be set free from the emotional bondage he'd been living with all his life. He dug his hands deep into the pockets of his jacket. Maybe he could be, he thought as he watched the ribbons of water flowing freely from the fountain on the wall.

Chapter Forty-four

Shari sat in front of the television set listening to the World Wide News anchorman. Although the city of Chicago had experienced their fair share of snow and below freezing temperatures, it was incomparable to the unprecedented snow and ice storms affecting the southern part of the country.

According to the anchorman, one of the largest airline carriers in the country had to cancel over 2,000 flights because of the storm. There had been twenty-two weather-related deaths, and over a million homes and businesses were now without power. According to reports from the utility company, more than 500,000 customers were still in the dark.

Shari looked at the $700 utility bill she was holding in her hand. Even though she and Tony still didn't have the money to pay the bill, and the moratorium would be ending in six weeks, her concern about her own family ending up in a cold, dark house seemed trivial in comparison to what she was hearing on TV.

A preview from the six o'clock news appeared on the screen, and Shari's jaw dropped. She picked up her cell phone and called Tia.

"Hey," Tia answered.

"Tia," Shari said urgently. "Turn to Channel Six. Hurry up. The news is about to come on."

"Why?" Tia asked as she pressed the down arrow on the remote control until she got to the channel.

"It's about our neighbor. I just saw the preview."

The theme song for the six o'clock news began playing as Tia turned up the volume. She sat glued to her seat as the words Breaking News Update spread big and bold across the screen. Then the female reporter began talking.

"Good evening, everyone," she began. "We've just received an update on the arrest of a man in his early fifties who had been posing as a teenager online in order to lure young girls to undisclosed locations."

A picture of the man who'd been arrested appeared on the screen, his frozen stare drew attention to his hazel eyes, and Tia cringed. She hated that she'd ever been drawn to them in the first place.

"Homer Woodard," the anchorwoman continued, "the man who is accused of allegedly kidnapping his neighbor's daughter, is now also being charged with child enticement and using a computer to facilitate a child sex crime. The charges were issued against the suspect after police combed through his laptop and discovered multiple online conversations he'd had with several underage girls.

"Police aren't providing any information pertaining to the nature of the conversations," the anchorwoman said, "but the suspect is believed to have met with several of the girls he met online. Currently, he is being held in the county jail on a $5,000 bail. We aren't releasing any of the victims' names due to their ages."

Tia remained speechless. To think Serenity had been held hostage by this monster! Her stomach began to feel queasy as she thought about how she had allowed herself to be intimate with Homer.

"In addition," the anchorwoman continued, "the suspect's mother is believed to have passed away in his home just days prior to the kidnapping incident."

"Mother?" Shari and Tia said at the same time.

"I didn't even know his mother lived with him," Shari said. "I never saw her."

Tia moved the phone to her other ear. She didn't bother to tell Shari that she had taken care of Homer's mother in the hospital, and how surprised she'd been when he'd shown up to take her home. She just wanted to put the memory of him and everything else that had to do with him behind her.

"I wonder when she died," Shari said. "I never saw any ambulance or anything."

"Well, obviously it happened while we weren't at home," Tia said. "Otherwise, I'm sure we would have seen or heard something."

"Lord have mercy. You just never know who's living next door to you, do you?"

"No," Tia said sadly, "you don't."

"I feel sorry for those other girls and their families, but let's thank God Serenity was able to escape!"

"Oh, I have," Tia said assuredly. "Believe me. I have."

"How is she doing anyway?"

Tia turned off the television set, thankful that the focus was shifting away from Homer. "All things considered, she's doing okay, I guess."

"How long are you going to keep dropping her off at school?"

"I'm just trying to give her some time to recuperate before I start letting her stand outside and wait for the school bus again. I just want her to feel safe."

"You probably need some time to feel the same way, huh?" Shari asked.

"Yeah, I do."

"Thanks for dropping Cookie off too."

"Well, they go to the same school so it only makes sense. And Lorenzo is finally making himself useful now by watching for the school bus when they come home."

"That's good," Shari said. "It's a start, don't you think?"

"I guess." A wave of sadness came over Tia as she recalled the conversation she'd had with Serenity the night she'd escaped from Homer's basement.

"Serenity thinks I don't care about her."

"Oh, no," Shari said pressing the mute button on the remote control, "that's just her adolescence talking. She knows you love her."

Tia looked outside at the frozen stillness. She would be so happy when they got past this cold front. "I don't know," she said. "We're not as close as we could be . . . should be. But I'm going to start spending more time with her."

"You haven't forgotten that all things are possible with God, right?"

"Right," Tia said. But how could she expect God to make everything right when she had done so much wrong? *

Chapter Forty-five

It had been four weeks since Lorenzo had begun attending group therapy sessions. He had finally found the courage to break his own vow, and had decided once again, to divulge what had happened to him as a boy. It hadn't been quite as hard as it had been when he'd told his parents; mainly because several of the men and women in the group of twelve had also been molested when they were younger. Lorenzo was finding out that his situation was not as isolated as he'd thought it to be for so long.

Lorenzo sat in his group therapy session listening to a female client talk. "Once you forgive your perpetrator," the woman said, directing her comments toward him, "God will take care of the rest."

She had just finished talking about her own childhood experience but Lorenzo could tell by the creases in her forehead and the way her jaw clenched while she spoke that she still had some forgiving of her own to do.

He tensed up. "You know this is supposed to be a group of transparency and truth, right?" he said.

She blinked and turned her head slightly. "What does that mean?"

Lorenzo leaned forward on his elbows. "That's what the counselor said." He hunched his shoulders. "I'm just saying."

"Saying *what?*" she asked defensively.

Lorenzo looked at the woman briefly, and then glanced around the room. "Well, you got your face all torn up like you're still mad. I'm just saying, are you sure you don't have some more forgiving to do?"

"Maybe I do. But what about you?"

A short man sitting next to Lorenzo turned to face him. "You know, man, the Lord can help you with your anger," he said. "But you gonna need to forgive the man who abused you just like God is willing to forgive you."

Lorenzo looked at him like he was crazy.

"He's partially right," Evan, the counselor who was facilitating the group, said. "God can help you with your anger." He scooted to the end of his seat. "You see, right now, you're being held hostage by your own dark emotions. You got this pent-up anger inside that you're walking around with every day, *and*," he leaned forward, "you got to deal with an unforgiving spirit on top of that."

"I bet the man who molested you probably don't even think he did anything wrong," another man in the group said. "He might not even have enough sense to ask for your forgiveness."

Lorenzo stood up, outraged by the comment. "What do you mean, he didn't do anything wrong?"

"Sit back down," Evan said calmly, "and listen. That's not what he said. He said the man probably doesn't *think* he did anything wrong."

Lorenzo sat down slowly.

"And he's right. The majority of molesters come up with what they think are justifiable reasons for doing what they do. And they try to twist the reality and make it seem like the ones they abuse were somehow willing participants. But the truth is they're sick individuals." Evan looked at all twelve clients in the room. "And the victim is never at fault. None of you are to blame."

Lorenzo's eyes glassed over. This was the first time he'd been told that what had happened to him was not his fault.

"Let me tell you something, man," Evan said. "Suppression can be a deadly thing. For me, it had me sniffing something up my nose every chance I got; for you it was popping pills." He continued to look at him. "You're not alone," he said. "Every one of us in this room has had to deal with the same emotions you're dealing with. We might have different situations that caused them, but we've had to deal with them just the same."

Lorenzo's eyes raced across the faces of the other clients. Almost every head in the room was nodding slowly.

"It's hard," Evan said. "I know. But when you turn it over to Jesus He takes the load from you."

Evan paused, and Lorenzo saw that familiar glow emanating from his face. This was the second person whose face seemed to transform into some kind of light whenever they began talking about Jesus and deliverance.

"God makes a way when you think there is no way," Evan said.

"Uh-huh," the man next to Lorenzo agreed.

"Just think about." Evan grabbed the Bible on the table and began flipping through the pages. "I don't know how much you know about the Bible," he said, "but there's a story in here about Jesus feeding more than 5,000 people with just two fishes and five loaves of bread. I believe that was put in there to show us how He makes a way out of no way."

"That's right," another member of the group said softly.

"He gives you strength you didn't even know you had," Evan said. "And it's God's kind of strength you're gonna need in order to forgive. Then, my brother, you can be set free."

Lorenzo shifted in his seat as an unwanted teardrop landed on his thigh. *God, how I want to be free!*

"What's done is done," the same woman who had been speaking earlier said. "When are you going to stop being so angry?"

Lorenzo looked at the woman's hands. They were curled up so tightly that they resembled the size of two small oranges. "I don't know," he said. "How about I'll get better when you get better?"

"I am better . . ."

"All right," Evan intervened. He scooted his chair closer into the circle. "Everybody, let's get ready for our closing prayer."

Everyone in the circle held hands and lowered their heads as Evan began to pray.

"Father, how thankful I am to You on this day. I'm still here because You brought me out of the darkness and into Your light. Your Word tells me that I can do all things through Christ who strengthens me. And I believe.

"It's my prayer today, Father, that everyone in this room will surrender their souls to You so that You can do for them what they cannot do for themselves. Give them the strength to turn to You not only for deliverance and healing but for the salvation of their souls, Lord.

"Set them free, Lord. Remove the bondage that's been holding them hostage. Right now. In the name of Jesus, I pray, amen."

Lorenzo wiped his eyes and raised his head.

"Step into the light, my brother," Evan said patting him on the back. "Let Jesus deliver you."

Lorenzo nodded his head.

Chapter Forty-six

It was Wednesday evening, and the green neon-colored numbers on the digital clock read 7:30 p.m. Tia had been in bed all day, paralyzed by an increasing feeling of sorrow and regret that had rendered her unable to rise up and get out of her bed.

It had been quite a month. Between Lorenzo's escalating addiction and Serenity's kidnapping it was a wonder she hadn't lost her mind. Although Lorenzo was finally getting the help he needed, they weren't in the clear yet. And there was still the infidelity she'd committed with Homer.

Infidelity . . . Tia hated that word! God forgive her but she hated Homer as well. She pulled the comforter over her shoulders. Did she really hate him or was it what she had allowed herself to do with him that she hated? She wondered if she would hate him any less had he not kidnapped her daughter.

She gripped the edges of the comforter and pulled it closer to her neck. The guilt was beginning to take a toll on her. Tia knew that what had happened to Serenity had not been her fault, still she felt that if she had never become intimate with Homer she would not have had to reject him later, and he would not have kidnapped Serenity in retaliation. Everything that happened had been caused by a domino effect, and Tia had knocked over the first tile.

The phone began to ring, and she opened her eyes.

She looked at the caller ID and answered the phone.

"Hello, Granddaughter. How are you feeling?"

"I'm fine," Tia lied.

Tia had told her grandmother and mother about what had happened to Serenity. Both of them, of course, were thankful that Serenity had escaped and that the perpetrator had been caught.

"How was work?" Mavis asked.

"I didn't go to work today."

"Why not?"

"I just didn't feel like it," Tia struggled to get the words out. "I just don't feel good."

"I thought you just said you were fine." Mavis was quiet for several seconds. "Something don't feel right," she said.

"I just don't feel good, Grandma. That's all."

"Where's the pain at?"

Tia wiped her eyes. How could she tell her that the pain was not physical? What words could she use to describe the ache she felt in her soul? There were no words to describe it. Only tears.

"What's wrong, child?"

"It's just too much," Tia said grabbing a tissue from the nightstand.

"What's too much?"

"Everything!" she cried out. "The stuff that happened with Serenity, the stuff that's *been* happening with Lorenzo, the neigh—" she stopped. She hadn't divulged everything to her grandmother and mother. They did not know she'd been unfaithful to Lorenzo or that the neighbor who'd kidnapped Serenity was also the man she'd been unfaithful with.

"Give it to the Lord," her grandmother said. "You got to give it to the Lord. Whatever it is, let it go."

"I know, Grandma," she said wearily.

"How are Serenity and Lorenzo doing?"

Tia grabbed another tissue and wiped the remaining moisture from her eyes. "Well," she said, "Lorenzo's getting counseling now at a Christian-based treatment center."

"Because of those pills he's been taking?"

"Yes."

"Praise the Lord," Mavis said, "because He *is* the true deliverer!"

Tia smiled slightly.

"And what about Serenity?"

"Serenity's at Bible Study right now, and I think she's getting back to her old self," Tia tried to chuckle. "I don't know if that's good or bad. But I'm trying to spend more time with her."

"Tell my baby I said hi."

"I will."

"And tell her to call me sometimes. That girl don't never pick up the phone and call nobody."

"I know," Tia said. "You're right. How's Mama doing?"

"She's doing all right. She's downstairs now keeping herself happy with all those flowers."

Tia smiled.

"You know, you've got a lot to be thankful for," her grandmother said. "I know you're going through some rough times right now, and I'm not trying to diminish that. But it could be a lot worse. So if you can't be thankful for nothing else, be thankful for that."

"I'll try, Grandma."

"Yeah, and get rid of those secrets."

Tia's eyebrows arched. Before she could say anything, Mavis continued.

"Secrets are a lot like sad souls. Both of them slowly eat at you from the inside, and either you gon' kill it or it's gon' kill you. It's your choice," she said. "It's always your choice."

***

Serenity sat in the makeshift classroom listening to the youth pastor at First Temple Church. The small room was filled to capacity with boys and girls ranging in age from twelve to seventeen. Everyone was seated at long tables or individual chairs as they began the weekly Bible Study.

It was hard for Serenity to stay focused in the chilly room, and she scooted closer to Cookie.

"I'm cold," she said. "Look." She pointed to the many raised bumps on her arm. "I need a sweater."

"Don't look at mine," Cookie said. "I told you to bring one."

"Hey, you're cold?" Jonathan, the boy sitting behind Serenity, asked.

She exchanged looks with Cookie before answering him. "Uh-huh," she said.

"Here, you wanna wear my jacket?" he asked.

"Yeah," Serenity said, waiting for him to take it off and give it to her.

He began to take off his jacket, then stopped. "Psych!" he said loudly and began laughing.

"Ooh!" Serenity said as she threw her pencil at him.

He dodged the flying object and laughed again.

"Excuse me," the youth pastor said, "but can I get some quiet back there?"

"Sorry," both Serenity and Jonathan said.

The youth pastor continued. "Like I was saying, we are not perfect people. That's why we need a Savior."

Some of Serenity's peers shifted in their seats.

"Just like you're not perfect," he said. "Neither are your parents."

Serenity exchanged a look of doubt with Cookie.

"Sometimes parents struggle with things just like you do."

Some of the kids frowned.

"What? Y'all think y'all special?" he asked jokingly, and everyone started laughing.

"We'll you ain't." He became serious. "Satan's gonna try you just like he tries your parents. Remember that. And the next time you want your parents to cut you some slack, try cutting them some slack," he said. "Because even when they make mistakes, they still love you. They do."

It had grown quiet in the room.

"Let us pray for each other," the pastor said. And everyone lowered their heads.

Chapter Forty-seven

Lorenzo was on his way to the treatment center for a one-on-one session with his counselor Mark. As part of the program requirements, he also had to provide a urine sample two times a week or whenever his counselor deemed it necessary. Lorenzo had no problem with that. His samples always came back clean because he had not taken any pills since he'd begun therapy after his fall.

Although Lorenzo had been attending group and individual therapy twice a week for a month, he was still in the initial phase of treatment and there were still times when he felt down. He mentioned this to Mark, during his therapy session.

"There'll be times when you're going to feel that way," Mark said. "But whatever you do, don't become discouraged," he warned him. "That's one of the enemy's biggest tools—discouragement."

Lorenzo nodded his head as he listened.

"It takes time to heal," Mark said. "Admitting your abuse and speaking out about it means that you've taken the first and most important step toward the healing process." He opened his drawer, pulled out a small notepad, and pushed it toward Lorenzo. "Today we're having a funeral," he said.

"Huh?" Lorenzo gave Mark a look of confusion.

"Write down every negative feeling or thought you've been carrying around with you since the day you were molested."

Lorenzo picked up the pencil and stared at the blank sheet of paper for several minutes. Finally, he looked up. "Nah, man, I can't," he said.

"You'll never be free until you can," Mark said.

Several more minutes passed before Lorenzo began to write slowly.

Ugly, shame, hate, denial, sad, rage, cold, worthless. . . . Those were some of the words Lorenzo wrote down. He knew he'd sheltered all of those emotions in his heart, but what he didn't know was how to release them. He'd forgotten, or maybe he'd shunned the answer—he wasn't sure which—when it had been presented to him by one of his Christian coworkers years ago.

Now for years, he had been battling with his emotions, forgetting that if he surrendered himself to the Lord, the battle would no longer be his to fight but the Lord's. Somehow, he'd made a detour, a wrong turn. He'd stepped off the path of righteousness and had become completely lost.

He looked at the self-destructive words he'd written on the piece of paper. Without warning, the damn inside of him broke, and his shoulders began to heave violently as twenty-seven years of pent-up tears were finally released.

Mark sat silently.

After some time, Lorenzo's tears began to subside. He grabbed a wad of tissue and blew his nose. "I'm sorry, man," he said.

"For what?" Mark asked gently. "For being human?"

Lorenzo blew his nose again. The words he'd written on the piece of paper had quickly become distorted from the tears that had fallen from his eyes.

Mark instructed him to fold up the piece of paper.

Lorenzo folded the paper in half, and then folded it again.

"It's time to say your last good-byes," Mark said. He placed his hand over the folded paper. "Lord," he began, "we put to death all these words of bondage that only serve to keep Lorenzo in the pit of depression he's been in for too long."

Lorenzo bowed his head.

"We cast down all words, thoughts, and actions that go against You, Father. Right now. And we ask that Your will be done, not ours. Lift up Lorenzo, Lord. And set him free from the things that have kept him bound. Thank you, Father. In the name of Jesus, we pray. Amen."

"Amen," Lorenzo whispered in agreement with his counselor.

"You're gonna make it," Mark said. "Believe that."

Lorenzo hesitated. "I believe," he said.

He left the treatment center and headed for his car. He drove home with the front windows slightly cracked. The cold front was passing, and Lorenzo noticed the tree branches beginning to relinquish the weight from the icy burial chamber they'd been encased in. As he drove, he saw the ice-paved sidewalks, which had sent many pedestrians to the emergency room, being transformed into a slushy mixture of icy crumbs.

Lorenzo turned into his driveway and pressed the button on the remote control. He waited while the garage door slowly rose and was relieved to see Tia's SUV parked inside. He parked his car next to hers and turned the engine off. He remained seated behind the steering wheel as he thought about the events that had taken place during his counseling session.

After the "funeral," Lorenzo realized not only had he been harboring a shame that did not belong to him but he had also been in mourning over what had happened to him and how his innocence had been forever lost.

"It will do you no good to wonder, why me?" Mark had said before Lorenzo left his office. "The only thing you can do now is get past it by turning it over to the Lord."

And that's exactly what Lorenzo intended to do. Bits and pieces of God's Word came back to him now as he reflected on how the past twenty-seven years of his life had been since the molestation. He recalled a verse from the Bible that held an undeniable truth:

"The thief comes only to steal and kill and destroy; I have come that they may have life, and have it to the full."

His inability to get past what had happened to him had cost him a great deal. It had come between him and his wife, and worst of all . . . it had interrupted his relationship with Jesus. He had allowed it to hinder him emotionally and physically, even costing him his job. Everything good had been stolen from him or destroyed. He, himself, had almost died.

He closed his eyes and bowed his head. "Father, forgive me for my sins," he whispered. "Forgive me as I forgive Brent for molesting me all those years ago." He stopped to catch his breath . . . that was the first time he had mentioned the perpetrator's name in twenty-seven years. "Forgive me for abandoning my duties as a husband, Lord. Forgive me for turning my back on you."

Lorenzo shook his head from side to side. "I've fallen short again, Father, but I know with You by my side I can also rise again." He clasped his hands together tightly. "I surrender my heart and my life to You, Lord. Help me to give You all the glory, all the honor, and all the praise. In Jesus' name, amen."

Today had been the turning point for Lorenzo. He had received the strength he needed. He was not going to subdue his grief any longer. There would be no more anesthetizing it and placing it in an unburiable grave. No. He relinquished the pain. Forever. Because he had been set free. Praise God! He had been set free. He remembered how Tony had reminded him of what Jesus said about freedom:

"So if the Son sets you free, you will be free indeed."

Lorenzo wiped his eyes and got out of the car. Hallelujah, he had been set free! Now, it was time to share the truth with his wife.

He let the garage door down as he got out of the car and went into the house. Tia was not in any of the rooms on the first level so he slowly walked up the stairs and headed for the bedroom.

"Hi," Lorenzo said as he peeked through the partially open door.

Tia grabbed a magazine and began flipping through the pages. "Hello," she said cautiously. Somewhere in her heart, a fractured piece of emotion still wanted to greet him with the eagerness of a child. But as she remembered all that he had withheld from her, her emotions remained in a distant and unobtainable state.

He stood in the doorway as Tia continued her pretense of browsing through the magazine. Finally, he took a deep breath. "I'd like to talk to you for a minute," he said nervously.

Even though Lorenzo had been faithful in attending his counseling sessions, they were still not on speaking terms. Her heartbeat quickened. What did he want to talk to her about? "Talk on," she said without looking at him. She wanted to give him some of his own medicine, treat him like he'd treated her on so many occasions when she'd wanted to talk to him. "I'm listening."

"Can I come in?"

Her body stiffened. "For what? You never want to come in any other time."

"I want to talk to you in private."

"Serenity's at school," she said as she continued to flip through the magazine.

Lorenzo sat down on the bed next to her and watched his wife flinch as he gently took the magazine out of her hands. "I have something to tell you," he said.

Tia's heartbeat sped up even faster. *What is it now? Another woman? Another man?* She looked at him. He was holding his head down, and she could tell something was wrong. "What is it?" she asked.

"I've been concentrating on a lot of negative things for a long time," Lorenzo said. "I had this automatic release shield in place. It was kind of like my own protective mechanism, but after awhile, I just kept it up all the time and it caused me to become cold and cynical."

"No kidding," Tia said sarcastically. "Is this what you learned in counseling?"

Lorenzo raised his head. "Please," he said softly, "don't make this any harder for me than it already is."

Tia's neck stiffened. There was something different in his tone. There was a tenderness in his voice that she hadn't heard in a long time. It made her feel uncomfortable, but she also sensed that it was genuine.

"God has a purpose for me," Lorenzo said. "I've been traveling on the wrong road for a long time. Now, I'm trying to get back on the right path, and I realize part of my journey is going to have be a solitary one." He looked at her with tears in his eyes. "But I realized something else too. It doesn't have to be a lonely and hostile one."

Tia's chest rose and fell quickly. "What are you talking about?"

"Tia," he took a deep breath and continued, "when I was eleven years old . . ."

Chapter Forty-eight

Hours later, Lorenzo was amazed at how cathartic it felt to relinquish his secret to his wife. It wasn't just the telling of it; he had already done that twice—once to his parents, once in counseling. It was finally being able to share it with her and discover that she was not going to judge him or blame him for what had happened.

He'd made the decision to trust her, and it had not been a mistake. After he had finished telling her his story, Tia cried with him and rocked him in her arms. She was his blessing, and had been all along, but he had been unable to see that. He held onto her tightly. It was an awful thing to throw away a blessing.

"Today," Lorenzo said, "my counselor told me things would get better with time. And they already have." He wiped the tears from Tia's face. "Now, it's about to get even better."

"What do you mean?" Tia asked.

"On Sunday, when the pastor offers the call for salvation I'm going to rededicate myself to Jesus," Lorenzo said. "And I want to be baptized again." He smiled. "All things new."

"That's beautiful," Tia said as her eyes became misty all over again.

"You know," Lorenzo said, "counseling helped me to look at the shredded pieces of our marriage, and my life in general . . . which caused the shredded pieces of our marriage." He pressed his lips together and shook his head.

"Instead of dealing with my issues, I took pills. Instead of trying to heal, I numbed up, and I pushed you and Serenity away in the process. But now," he pointed to his forehead with his index finger, "now I realize that I just can't afford to keep letting my mind stay weighted down with all these dark and gloomy memories from my past."

Tia sat with her hands in her lap and listened.

"It's like the counselor said," he continued, "if I'm going to live in the past, then I may as well still be there or be dead because that's not living." He paused. "The funny thing is, after I fell and ended up in the hospital, I was wishing God had just let me die.

"Now, I want to live," he said. "And if I'm going to live, then I need to live freely!"

Tia marveled at the change in his demeanor. He'd left the house one way and had returned a completely different person. She wanted to hug him, but doubt crept in. Had he really changed that much? She remembered his reaction the last time she tried to hug him in the hospital and decided against it.

Her grandmother's words came back to her: *"get rid of those secrets."* Tia had seen and been a recipient of the damage caused by secrets. Now, after hearing Lorenzo let go of a secret he'd carried around with him for practically all of his life, Tia knew she would have to confess her wrongdoing if she were ever to have a chance at living freely . . . with or without Lorenzo.

Her heart was beating way too fast. "I'm proud of you, Lorenzo," she said. And before she knew it, she was crying heavily.

"What's wrong?" he asked gently. "Why are you crying so hard?"

She started to hyperventilate. "I . . . did . . . a . . . terrible . . . thing."

"Tia, calm down," he said, placing his hand on her back. "What did you do?"

"Something . . . really . . . wrong."

"What?"

"I . . . met . . . another . . . man."

"You met another man?"

She nodded her head.

"Did you sleep with him?"

She lowered her head.

"Did you sleep with him?" he repeated firmly.

"Yes," she said without looking up.

Lorenzo remained silent. "When?"

"Back in January," she said softly.

"Do you want to be with him?"

She raised her head quickly. Her eyes widened. "No," she said. "It only happened once, and I realized it was a mistake." She stopped crying. "I realized that no matter how bad our marriage was that still didn't give me the right to be unfaithful to you." The tears returned. "I just wanted you to love me, but you kept pushing me away."

"Don't cry," he said. "I'm partially to blame for this too. I know I abandoned you emotionally. I checked out. I wasn't there when you needed me, and I'm sorry. Some people might say I cheated on you too because I chose pills over you. That's all I wanted. Some people might even say the drugs became my lover. You just had one in the flesh and blood."

"Oh my God," she cried, covering her face with her hands.

"What? What is it now, Tia?"

She continued to cry. How could she tell him that the man she'd slept with was the same man who had kidnapped their daughter? "I'm so sorry, Lorenzo. I'm so sorry. Please forgive me."

He moved her hands from her face. "Look at me," he said.

She kept her head down.

"Look at me," he said again as he gently lifted her head up.

"I'll forgive you. If you . . ."

"No, wait," she said solemnly. "You don't know the rest of the story."

"Then tell me."

"The man was our neighbor."

Lorenzo's mind began to race. "Tony?" He shook his head. "Please tell me it wasn't Tony."

"It wasn't Tony. It was the man next door to Tony."

Lorenzo put one hand on his forehead and stretched out his other arm. "Stop! Hold up! You mean the same man who kidnapped Serenity?"

"I didn't know," Tia said. She couldn't stop crying.

"Homer?" Lorenzo jumped up from the bed.

"Lorenzo, wait," she said. "I didn't know."

He stood breathing heavily as he stared down at her. "I need some time to process this," he said and stormed out of the room.

Chapter Forty-nine

Lorenzo grabbed his coat and went back out to the garage. He got in his car and called Mark, his counselor.

"Hello, this is Mark speaking."

"Mark," Lorenzo said to the calm voice on the other end of the line, "this is Lorenzo."

"Hey, what's up, man? Is everything okay?"

"No, not really," Lorenzo said, still breathing heavily. "My wife just told me she had an affair with the same man who kidnapped our daughter." He gripped his cell phone and shook his head. "I don't know if I can handle this, man."

"Let's start at the beginning," Mark said calmly. "When did this happen?"

"She said back in January."

"And what were you doing during this time?"

Creases appeared in Lorenzo's forehead. He looked at the phone. "What kind of question is that, man? You know what I was doing."

"Tell me."

Lorenzo was silent.

"Come on, now," Mark encouraged. "Don't get quiet on me now. You've been making excellent progress. And you should know by now, communication is the key. So I'm going to ask you again—what were you doing during this time?"

A lump formed in Lorenzo's throat. He swallowed hard. "I was getting high," he said as a heavy sensation settled in the core of his soul.

"Which means what?"

Lorenzo hesitated, but he knew where Mark was heading. Lorenzo had come this far and had faced his demons. He could not go backward now. "I wasn't there when she needed me," he said quietly.

"Where were you?"

"I mean, I was there. But emotionally, I wasn't."

"And do you think your wife knew this man would end up kidnapping your daughter?"

"I doubt it," Lorenzo said, "but if she wouldn't have been messing with him none of this would have happened."

"How do you know? How do you know this man didn't already have his mind set on your daughter? He could have been using your wife to get to your daughter."

"I don't know, but it's still messed up."

"I agree," Mark said. "That's why God tells us we reap what we sow. There's a consequence for every negative action . . . for all of us. For me, it was years of trying to mend all the hearts I broke and the relationships I damaged during my years of addiction." He spoke slowly into the mouthpiece. "You checked out of life, man. You numbed yourself with pills and neglected your family in the process. What did you think would happen?"

Lorenzo's heart felt too big for his chest. "So you're saying this is all my fault?"

"Of course not. There you go getting defensive again."

"Well, what are you saying?"

"I'm saying your wife has to own up to her wrongdoing as well. And the bottom line is that both of you will have to make up your mind to either come together as a united front or go ahead and give the enemy what he wants, which is to see your marriage completely dissolved."

Lorenzo painfully remembered how, when the pain of his past had become too much to bear, he had turned away from God instead of turning *to* Him. He'd also rejected Tia and Serenity as well. His counselor was right. What *did* he think would happen? The problem was . . . he hadn't thought at all. If ever he needed the Lord's strength—and he had—he would certainly need to call on it now if he and Tia were going to get through this.

Lorenzo stayed on the phone with Mark a little while longer. The conversation ended with a prayer, and then Lorenzo thanked Mark and hung up. He gripped the steering wheel and stared straight-ahead at the dingy garage wall. He looked at the other two walls on both sides of him; they were just as dingy. He remembered painting each of the walls white shortly after moving into the house. Now, he couldn't even remember how or when the walls had gotten so dirty.

Lorenzo got out of his car and went back into the house. He walked into the living room and sat down.

Tia heard him come in and slowly walked down the steps.

His back was turned to her as he sat on the couch.

"Lorenzo," she said.

"Don't talk to me right now," he said. "Not now."

She crossed her arms. "When you talked to me, I listened. Now I need to talk and have you listen. After that, we don't have to talk anymore." She shifted her weight. "It's not like it'll be the first time."

He turned briefly to look at her, then turned back around.

She shifted her weight again. "For most of our marriage," she said, "I always wondered if there was something wrong with me. After we got married, you changed . . . or I guess you were always that way. I just didn't know it at the time." She stared at his back. "You kept it hidden."

Lorenzo lowered his head slightly as she continued.

"When you would have your up-and-down moods, I always thought it was because of me." She placed a finger on the side of her cheek. "Now, I know it wasn't. Now, I know what you were dealing with. But back then, I didn't, so I blamed myself. And I never knew what to do to make it better."

Tia watched the rise and fall of Lorenzo's shoulders as she leaned back against the wall. "I tried to be a good wife even when you rejected me over and over again, even when you made me feel like I wasn't enough for you. But a person can only be rejected for so long. I started feeling like a failure because of your rejection and all the things I told myself it meant." She rubbed the sides of her forehead. "Then I just got tired of trying to please you and be what you needed." She threw her arms up into the air, "Especially when I didn't even know what that was."

She walked around to face him. "Can you believe I was actually afraid that you would leave me? That's how much in denial I was." She put her hand over her heart. "I couldn't even admit that, emotionally, you had left me a long time ago. And then I told myself I should have left you right after Serenity was born like I had planned to do. But you said things would be different, and I believed you. So I stayed." She sighed.

"Our marriage never really had a fair start to begin with. It's been lopsided for so long that I'm not sure if it's ever really been balanced. All I know, Lorenzo, is that I loved you, and I would have done anything for you. But you made it clear for years that the feeling was not reciprocal." She stood in front of him staring at his semilowered head.

"And now," she said wearily, "thirteen years later, I find out why. I'm sorry for what I've done. I hope you can forgive me just as I'm willing to forgive you." She did not wait for a response from him. She wasn't expecting one. She turned to leave the room. "Now," she said, "I'm done."

Lorenzo remained still. The only thing moving was the increasing rise and fall of his shoulders. *Done?* He looked down at his clenched fist. What did she mean, she was done? It couldn't be over now. Not when he had finally taken the first steps to get back on the right path. He looked out the window. "You're going to have to help me through this, Lord," he whispered.

He watched the melting ice continue to drip from the gutter just above the living-room window. How many times would he keep messing up? How many times would he have to say he was sorry? He was ready to let it go . . . every burden, every worry, every fear. He wanted it all dissolved—once and for all. He was so tired. "Lord, give me strength," he said as he slowly rose from the sofa.

He walked toward the stairs and stopped. What if she was up there packing? What would he say? He held onto the banister and ascended the stairs one by one. The bedroom door was open and he saw her sitting on the side of the bed staring out the window. He quickly scanned the room. There was no suitcase in sight.

He sat down next to her. "This is messed up," he said.

"Which part?" she asked as she continued looking out the window.

He smiled sadly. "All of it. So much time has been wasted. So many mistakes have been made."

"I know." She took a deep breath. "I understand if you can't forgive me. I might not forgive me either . . . at least not right away."

"Well, like I said," he began patting the top of his knee, "I've made my mistakes too." He slowly took her hand and covered it with his own. "But I meant what I said earlier about living and being free. You and me," he said, "we need to make a fresh start. We did things wrong for thirteen years. Now, we're going to do it right. This time, we're going to let God be in control all the way."

"Like we should have let Him all along," Tia said.

Lorenzo squeezed her hand. "You're right."

The icicles continued to melt away, disintegrating as the freezing temperatures outside began to subside. That night Lorenzo did something he hadn't done in a long time—he slept in the bedroom, in the bed, with his wife.

Chapter Fifty

It had been a cold and brutal winter. Everyone was thanking God that April had finally arrived. The Sparks family was especially thankful to God as they walked through the doors of the First Temple Church. Lorenzo led Tia and Serenity down the aisle to the second row where Tony and his family sat. After she sat down, Tia took a prayer card out of the holder on the back of the seat in front of her. She began writing on it as the choir started to sing:

> *"No tears in heaven, no sorrows given.*
> *All will be glory in that land; . . ."*

As the song ended, the pastor walked up to the podium. "Yes," he said, "no tears in heaven. Can I get an amen?"

"Amen," Lorenzo said louder than everyone else. He looked down the row at Tony. Tony had risen above the pain and misery of addiction and had stayed that way for more than twenty years. To Lorenzo, that really did equate to being delivered as Tony said he was. And that was exactly the kind of freedom Lorenzo wanted.

He thought about the God-filled testimonies of the others at the Christian-based treatment center. Ironically, it was their strength that had helped him to admit his weakness. It was their willingness to move past their own personal trauma that had given him the courage to speak out about what had happened to him so many years ago.

It had been the beginning of his healing, and Lorenzo knew God was all up in that.

As the service came to an end, the pastor offered the invitation to anyone wanting to accept Jesus Christ into their life.

"Are you ready?" he asked everyone sitting in the pews. "If you die today, do you have your ticket? Romans 10:17 says, 'Consequently, faith comes from hearing the message, and the message is heard through the word about Christ.'

"And Hebrews 11:6 tells us, '. . . without faith it is impossible to please God, because anyone who comes to him must believe that he exists and that he rewards those who earnestly seek him.'"

Lorenzo stood up. He looked down at Tia and extended his hand. She smiled up at him, then stood and took his hand. Together, they walked to the front of the pulpit.

The pastor continued. "Acts 2:38 says, 'Repent and be baptized, every one of you, in the name of Jesus Christ for the forgiveness of your sins. And you will receive the gift of the Holy Spirit.'"

More people joined Tia and Lorenzo at the altar, ready to answer the call, eager to accept Jesus Christ as their Lord and Savior. The pastor began confirming each person's public declaration. When he got to Lorenzo he took his hand. "Matthew 10:32 said, 'Whoever acknowledges me before others, I will also acknowledge before my Father in heaven,'" he said.

The pastor looked at Lorenzo. "Do you believe that Jesus Christ is the son of God and that He died on the cross for your sins?"

"I do."

"Do you believe that on the third day, He rose from that death and now lives in heaven with God the Father?"

"I do."

"Do you admit you're a sinner, and have you repented of your sins?"

"Oh yes," Lorenzo said nodding his head fully. He squeezed Tia's hand.

The pastor continued. "Mark 16:16 said, 'Whoever believes and is baptized will be saved, but whoever does not believe will be condemned.' Have you been baptized, brother?"

"I have," Lorenzo said. "But I want to be baptized again and rededicate myself to the Lord."

"Praise the Lord," the pastor said shaking his hand. He motioned to Tony and another member of the congregation. "Please take Lorenzo and prepare him for water baptism." The congregation began clapping their hands and praising God.

The pastor approached Tia, and she gave him the card she'd filled out earlier. After he read it, he spoke. "Brothers and sisters," he said, "Tia Sparks stands before God in repentance." He looked at the card again. "And she's rededicating herself to the Lord. Let us praise God for her decision."

The congregation began clapping again as Tia shook the pastor's hand. She smiled at Serenity as she returned to her seat. After she sat down, Shari reached over and squeezed her hand.

The past few months had been an accumulation of all that had been going on in Tia's life. She knew she hadn't done so well spiritually or emotionally. She had strayed from the path and taken a detour which had only led her to a cold and dark place.

Her thoughts were interrupted by the opening of the curtains behind the pulpit. She saw Lorenzo standing in a long white robe. Then Tony led him into the pond of water as the sanctuary grew silent.

"Brothers and sisters," Tony began, "Lorenzo Sparks has confessed that Jesus Christ is the Son of God, and upon this confession I baptize him in the name of the Father, the Son, and the Holy Spirit."

He lowered Lorenzo into the water and brought him back up swiftly.

Applause broke out again as the congregation began to sing:

> *"What can wash away my sins,*
> *nothing but the blood of Jesus . . ."*

After the church services ended, members of the congregation stopped to give Lorenzo a hug or handshake as they congratulated him on his baptism. They hugged Tia and all the other members who had rededicated themselves to Jesus, offering them many words of encouragement.

"Praise the Lord," Tony said giving Lorenzo a hug.

Before he could say anything, Shari was next in line. "Congratulations," she said as she gave him another hug.

"Thank you," he said. Lorenzo was elated. He couldn't remember ever feeling so free. For the first time in his life he actually felt right . . . like what he was doing was the right thing to do. And this was only the beginning. He wouldn't stop with just being baptized. This time, he intended to live a life that fully reflected his love, reverence, and praise for Jesus Christ. He would be the example of a man, a Christian man, that his family had needed for so long.

Chapter Fifty-one

Tony and Lorenzo lingered behind as Shari and Tia headed to the church parking lot with the girls.

"So, I guess I won't be seeing you at the clinic anymore." Lorenzo said to Tony.

"Nope," Tony said adjusting the wool collar on his coat. "Tomorrow I start my new full-time job."

The counseling position at the Christian-based treatment center in Waukegan had reviewed Tony's online application and had called him in for an interview. During the interview, Tony had been up front about his five-year crack addiction. That, along with his testimony of having been delivered, and then staying clean for more than twenty-two years, resonated well with the director of the clinic. Days later, when Tony's cell phone rang, he heard the words he'd been praying to hear.

Not only had the director presented him with an offer for the job, but the position also came with an increase in pay. Now, he and Shari could get caught up on their bills a little faster . . . including the utility bill set for disconnection.

"God is good," Tony said smiling.

"Yes, He is," Lorenzo said. "Congratulations, man."

"I may not be at the clinic," Tony said pulling on his leather gloves, "but I'm still just two houses down from you, and you know you can call me anytime."

"I know, and I do appreciate that."

"I mean I was never your counselor anyway," Tony continued. "But now that I'm not working there, it'll be easier to talk to you and support you without me having to worry about any kind of conflict of interest."

"Yeah, I hear you, man."

They opened the church doors and exited the building. The snow that had once covered the branches on the trees had dissipated into a thin layer. Lorenzo looked up toward the sky. Soon, the promising warmth from the sun would remove all visible traces of the icy remnants.

"Talk to you later," he said to Tony as he hurried to the car and opened the passenger door for Tia. He listened to her giggle—a sound he hadn't heard in a long time—and he knew that not only was God giving him a second chance at life, He was giving him a second chance at his marriage.

Lorenzo knew it would take a lot of work and effort on his part, but God, in His awesome mercy and grace, had heard his cries and had forgiven him. And Lorenzo would not take that for granted.

Serenity ran to the car and climbed into the backseat. She looked at the back of her father's head, and the image of him lying unconscious on the living-room floor suddenly returned to her memory. That's what had started it all. She'd been scared, and in her panic, she'd ended up in front of that crazy man's house. If her father hadn't been on drugs she would have never . . . She stopped herself.

She could see that Lorenzo was changing. She'd been watching him since he'd started going to the treatment center. She noticed how he didn't slur his words anymore and how he wasn't always sleeping on the couch like he used to. Since the kidnapping, her father had actually begun standing at the front door every day waiting for the school bus she rode on to pull into the cul-de-sac.

"You don't have to do this every day," she'd told him. "It's okay."

"Yes, I do," he'd responded. "This is my way of making sure I stay on top of what's going on."

She remembered his sad smile, and she'd wanted to believe what the youth pastor had said—that parents weren't perfect but really did love their children.

"I should have been doing it anyway," he'd mumbled as she'd shrugged and walked past him into the house.

Lorenzo turned to look at Serenity. "Got your seat belt on?"

She pulled the latch down and across her waist until it caught in the holder. "Yep," she said.

"What's the matter?" he looked at her intensely. "Why are you looking like that?"

"Looking like what?"

"Like you're thinking about something real serious."

She shrugged. "I don't know."

"Well, remember what I told you," he said.

"What?"

"About my story."

"Oh, that," Serenity said. Lorenzo had revealed his story of abuse to Serenity shortly after he'd told Tia. "I wasn't thinking about that."

"Okay, I just want to make sure. Because that's what I was doing—thinking about that for twenty-seven years—and look where it got me."

She nodded her head.

He reached back and gently squeezed her cheek. "Thank God for delivering me," he said.

Serenity smiled as he turned back around. Something her grandmother had said to her during one of their visits suddenly returned to her memory.

"A sad soul can kill you," her grandmother had said. "You remember that."

Somehow Serenity knew she always would, and in the backseat of the car she whispered "thank you" to God for keeping her father alive.

Tia sat in the front seat next to Lorenzo silently thanking God as well. Her emotions, fractured as they were, had begun to reconnect. Her heart expanded as she looked over at him. And she thanked God again for what she was feeling.

Through her darkest days, God had continued to love and nurture her like no one else could. He had placed her feet back on solid ground, and she would not make the same mistake twice. Her soul had been replenished, her strength renewed. She knew that whatever else was to come she would overcome it just as long as she called on the name of the Lord for her strength.

Tia turned the volume up on the radio as Lorenzo pulled out of the parking lot. The sound of a woman's powerful voice sang in an upbeat tempo, and halfway through the song Tia joined in with the singer.

Both Serenity and Lorenzo listened to Tia's voice, strong and clear, as she sang "I Got The Victory" from the bottom of her soul.

Chapter Fifty-two

The following week, Tia and Lorenzo were on their way to their first counseling session together. As Tia drove past the cemetery, Lorenzo's thoughts returned to the water baptism he'd received on Sunday.

"You know what was odd about my baptism?" he asked Tia.

"No, what?"

"The water."

"The water?"

"Yeah," he said passionately. "It was ice cold going under, but I kid you not . . ." he repositioned himself, ". . . I felt this warm sensation when I came back up."

Tia continued driving as Lorenzo silently watched the tombstones erected above the ground pass swiftly before his eyes. He turned his head until he could no longer see any of the grave sites.

"There but for the grace of God go I," he said.

"Amen," Tia said in agreement.

Lorenzo turned his attention back to the counseling session he and Tia would soon have. "Now that Tony's been offered a full-time position at the treatment center in Waukegan, I guess I won't be seeing him at the clinic anymore."

"You sound like you're a little sad about that," Tia said poking him softly in the side.

"Maybe a little. I mean, he wasn't my counselor or anything, but he was the one who did the initial intake, and, I don't know, he really made me feel comfortable." He stared out the window. "Especially when I found out he used to be on drugs." He turned back to face Tia. "Did you know that?"

"No, I didn't. Shari never told me."

"I guess the past is the past," Lorenzo said. "Unless you're using it to help somebody else, there's no point in going around saying, 'Hey, look at me. I used to be a drug addict!'"

They both laughed at the silliness of what he was saying. But the part about using the past to help someone else remained in Lorenzo's thoughts.

Fifteen minutes later, they entered the clinic, and Lorenzo checked them both in at the front desk. He sat down next to Tia and noticed a man sitting in the chair right across from him. Lorenzo recognized the look of despair in the man's eyes; a little over a month ago, he might have been looking at a reflection of himself.

Since he'd started counseling, Lorenzo had come to understand that his addiction to the pills was really just a symptom of his underlying issue—one that had gone unresolved for too many years. Turning to pills may have started out as a method of escapism from a painful past, but once the pills became a habit, his escapism quickly transpired into a ball and chain.

He'd come to realize that all he'd ended up doing was trading the memory of a painful past for a recurring and unpleasant experience in the here and now. And he hadn't even had enough sense to see that.

But for the grace of God he would still be imprisoned. He knew Jesus was the answer just like Tony, the other counselors, and all the members in his group meetings said He was. Jesus held the key. Lorenzo may have opened the door at some point, but he never really let Him in.

A counselor came to the door and called out a name. The man sitting across from Lorenzo stood up and walked slowly toward the counselor. Lorenzo watched him until the door swung close behind him. Then Lorenzo leaned toward Tia. "Guess what."

She turned toward him. "What?"

"I think I want to be a counselor."

She arched her eyebrows. "Really?"

"Yeah," Lorenzo said as he scanned the room. "I do." He counted twenty-one other clients all waiting to be seen by a counselor. They stood or sat with their shoulders slumped and their spirits broken, making small talk and joking with one another while their eyes conveyed a message of lost hope. "I want to do what Tony and all the other counselors did for me."

"You mean getting you off those pills?"

"No, that was God," he said staring off into space. "Tony and the other counselors were just the tools God used to get to me. Now, I want Him to use me to do the same thing for other people."

"I think that's beautiful," Tia said.

"Yeah, and with God's help, I'm going to get my act together so I can counsel others and share my testimony too." He began nodding his head. "One day, I'm going to be the light for somebody else."

"You already are," Tia said and squeezed his hand.

Lorenzo smiled. Yes, God had delivered him out of the darkness, and he was going to be a living testimony to what the power of God can do for anyone who calls in earnest on His name.

God was the true path to deliverance and freedom. It was a proven truth, a proven cure, and Lorenzo knew he couldn't keep that to himself. His heart and soul would not allow it. Not this time.

Epilogue

Homer sat at the table in the county jail and looked at the attorney the court had appointed for him. He took note of her polished ability to stare him straight in the eye and try to fool him with her smile. He didn't trust her. He knew she was just like everyone else . . . smiling in his face while determining which part of his back that knife she kept sharpened would go into. And just because she was all dressed up and called herself an attorney didn't make her any different. That's just the way women were, and that's exactly why he wasn't going to admit to any wrongdoing.

"I'm not pleading guilty," he said to the attorney. "Let's get that clear now."

"If you go for a trial jury," she said, "it's not going to look good for you."

Homer was adamant. "I'm not pleading guilty. I didn't do anything wrong. I didn't do anything those girls didn't want me to do."

The attorney sighed. "You realize they were minors, and that makes it against the law, right?"

"I didn't do anything they didn't want me to do," Homer repeated.

The attorney closed her notebook and stuffed it, along with all her other papers, into her briefcase. She looked at him once more before she stood up to leave. "We'll talk again next week," she said before leaving the visitor's room.

Homer snickered to himself as he watched her walk away. He was escorted back to the common room and walked slowly to one of several round tables that were scattered throughout the room. The tables, with four metal legs connected to small round areas for sitting, reminded Homer of silver spiders bolted to the floor.

He sat down at an empty table in the corner of the room and began to look at the books situated on an antiquated bookshelf several feet away. He scanned the variety of paperback and hardcover books on the shelf and suspected they were just as old as the piece of furniture they sat on. He heard a voice behind him and turned around quickly.

Three inmates were lowering themselves down onto the remaining round metal seats. One of them was a tall, athletic man who the other two inmates referred to as Big Butch. The second one was just as tall but slender, and the third inmate was short with a stocky build.

The voices blaring from the television bolted on the wall blended in with the voices of all the inmates. Homer pointed to his ear.

"I said what are you in here for?" Big Butch repeated.

Homer waved his hand. "Just some bogus charges," he said.

"What kind of charges?"

Homer studied the massive bulge created in the inmate's arms when he placed his elbows on the table. "Some girls accused me of doing some things I didn't do."

"Oh yeah?" the short stocky inmate said and glanced at Big Butch. "What kind of things?"

"Wait a minute, wait a minute," the slender inmate said. "We're being rude. We didn't even introduce ourselves. I'm Stony," he said. He pointed to the short, stocky inmate. "This here is Chunky."

"And they call me Big Butch," the tall, athletic inmate said. He stared hard at Homer. "You can see why."

Homer nodded his head. "Yeah, I can. I'm Homer," he said holding out his hand.

Big Butch ignored Homer's extended hand. "I know who you are. You the dude who likes to mess with little girls. I heard about you."

Several other inmates had migrated to the table where Homer and the other three men sat. Homer relished the attention he was getting. For the first time in his life, he felt important, like people wanted to hear what he had to say, and so he continued to talk.

"Well, they weren't that little," he said with a smile. "They were old enough to know what they were doing."

"Yeah, but you said girls," Stony said. "How old were they?"

"Let's just say they were younger than me," Homer said and chuckled as he looked around the table.

"How much younger?" Stony continued to probe.

The looks of repulsion on the faces of the other inmates caused an uneasy feeling to sweep over Homer. He tried to brush it off by continuing to talk. "They weren't too young to know what they were doing," he said. "And then they tried to say that I forced them to, you know, do things with me." He laughed. "But they're lying." He looked around the table. "We know how girls are, right?"

No one answered.

"Continue," Big Butch said with a tense look on his face.

"Yeah, so I met this one girl," Homer said. "And she just begged me to show her the ropes. You know, teach her the tricks of the trade." He sat up straight. "So I did."

"What kind of tricks did you teach her?" Chunky asked.

"Forget that," Stony said backhanding the air. He glared at Homer. "Man, you making this seem like you was some kind of angel exalted in the sky."

"More like a fallen angel," Chunky said. "And you getting closer and closer to the ground as you speak."

Homer tried to mask his nervousness. "What are you talking about? Those girls liked it, and I just told you they wanted it." He looked at Big Butch. "You know what I mean, right?" He elbowed the side of his arm.

Big Butch looked at his arm, then at Homer. "No, man, I don't know what you mean."

"Aw, come on. Why else would they have agreed to meet me?" He sighed and shook his head. "That's why I can't figure out why they're complaining now."

"Maybe because they were little girls," Stony said, staring straight-ahead.

"They weren't that little," Homer said, elbowing Big Butch's arm a second time.

"Don't do that again," Big Butch said.

"Don't do what?"

"Elbow me. As a matter of fact," he said, standing up, and the other two inmates stood up as well, "don't touch me at all. Those little girls might have 'liked' it as you say, but I don't."

They all walked away and the rest of the inmates dispersed, leaving Homer as he had begun—alone at the table.

"Hey, what's wrong with that dude?" Stony asked. "He's limping around here bragging about what he did to those girls like it's cool or something."

"Nah," Chunky said, "that ain't cool. That ain't cool at all."

"Yeah," Big Butch said. His face hardened. "Old short leg gon' need some schoolin'."

"Who gon' be the teacher?" Chunky asked.

"I'll let you know," Big Butch said as he looked over in Homer's direction.

***

When the "lights out" call rang out, Homer had long stopped talking. He lay down on the thin mattress, and as soon as he closed his eyes he saw the disapproving looks that had been on the faces of the other inmates earlier.

The story about the girls he'd told them in the common room had been meant to impress them. But the looks on the faces of Big Butch, Stony, and Chunky reflected anything but that. Homer tried to reason away their expressions as just the look of a hardened criminal. But no matter how hard he tried to pretend, his instinct told him something different.

An uneasy feeling came over him as he struggled to remove the visual images of their faces from his memory. Had he told too much? His mind began to race. What would they do to him? Homer had heard many stories about terrible things happening to inmates in jail. Was he about to be one of them? He thought about what the police officer had said to him earlier while he was conducting the strip search.

Homer, along with the rest of the newly admitted inmates, had been ordered to get undressed. He had carefully removed his shirt and pants and had stood with his socks and boxers still on.

"Everything off!" the officer had yelled.

Seconds later, the officer had approached Homer with a hateful glare in his eyes. "You're the one who likes messing with little girls, huh?" he'd whispered in a slow and deliberate manner.

Homer remembered standing there, completely naked in front of the officer. "I don't know what you're talking about," he'd said.

"You will," the officer had chuckled.

Now, Homer's heart, once hardened under the guise of self-innocence, was beginning to crack. *What had the officer meant? Why had he laughed?* Homer began breathing rapidly as he imagined the worst scenarios for himself.

He turned onto his back and looked at the ceiling. Although his own voice had quieted, he could hear another voice emerging from within him. It came from a deep and long ignored place, and hinted of many sleepless nights to come. He stiffened as he realized what his court-appointed attorney had said was true—if he didn't plead guilty, he would probably end up in a prison cell just like this one for a very long time.

He kicked back the thin, sweat-soaked bedspread he'd been lying under and sat up. He looked around the cell that was smaller than the average college dorm room. It was surrounded by cement blocks that served as walls, and the steel bars that kept him caged in like an animal may as well have been a metal noose around his neck.

A spasm of pain rippled across his stomach. It had become a familiar pain ever since his wife, Sandra, had left him. *Or had he felt it before then?* He was no longer sure. But one thing he was sure of was that he didn't have what it took to be locked up day in and day out with people he would never spend one second with on the outside of jail. It was too much for him to bear.

He envisioned his life—no, his existence—as an inmate. The days turned into months, and the months turned into years. He stood up slowly and took his government-issued sheet off the mattress. He didn't belong there, and he was not going to give Big Butch or any of his cohorts the chance to do him harm.

Homer stood up on the wooden chair in his cell.

Perhaps if his mother had not abandoned him at birth . . .

He threw the sheet over the ceiling pipe above him.

Maybe if his wife hadn't left him . . .

He calmly tied both ends of the sheet around his neck.

If Tia hadn't rejected him . . .

He jumped off the chair.

If *anyone* would have cared about his feelings just once . . .

Soon, Homer's feet began kicking viciously at the air. Just as he was losing consciousness, he felt someone pulling him down, and then he immediately felt a sharp object pierce his chest. He struggled as the object penetrated his upper body a second and a third time. After the fourth time, Homer lay limp.

He closed his eyes right after Big Butch whispered "guilty" into his ear, spreading the conviction throughout his sad soul.

Discussion Questions

1. Why do you think Tia was so attracted to Homer?
2. Do you think Homer's attraction to young girls had anything to do with his mother abandoning him?
3. Why do you think Homer was so mean to the squirrel?
4. If you were Franny, would you have called your son for help or would you have chosen to sleep in a shelter?
5. Should Homer have forgiven Franny?
6. Do you think Homer got what he deserved, or should he be forgiven?
7. Even though Tia tried not to, do you think she unknowingly passed on the legacy of emotional detachment to her daughter Serenity?
8. Do you think there are similarities between Serenity's behavior and that of her mother?
9. Do you believe Jesus is the ultimate healer and deliverer from any and all addictions?
10. Why do you think Lorenzo waited twenty-seven years before telling his parents what happened to him as a young boy?
11. What secrets, if any, are you still harboring?

About the Author

Wisconsin native Catherine Flowers is the creator of the Christian blog, www.freefrombondage.com. When she's not fully engrossed in her own projects, she enjoys working as a freelance content editor and writing content for other Web sites. For more information about the author, please visit www.freefrombondage.com or send an e-mail to authorcatherineflowers@aol.com.

UC HIS GLORY BOOK CLUB!

www.uchisglorybookclub.net

UC His Glory Book Club is the spirit-inspired brain-child of Joylynn Ross, Author and Acquisitions Editor of Urban Christian, and Kendra Norman-Bellamy, Author for Urban Christian. This is an online book club that hosts authors of Urban Christian. We welcome as members all men and women who have a passion for reading Christian-based fiction.

UC His Glory Book Club pledges our commitment to provide support, positive feedback, encouragement, and a forum whereby members can openly discuss and review the literary works of Urban Christian authors.

There is no membership fee associated with UC His Glory Book Club; however, we do ask that you support the authors through purchasing, encouraging, providing book reviews, and of course, your prayers. We also ask that you respect our beliefs and follow the guidelines of the book club. We hope to receive your valuable input, opinions, and reviews that build up, rather than tear down our authors.

What We Believe:

—We believe that Jesus is the Christ, Son of the Living God.

—We believe the Bible is the true, living Word of God.

—We believe all Urban Christian authors should use their God-given writing abilities to honor God and share the message of the written word God has given to each of them uniquely.

—We believe in supporting Urban Christian authors in their literary endeavors by reading, purchasing and sharing their titles with our online community.

—We believe that in everything we do in our literary arena should be done in a manner that will lead to God being glorified and honored.

We look forward to the online fellowship with you.

Please visit us often at:

www.uchisglorybookclub.net.

Many Blessing to You!

Shelia E. Lipsey,
President, UC His Glory Book Club